For more than 40 years, Nick worked as a librarian, mainly in educational and legal libraries. Writing short stories was one of his hobbies throughout his career and he has continued to write since his retirement in 2021. In his spare time, he also enjoys volunteering in his local parks, where he does conservation work.

Nick was born in Norwich. For the last 30 years, he has been living near Crystal Palace.

Nick Fox

BE RULED BY ME, AND OTHER STORIES

AUSTIN MACAULEY PUBLISHERS

LONDON * CAMBRIDGE * NEW YORK * SHARJAH

ISBN 9781035868995 (Paperback)
ISBN 9781035869008 (ePub e-book)

www.austinmacauley.com

First Published 2024
Austin Macauley Publishers Ltd®
1 Canada Square
Canary Wharf
London
E14 5AA

Table of Contents

Be Ruled by Me

Be ruled by me, and we will rule the realm.
Roger de Mortimer in "Edward II" by Christopher Marlowe

By the time they reached the final room, Alex was exhausted. He had enjoyed the exhibition. He had entered a world of flat, rugged landscapes, pitted with windmills; he had wandered over sand dunes by stormy seas; he had mingled with drinkers in taverns and shoppers in the marketplace; he had visited servants in their masters' homes. For two hours, he had been living in Holland in the 16th and 17th centuries.

But the last room was devoted to portraits of dignitaries he had never heard of. Who was *Emmanuel Philibert of Savoy, Prince of Oneglia*? Did he need to study a picture of *Diana Cecil, Countess of Oxford*? Passing the portraits with only a casual glance, he was nearing the exit when he saw that Kath was lingering in front of one of them.

'This can't be right,' she said as he returned to her. She was looking at a portrait of a plump, fair-haired man, standing on a rocky path at sunrise. It was an allegorical picture: angels circled his head, while he pointed upwards to a cross, suspended above the mountains. According to the notice, it was a portrait of Laurens II, King of Favonia, painted by Konrad Brassens in Nördlingen in 1634.

'What's wrong with it?' asked Alex.

'Well, it's not Laurence. You must have seen Quorino's portraits of him. He painted dozens. He didn't look anything like that.'

***

'Yes, here's the Wikipedia entry for Quorino. It's got links to almost all his paintings. Look.'

They were drinking tea in the gallery café. Kath held out her smartphone.

'He must have painted Laurence just about every year. *Laurencio II armado*—Laurence in armour; *Laurencio II in cavallo*—Laurence on horseback; *Laurencio II com la Enfanta, Maria Luisa*—Laurence with the princess. Can you see any resemblance to the man in the exhibition?'

'No, you're right.' Alex studied the face—darker hair, lean features with high cheekbones. 'So, what do you think's happened?'

'Don't know.'

There was silence. Alex had hoped they would have a relaxing chat in the café. It was meant to be a chance to get to know each other better. Instead, she was ignoring him, tapping on her phone, pausing only to brush her hair out of her eyes. He picked up the exhibition guide and skimmed through the entries. It served him right, he thought. He had been showing off to her by explaining what was happening in Horst's *Isaac blessing Jacob* and in Rubens' *Mercury and Argus*. His dilettante knowledge was insignificant beside her historical expertise. He had forgotten that her thesis had been on Favonia.

'That's interesting,' she said at last. 'Quorino was appointed *pintoro del rego*—the king's painter. That meant he had to paint the king's portrait whenever he was asked to. Plus, nobody else was allowed to paint him. You see what that means, don't you?'

'I suppose so. Brassens must have painted him before Quorino's appointment.'

'No, he was appointed to the post in 1614, when Laurence's grandfather was still king. And he carried on until his death in 1649—fifteen years after the date of Brassens' portrait. No, what interests me is that Quorino is our only source for what Laurence looked like. He created our image of him. How do we know he looked like that?'

'You mean his pictures were propaganda?'

'Yes, inevitably. Laurence would have wanted to project a particular image—somebody serious and statesman-like. Because in fact he was quite frivolous. He wasted vast sums of money. And as for his sex-life—he had no end of mistresses and lots of illegitimate children.'

'So, you think Brassens might have painted a more accurate portrait?'

'Mm, I wonder. I still don't understand how he *could* have painted him. It wasn't like today. You couldn't have snapped a quick photo of him. And surely he wouldn't have posed for Brassens. Perhaps the picture was wrongly attributed.'

'But it's not a naturalistic portrait. Couldn't the king be representing something? I don't know—victory or something like that?'

'You think so? But wouldn't he have painted a stronger, more powerful image—a god-like figure?'

'I suppose so. Could it be the portrait of someone who claimed to be the king?'

'A pretender? I suppose it's possible, but I don't think so. Laurence was the only son of King Mark—Marco IV. There was nothing controversial about his succession.'

'Was it likely that Laurence would have been in—where was it?'

'In Nördlingen? Yes, maybe. There was a battle there in the middle of the Thirty Years War. Two battles actually.' She tapped at her phone. 'Yes, the first was in 1634—the same year the portrait was painted. Favonia sent a small army to support the Spaniards, who won the battle. I don't know if Laurence was there—I suppose he might have been.'

Alex could sense Kath's excitement. Her first glimpse of the picture had changed her destiny. He knew that her temporary job at his workplace was inconsequential for her—just a break in her academic career with the aim of earning a little money. Now, suddenly, her PhD thesis was spreading out before her. Perhaps she was mentally drafting the summary already.

They parted ten minutes later—ten minutes of silence apart from the tapping on her phone.

'Thanks ever so much for inviting me here, Alex. I loved the exhibition and now you've found me some research I can really get my teeth into.'

She kissed him. It was a friendly kiss, affectionate even. But it was also a dismissive kiss. Of course, they would continue to chat at work—for as long as she stayed there—but he could abandon all thoughts of any deeper relationship. He had shown her a path to her aspirations. Now he had served his purpose.

As he waited for the bus, he thought again about the portrait. If only he could help resolve the enigma. If only he had some of Kath's specialist knowledge, her acquaintance with expert tutors, her access to the university library. It was arrogant to dream that he could contribute anything worthwhile.

He pondered why he wanted to help. Did he have a disinterested desire to find out the truth or did he merely want to impress Kath?

But even as he stood, glumly waiting, an idea was piercing through his self-pity. He still had a week's leave owing to him. Perhaps he could book a flight to Favonia and see what he could find there in the galleries and museums…

***

'Uni bigleti, favore.'

He looked up from his phrasebook. To his relief, the man at the desk understood and handed him a ticket for the gallery. As he counted out the unfamiliar money, he noticed an elderly woman just ahead of him, smiling. She must have heard his poor attempt at Favonian.

'It is your first visit to the gallery?' She spoke English perfectly, with only a trace of an accent.

'Yes, I want to see Quorino's portraits.'

'You choose well. Follow me.'

Despite her age, his new friend almost ran up the flight of steps to the first floor. There she ushered him into the room facing them.

'See,' she said. 'Favonia's greatest painter.'

There must have been sixty paintings around the walls. Most were portraits, but there were two mythological scenes that attracted him. He looked at his companion to see if she intended to give him a guided tour, but she gestured him away.

'Go. Look. But ask me anything.'

He approached *Leda and the swan*. The young woman's expression mingled fascination, fear and sexual excitement as she surrendered to the arrogant power of the disguised god. Next to it was *Orpheus and Eurydice*. Here the anguish and disappointment on the woman's face was heart-breaking. Yet it was her lover's remorse, as he watched her recoil back into Hades, that was even more tortured. How could Quorino make a back view so expressive?

He had come to look at the portraits of Laurence. According to Kath, Quorino was a propagandist for the king and he could understand what she meant. In the early paintings, he was dressed in black; in one, he was holding a sealed document. The artist was emphasising his seriousness and his concern with affairs of state. In the later paintings, he wore a crown and was sometimes riding a horse. Always he stood against a bare background: no scenery, just grey brushstrokes giving emphasis to the figure in front. However, Alex didn't think the portraits were flattering: despite his imposing figure, Laurence looked awkward and uncomfortable, as though he hated the role of monarch.

'Favonia's greatest painter,' repeated his companion (how long had she been standing beside him?), 'and Favonia's handsomest king.'

He turned to smile at her.

'It is rare that the English care about our Laurencio,' she said.

'Yes, but you see, I went to an exhibition in London recently where I saw a portrait of him by another artist. He didn't look like that. I wanted to find out more about him.'

'Ah yes, Konrad Brassens. I have seen that portrait. You liked the picture?'

'It was very different. We call the style Baroque in English. A lot of swirling clouds and…'

'And angels and trumpets. Yes, it amuses me.'

'But who was he painting? It was a different man.'

'Indeed. It is a mystery, no? But there is the man who could solve it.' She pointed at another of Quorino's portraits: a stern, middle-aged man, with a flowing black wig. Underneath were the words: *Domenco Sevolles, Condo di Maronto*.

'Who's he?'

'He was Laurencio's First Minister. I liked him once. Now I hate him.'

'Yes, that can happen with historical characters. As you read more about them, you find out things you don't want to know.'

He felt foolishly proud of that remark. It combined, he thought, a sympathy with the woman's emotions and a reflective assessment of the effects of study. Her response disconcerted him.

'Perhaps. But for me he is not historical.'

***

'You know Laurencio better now?'

They were sitting in the gallery café. How different from the café in London. This woman didn't fiddle with her phone. She asked questions and listened carefully to his answers.

'Yes, I think so. But I still don't understand about that other portrait.'

'You have ideas about it?'

11

'Well, I expect it was just a mistake on the notice. I did wonder if the two Laurencios were rivals to the throne, but my friend, Katherine, said there was no dispute over the succession. Laurencio was the only son of King Marco.'

'Are you sure?' She smiled.

'No. But Kath said so. She's studied the history.'

'And Marco was the son of Laurencio I, who was the son of Eduardo III, but Eduardo was not the son of Marco III. He was his uncle. Marco had no sons.'

'I see, but that must have been a long time before.'

'Not long. Eduardo was an old man when he became king. He died two years later in 1601. Then Laurencio reigned until 1615. Then Marco IV was king.'

'You remember the dates well. I'm impressed.'

'Yes, I studied them much. Those three kings—Eduardo, Laurencio and Marco—were all older than the true heir to the throne: the child of Marco III.'

'Hang on. I thought you said Marco III didn't have any children.'

'He had no sons, but he had one daughter—Juliana.' Her eyes blazed with anger. 'They said a woman could not inherit. But Domenco—the man in the portrait—he said the laws allowed it.'

'So, Juliana should have been queen all the time?'

'Indeed. And Domenco plotted all the time that she be queen. He was her chamberlain, you understand.'

'So that's why you used to like him. What made you change your mind?'

She was silent. Her agitation had suddenly aged her. At first, because of her grey hair, he had thought she was elderly, but her vivacity in the gallery had made her look younger. Now she seemed old again. He sensed a latent fear and anger in her blazing eyes, perhaps unexpressed for decades. He had to change the subject.

'Where did you learn to speak such perfect English?'

'My tutors taught me English. Then I travelled to England to meet the Prince of Wales.'

'You met Prince Charles?'

'Who? Carlo, the Enfanto? Yes, we met, but he was a boy. I knew Enriquo, his brother. I liked Enriquo. 'My little Henry,' I called him. He was not little, but he was very young—two years younger than I.'

She was so thrilled about the memory of the meeting that he didn't try to correct her confusion. Why should she have a detailed knowledge of the British Royal Family?

'Of course, we were never alone together. Always Domenco was with me and the Sinor Challoner was with Henry.'

'Who?'

'Domenco Sevolles. You saw his portrait.'

'Yes, but that was 400 years ago.'

'400 years is not so long.'

'And who was the other man you mentioned?'

'Challoner? Thomas Challoner, the Chamberlain of the Prince and friend of the king.'

'Which king?'

'Jacobo, of course. King James I.'

What was she talking about? At first, he had been enjoying her company. After struggling to speak a few, stumbling words of Favonian at the airport, at the hotel reception, on the metro, he had succumbed to her easy command of English and her apparent concern to satisfy his curiosity about King Laurence. But her interest had veered off into fantasy—a fantasy which she appeared to believe. How should he respond? Perhaps he should simply stand up, shake her hand and leave her on her own. Eventually, he would have to do that, but in the meantime, he decided to humour her. There was something compelling about her confused, incoherent narrative.

'And did you meet King James?'

'Oh yes, he was very sympathetic. I know he preferred boys, but he wanted a good bride for his son. And I had a big dowry. My religion was wrong, but Domenco thought we could agree. I remember the king showed us the tigers in Paris Garden. He was proud of his savage animals.'

'He took you to Paris?'

'No, Paris Garden. In London.'

'I think you had better start the story from the beginning. I'm getting confused.'

'I thought I told you already. All right, I begin again…

'I was born in 1592 in the Royal Palace—here, in this building.'

Suddenly Alex remembered. He had read about it in the guidebook. After the civil war which led to the establishment of the Republic, the old palace had fallen into disuse and decay. Then, many years later, it had been restored and transformed into the National Gallery of Favonia. He had admired the majestic entrance: the large courtyard, the marble steps leading up to the main door, framed by Ionic columns. Once inside, he had forgotten all that in the midst of the modern interior.

He thought he understood now. This woman must be a tour guide, employed to bring to life the history of the palace in the guise of an important character in that history. But it was strange. Why had she adopted only one tourist? And why was she not dressed in costume? He looked at her green blouse, her black cardigan and trousers.

'My mother died in childbirth. I was the only child. My father, King Marco III, always said I was heir to the throne. When he died, I was only seven. Domenco Sevolles, the Count of Maronto who was my tutor and my father's chief counsellor, said I was now Queen of Favonia, but others said no—it was impossible because of the Lex Salica. You understand?'

'The Salic Law? Yes, I think so. It meant that no woman could inherit the throne.'

'Yes, but Domenco said it not apply in Favonia. But he had enemies who said yes. So, my father's uncle became King Eduardo III. He was an old man. I don't think he wanted to be king, but his sons insisted.'

'Because the son wanted to succeed, I suppose?'

'Yes, although it was the younger son who wanted the power: Federico, Cardinal of Montello. In effect, he ruled Favonia from the time of my father's death until 1611—twelve years. He and Domenco were enemies, but Federico had the Pope's blessing. No one could stop him.'

'And what happened to you?'

'I had to move out of this building. I lived in a small palace in the countryside—twenty-five kilometres from Montello. Domenco organised my education. Men taught me English, French, Latin, natural philosophy…'

'I'm not sure if I know what that is.'

'Science and magic. But do not worry. My tutor, Orostel, taught me little. Always he was in his workshop, surrounded by his equipment: crucibles, aludels, alembics. Trying to turn base metals into noble ones. Sometimes he showed me the different liquids: aqua fortis, aqua regis, aqua vitae. He taught me the stages from imperfection to perfection: projection, putrefaction, incineration and so on. It meant nothing to me. He taught me the names of the plants I could smell in the room: aconitum, mandragora, spigelia anthelmia. He showed me the egg of a cockatrice, the horn of a unicorn. But it was all nonsense… And then I learnt statecraft. Domenco taught me that himself, because he still wanted that I be queen.'

'It sounds very serious. Did you have any fun?'

'A little. I learnt dancing too. And horse-riding. I liked the grounds of that palace. They were more wild than here, without terraces or classical statues. But I played no games; I had no friends—only my chambermaids. They were sympathetic, but it was not the same.'

'How long did this last?'

'Until I was fifteen. Then Domenco took me out in my carriage to show me off. He took me to banquets where I could dance. I was a success. People liked me. People cheered me. Courtiers danced with me. And Domenco was plotting with some of the ministers. Eduardo had died by now and his son, Laurencio, was King. He was not popular. His brother, the Cardinal, neither. They spent money on silly wars. They sent soldiers to fight with Spain against England. They were brutal with the Huguenots who had fled from France after the massacre. The Cardinal even introduced the Inquisition. It was a time of great fear.

'And no one liked Prince Marco. He was an invalid. He had much pain—in the chest, the back, the legs. Sometimes breathing was difficult. Sometimes he had seizures. No one thought he would live long. He wore a smock with amulets pinned to it to ward off evil. I felt sorry for him, of course. But I couldn't like him, because he liked no one—no one except his mother.'

'So was Domenco plotting a coup?'

'Perhaps. But first he wanted that I marry. I think he hoped that I marry Prince Marco, but the Cardinal would never agree to that. Then Domenco sent a delegation to Austria. He hoped that I marry Ferdinand, the son of the Archduke, but he married his cousin, Maria Anna. So Domenco arranged that I meet Henri de Bourbon. But no. Henri married Charlotte Marguerite de Montmorency. All the courtiers were excited about who I marry. No one cared about Prince Marco.'

'The Cardinal must have been angry.'

'He was furious. He forbade that I leave my palace. I was locked in there for six months, with the palace staff. Only Domenco was allowed out.'

'You were a prisoner?'

'Yes, my servants looked after me and I could walk and ride in the grounds, but the gates were locked and a guard was there always.'

'So how did you get out at last?'

'Tradesmen and labourers were coming often to work in the fields or care for the horses. In February 1611, a wheelwright and his apprentice came to repair some of the farm vehicles. Domenco made me change clothes with the apprentice. I was dressed as a common man, with a jerkin, hose and beret. I left in the wheelwright's cart. He took me to an inn far away. I stayed there for the night. Domenco came early next morning with horses. He was disguised too. He was dressed as a merchant. I became his male servant, with a short travelling coat with fur trimmings. We rode south along the main highway. We saw few people: a horse and cart, a farmer driving a flock of sheep to market, occasionally a carriage. Then we turned off on to a small track going north through a dark forest. We changed clothes again. Again, I was a peasant. We rode quickly until we crossed the border into France. I was exhausted, but Domenco had arranged everything. At the inn next morning, a small carriage arrived, with a coachman and maidservant. Now we could travel in more comfort and I was a woman once more. We travelled north again, staying at inns. I spoke little. People stared at us. Did they know who I was? Or only that I was a foreigner?

'I was scared, but the journey was exciting. Then we reached the coast. I loved the sea. I had not seen it before. It looked wild, the waves crashing on the shore. We rode along the coast until the towers of a city appeared on a hill above the sea. It was the first city I had seen on the journey. Boulogne—you know it?'

'Yes, I've been there, but it's different now. Supermarkets and offices at the lower level. But the old city is still there. It's quite a climb to get there.' Alex was surprised to find that he had accepted the pretence that they were speaking from different centuries.

'Well, we stayed there two nights, while Domenco found a commercial ship which could take us to England.'

'Did he think you would be safe there?'

'He wanted to arrange the marriage between Prince Henry and me. Britain was no longer at war with Spain. We hoped they would forget our part in that war. In the past, our nations had been friendly. Queen Elizabel—Queen Elizabeth—had been my godmother, although she attended not my christening. She sent some minor courtier instead. But at least there was a bond.

'We had planned to set sail in the evening, but the sea was too stormy. At last, we left at 5 o'clock in the morning. The ship was tossing on the waves, the wind howled in the sails. I stayed below, feeling awful. Often I was sick. I thought the voyage would never end.

'We arrived in Dover nine hours later. I staggered ashore. Domenco and our servants were as ill as I. We were led to an inn and I went to bed.

'The next morning, my maidservant brought me regal clothes and helped me to dress as if we were in the palace again. She guided me downstairs where Domenco greeted me with a kiss on the hand. He was dressed as a courtier. After breakfast, he conducted me outside. A carriage was waiting with the Favonian royal coat of arms: a swan with two long necks looped around the golden crown. I know not how Domenco had organised everything. He must have been sending messages to his agents in England while we were travelling through France. We sat in comfort while the horses pulled us quickly.

'We arrived in London the next evening. I remember my first sight of the city: the large church of St Saviour as we approached the river and all the towers on the other side. So many churches. And rising above all the others was St Paul's, with its square tower and tall spire. We crossed the bridge, with houses on each side of it. Then we turned left along the main highway. We passed tiny streets with small cottages and taverns squeezed together. People stared at our carriage. Did they recognise the royal arms? I think not, but they knew we were important.

'We drove below the cathedral, through the arches of Ludgate and Temple Bar, crossing over the ditch between them. We passed the enormous Denmark House. At last, we stopped in the Strand at the sign of the Black Eagle. Do you know it?'

'I know the Strand, but not the pub. I don't think it's there anymore.'

'Perhaps not. We stayed in rooms there. Domenco told me nothing. He left early each morning and I saw him only at evening. Servants cared for me. I had everything I needed, but I was lonely again.

'On the fourth day, my servant dressed me in a black satin gown, trimmed with silver braid. Then Domenco led me to the carriage and we drove along the Strand, past Charing Cross. I remember the smell of horses from the Royal Mews. We passed through the Holbein Gate to the Palace of Whitehall. I had lived in two palaces, but this was larger than the two together. Servants bowed in greeting; they conducted us into the great hall. I had never seen so many noblemen and ladies, wearing long, coloured cloaks, all talking loudly, trying to be heard above the music.

'At one end of the hall was a canopy of cloth of gold. Seated under this were the King and Queen with the two princes and the princess. Prince Henry was dressed in red velvet and there was a redness too in his hair. He was quite tall with broad shoulders. As I looked at him, I think he smiled at me.

'A courtier ushered me towards the King. We approached and knelt before him. "Arise, Juliana, rightful Queen of Favonia. You are welcome here."'

'That wasn't very diplomatic of him, was it?' asked Alex. 'The king in Favonia would have been furious if he heard.'

'You are right. I don't know how Domenco had persuaded him to address me thus. I'm sure the Cardinal had spies in the English court. He had them everywhere. But you see, I was useless to King James unless I were Queen. He didn't want his son to marry a minor princess. He wanted to add Favonia to his realm. He was a lover of peace. He hoped to build his empire by marriages rather than war.

'Domenco and I withdrew into the throng and soon we returned to the Black Eagle. There I stayed for several days while Domenco was negotiating with I know not whom.

'At last, he told me that we were to meet the prince at Richmond Palace. We were to travel there by the king's barge. I was excited as we boarded at the Westminster water-gate. The Palace of Westminster was beside us. Behind that was the abbey, with its strange, unfinished towers. Another palace was on the opposite side of the river. We sailed slowly. Soon we were out of London. Green fields stretched out on either bank. We passed villages and churches and one more palace. The river wound past little islands. Swans swam out of our way. Then a huge building appeared in front of us. It was the colour of corn, with red chimneys and turrets. How many rooms did it have? Why were they needed?

'Prince Henry, surrounded by courtiers, was waiting for us at the landing stage. As I was helped on to the bank, he approached and kissed my hand. He was wearing black with a white ruff. He conducted us into the palace, as servants bowed to us, holding open the doors. I had never felt so important. We went into a small chamber on the ground floor, where Henry dismissed everyone apart from Sir Thomas Challoner (his Lord Chamberlain) and Domenco.

'We sat down at the table on which were wine and sweetmeats. Henry asked us about our journey by barge and then about our longer journey from Favonia. He approved of the adventure: "You, a woman, have travelled where many men would not have dared." He asked about my claim to the throne and looked outraged when I told him how my father's uncle had usurped it. When I talked about the Cardinal, the king's brother, he stood up in anger. "So, it was a papist plot. It is my mission to cleanse the continent of papacy."

'I felt uncomfortable, because I knew what was coming next. "You, Madam, will convert to the true faith?"

'Domenco spoke for me. "Indeed, Your Highness. The princess is already taking instruction."

'He had warned me about this. I also knew that he had met the Nuncio in Favonia to ask for a papal dispensation for me to marry a heretic. Domenco hadn't decided which option would be politically safer: for me to convert to Protestantism or for Henry to convert to Catholicism.'

'But what about you?' asked Alex. 'Didn't you care whether you were Catholic or Protestant?'

'Yes, I did. I cared little about the Holy Father, but I keep always my icon of the Blessed Virgin. I keep also my rosary. Always they console me.' She reached under her jacket to clutch her necklace. 'There was another Catholic suitor for Henry: Isabella of Savoy… Was she going to convert? But there was a passion about Henry's religion. It would be difficult. Yet I liked him, despite everything.

'He led me into another room and showed me his model army, laid out on a large table: brass soldiers, horses, carriages, weapons, scaling ladders. "Here I plan my battles," he said. "But come outside."

'We walked to the riverside. He told me of his plans for the navy and of his flagship, the *Prince Royal*. We strolled downstream and he pointed to the trees ahead. "There is the deer park. There we go hunting. My father loves to hunt too, but for him, the hunt is everything. For me, it is a preparation for war."

'I didn't like to hear him speak so much of war, but his words were familiar. "My father thought as you do," I said. "He used to say, 'La cazza es imago de guera'—The hunt is the image of war."

'"Your father was right," shouted the prince.

'We didn't stay long. Domenco and Challoner made it clear that it was time to part. Henry kissed my hand as I boarded the barge and stood waving as we sailed away. I had enjoyed the visit. I liked not Henry's Protestantism nor his enthusiasm for war. But he was young—young and passionate. I would have liked to marry him.'

She looked wistful.

'What went wrong?' asked Alex.

'We were in England only three more days. The king sent me courtiers to show me around the New Exchange near our rooms on the Strand. So many goods were displayed there: jewellery, linen, silk, hats, perfumes. I bought a gold model warship for Henry. Then the king himself took me to Paris Garden to see the wild animals.

'Back in the inn, the king sent me his personal physician to examine me. I had to undress in front of that fat Frenchman, so that he could prod and feel me all over to make sure I was suitable for the prince.

'On the last night, Domenco and I returned to the Palace of Whitehall. I met Henry again and we exchanged gifts. I think he liked the warship; I liked his present to me: a beautiful pomander-bracelet. Then he left me to prepare for the masque.

'The great hall was laid out for the performance. At the far end was the stage, with the king, the queen and Carlo and Elizabel seated in front of it. Henry went to join them. The courtiers were all assembled at the near end. Many of the women were dressed shamelessly. They wore translucent gauze, revealing their bodies underneath. I knew they wanted to impress the prince. Would he notice me amongst them?

'Lackeys snuffed out the candles around the stage and everyone was silent. Then, slowly, the candles were lit again. The stage was an island, with green grass and trees. Waves were breaking on the shore. It was so clever. I could not see the machine which pulled them back and forth. The sun rose on the back wall and the masquers walked on to the stage. They began to dance to the fiddlers' tunes until the figure of Aurora appeared, wearing a gold cloak and looking out to sea. She sang of joy and peace and triumph. But over the sea came Spanish ships, drawn by invisible cords. The masquers drew their swords and stood either side of Aurora. She raised her arm and the ships sank through trapdoors. There were crashes and shouts of dying men. The audience cheered and the candles were dimmed again. Then the sun rose once more. Aurora stepped down and approached the royal party. She bowed, took Henry by the hand and led him back on to the stage. A throne was lowered and Aurora sang:

Come, Meliadus, take thy seat,
Where Arthur sat of old.
Here, at thy kingly father's feet,
Reclaim the realm of gold.
The cries of faithless foes shall cease
And Albion's son shall reign in peace.

'The performance finished and the masquers invited the ladies of the court to dance. I hoped the prince would ask me; many other ladies were staring at him with beseeching eyes. But he danced only with the queen, his mother. Round and round they whirled, while the other ladies reluctantly accepted inferior partners. Domenco led me in a coranto, but we stepped aside when the galliards started. These were dances for younger men than Domenco, but still Henry and his mother danced.

'They were still dancing when a servant entered and handed a message to Domenco. He looked shocked when he read it, but he had a gleam of triumph in his eye too. Immediately, he told me that we must leave. He led me to the king, kissed his hand and whispered a few words to him. The king turned to me and wished me well. Then we walked out into the cold night and climbed into our carriage. I cried as we drove to our rooms. I had not said farewell to Henry.

'I never saw him again. He died a year later.'

'But what had happened?' asked Alex.

'Federico, the Cardinal, was dead. Assassinated by a Huguenot outside the cathedral.'

'That's terrible. But Domenco didn't like him, you said.'

'He hated him. That's why we had to leave so quickly. Without the Cardinal, Domenco could have power.

'That night, my maidservant helped me to pack, while Domenco wrote letters. We left at dawn. I was miserable all the way. I do not know if Henry and I could have married or whether I could have loved him. He was still so young. But I liked him much. And I knew what Domenco planned for me. He wanted me to marry Marco. Without the Cardinal, he thought no one would stop us.'

'But you said he was horrible.'

'He *was* horrible. But he was the Crown Prince. When his father died, his wife would be Queen Consort—although I should have been Queen in my own right.'

'Was it so important for you?'

'For me, no. For Domenco, yes. And I liked Domenco then. Always he treated me with respect. He wished that we return to Montello quickly. We drove to Dover and travelled overnight to Boulogne. The sea was calmer this time, but I felt sicker. Then we boarded another carriage and drove through France. There was no secrecy this time. It mattered not who saw us. At last, we crossed the frontier into Favonia and stopped at an inn. Here a message was waiting for Domenco. It told that Marco was already married.'

'Were you relieved?'

'Indeed. But Domenco was furious. I hoped that was the end. But he still had plans. You see, Marco had married a Huguenot—a cousin of the Duke of Rohan.'

'What? A Protestant? And after a Huguenot had assassinated his uncle?'

'Exactly. It was a political marriage. The Huguenots had negotiated a settlement with the king. They promised no more assassinations in return for marriage. He had no one to advise him—no one wise or powerful. He just agreed. His brother had always made the decisions. Now the Huguenots told him what to do. They wanted to spread Protestantism throughout Favonia. I heard that there were preachers in the marketplace every day, denouncing the corruption of Mother Church.'

'So, what did Domenco do?'

'He told me nothing. But next morning, he had already left. I learnt later that he was riding fast to Montello. I followed slowly in the carriage with my servants. We arrived the next day and returned to my palace outside the city. I felt strange. I had not been happy there as an exile, but I was pleased to see the staff again. Rosamaria, my Lady of the Bedchamber, cried when we met. If I could stay there—far from the city, far from my royal cousins—I thought I could be content.

'But Domenco returned a few days later. He had met the Nuncio, who told him that the Pope was furious that Marco had married a heretic. He had sent his Legate to forbid the marriage, but he arrived too late. The Pope was angry too about the nature of the wedding. The pair had exchanged vows in the cathedral porch, according to Huguenot custom. There had been no nuptial Mass. Now the Nuncio said that the marriage should be annulled, provided that it had not been consummated.'

'But how would anyone know if it had been consummated?'

'I told you that the Cardinal had introduced the Inquisition. Domenco spoke to the Inquisitor General who then interviewed Mathilde, Marco's wife. She confessed that she had never touched Marco. She wore her hair unbound—like a virgin's. The Inquisitor was very persuasive. Maybe she spoke truth—how could anyone have sex with Marco? But the interview would have continued until she confessed—whether it was truth or lie.'

'So, the marriage was annulled?'

'It was annulled and Mathilde was banished. Domenco was delighted. He was suddenly friends with the Catholic hierarchy, who had ignored him before. The king's Council was disbanded and a new Council of Purity was established, with Domenco as First Minister. Now he was the most powerful man in the land. Of course, I know not how many people he had bribed.'

'And what about the king?'

'He was never close to Domenco, but I think he was happy to have someone to make decisions for him. He didn't want his son married to a Protestant. Nor did the queen, Sophia, although she was a strong and clever woman. She never liked me. She was daughter of another of my father's uncles—Alphonso. And Alphonso was older than Eduardo, the brother who became king after my father. Alphonso was dead by that time, but I think Sophia thought that she should reign as his heir—except that would mean that I should have reigned before her as Marco III's heir. So, she married her cousin and ruled as his Queen Consort.'

'It can't have been healthy—all this inbreeding.'

'You are right. And Marco was the result.'

'And what about the Huguenots? They must have been up in arms.'

'The Inquisitor General threatened an auto-da-fé for any Protestant who didn't convert to Catholicism. Domenco opposed him. He said there should be freedom of worship for Huguenots, but no ministerial office. The Inquisitor overruled him. I think Domenco wanted to be overruled. He wanted to be seen as tolerant, but also he wanted the Huguenots out of the country. He paid much money to give them safe passage to France. There was protection for them there after the Edict of Nantes. He arranged a ceremonial escort for any who chose to leave, including Mathilde, after the annulment of her marriage. Those who stayed, but did not convert, did not live long. Their bodies dangled from the city walls.'

'Yuk! … So, then you were free to marry Marco?'

'Yes, it disgusted me. But we had a papal dispensation—even though it was not necessary, as the first marriage had not been consummated. It all happened so quickly. I was to be married only three months after my return to Favonia.

'But it was strange… I woke up on my wedding day, feeling excited. Yes, I disliked Marco; I hated the thought of marriage to him; I feared another Huguenot assassination. But still I enjoyed that morning. My maidservant dressed me in a purple corsage of velvet, edged with ermine. Over that, I wore robes of gold silk. And I had a small gold coronet. The coach, draped in red velvet, arrived in the courtyard and Domenco led me into it. Two pages rode in front of the coach and two behind, their horses adorned with scarlet and gold. As we rode through the palace gates, crowds of people were cheering. Of course, I was excited. I tried to forget about the man I would be marrying. Perhaps he was not so bad now. I had not seen him since two years. He was twenty now. He was a clumsy boy no longer. Perhaps.

'We rode first to the archbishop's palace for the signing of the marriage contract. Domenco led me into the great hall, while the king brought in Marco.'

She paused. A look of disgust spread over her face.

'So, he hadn't improved?' asked Alex.

'I cared not that he was ugly. I was sorry that he was weak and unwell. But he did not look at me. I was no one to him. We signed the papers. The archbishop blessed us and we had to embrace. There was cheering and a fanfare of trumpets. Marco scowled, standing there in his white satin, a cloak of gold cloth and a crown. I cried. Then we parted—I wished forever, but it was not to be. I was led back to my coach and we drove to the cathedral for the nuptial Mass in the Lady Chapel. Marco appeared again. We exchanged rings and vows in front of the altar with the reliquary which held the jawbone of St Adriano, the Patron Saint of Favonia. I was now married to the heir to the throne—I who had been heir presumptive fifteen years before.

'That night, the king gave a wedding banquet in his palace. This was followed by a masked ball. Of course, you always recognise everyone despite their masks. But it gave me an excuse to avoid Marco without I seemed to do so deliberately. I danced with several men, wishing that each was my bridegroom.

'The ball continued long into the night, but Marco and I were not allowed to stay. Before midnight, we were led away to the bridal chamber for the disgusting ceremony of the *couchado*. I remember the bed—it was very ornate, with ivory posts. Marco and I got in, but there was no privacy. The purple curtains were drawn back, so that the king, the archbishop, Domenco and other courtiers could make sure that the marriage was consummated. Of course, there was no sex—we hated each other too much. But we put our arms around each other reluctantly and Domenco persuaded the others that we had done what was necessary. As the archbishop left, he whispered in my ear, "It is a princess's duty to bear many children."

'The next morning, the courtiers returned for the *levanto*. Domenco arrived first, with a sheet stained with a calf's blood from the kitchen. He inserted it into the bed. Then, when the others arrived, we stood up and Domenco pulled out the sheet and held it up as proof. Some people are easy to convince.

'Marco and I had to pretend to the courtiers, but we didn't pretend to each other. Soon we devised a strategy. We stayed in bed together for the *couchado*. Then I left and walked along the corridor in my nightgown to spend the night in my own chamber, returning in time for the *levanto*. I know not how many people knew what was happening. Most of the servants knew, but they said nothing. And of course, Domenco knew everything. He would come to see me in my chamber. He comforted me. I had known him all my life; he had been like a father to me. It seemed natural that we should be together at night. I thought he loved me.

'Quickly I learnt the truth. As soon as I was pregnant, Domenco left me. He left me to marry a countess. They lived in rooms in another wing of the palace.'

'So, he abandoned you?'

'Yes. Suddenly I learnt that he cared not for me; he cared not that I be Queen. He cared only that he could rule in in my name. Of course, it was complicated. It was necessary that we pretend that Marco was the father. And adultery for a queen meant punishment by death. It is different for a king. My father had a son out of wedlock. So did my Laurencio. But for me, no. So, I told no one—not even my confessor. No one must suspect Domenco.'

'And *did* anyone suspect him?'

'It was treason to suspect. Of course, many servants knew. But what could anyone prove? And there was rejoicing when my Laurencio was born. He was born in the early morning. They said that the hawthorn in the palace garden was in bloom, although the month was December. I cared not. I was groaning in agony. But I was pleased to have a son.'

'What if you had had a girl?'

'Often I have wondered that. Would Domenco have been unfaithful to his new wife? But Laurencio was a healthy boy.

'My lady-in-waiting carried him from the birthing chamber to the royal nursery. He was tied in swaddling bands to keep his limbs straight. Like Marco, he had amulets pinned to his garments to ward off evil and sickness. He was baptised quickly—with water brought by friars from the River Jordan. After that I saw him little. His wet-nurse and the ladies of the bedchamber looked after him. When he could stand upright, they strapped him into a wooden walker on wheels. They did well. He grew tall and strong.'

'Was Marco pleased to see him?'

'Marco hated him. He knew who the father was, but he could tell no one. He needed that the pretence continue. How could he admit that his wife was unfaithful?'

'And what about the King and Queen?'

'Oh, the queen knew her son was not the father. And she hated me. But the king? I think he suspected nothing. He liked the baby. It delighted him that the future of the dynasty was assured. And the baby had his own name: Laurencio. He was an old man by this time. A foolish old man, but sympathetic. Without his brother to command him, he was lost. But I liked him. With a grandson, he could die happy. I knew not which would die first: the father or the son.'

'And did Domenco keep away?'

'Away from me, but he was always busy. It was at that time that he commissioned Quorino to paint in the court.'

'I'd forgotten about him.'

'His first painting was of the king on his throne, his son standing on one side, his "grandson" on the other. Did you see it in the gallery? Of course, Domenco arranged the pose. It showed the legitimacy of the succession. He made Quorino hasten, afraid that either the king or Marco would die before it was completed. But all was well. It is an intimate picture, yes? The king and his son are dressed simply in doublet and ruff, with no regalia, except that the king wears his chain of the Order of Hesperides. (Did you notice the golden apple?) Quorino painted Marco looking up at his father, so you cannot see his full face. And my Laurencio is so cute. He had learnt to stand only recently. The king loved the picture and Domenco persuaded him to appoint Quorino as *pintoro del rego*—the king's painter.

'It was one of his last decrees. He fell sick of the fever soon afterwards. The doctors bled him and purged him; they gave him barley gruel. But nothing did any good. The archbishop came to his bedside to grant absolution and he died soon afterwards. Six requiem masses were said for him as he lay in the chapel beneath the sanctuary in the cathedral. Then he was moved to the vaults to lie with our ancestors.'

'So, Marco was now King?'

'Yes, a herald announced the news from the palace steps: "The king is dead! Long live the King!" Beside him stood the archbishop, holding aloft the Blessed Sacrament.

'But there was no coronation for Marco. Domenco delayed it, because of the expense. I had thought we were rich, but he had spent so much on our journey to England and so much more since we returned. The Crown had little remaining. He raised taxes on cloth and imports; he negotiated loans with the Royal Bank. He sold honours—mayors, justices, town criers. He introduced new copper coins and ordered that the old silver ones be melted down. Of course, the church was rich, but he dared not tax the clergy.'

'But even without a coronation, you must have been recognised as Queen?'

'Yes, I was the Queen Consort. Of course, Domenco did everything. Marco simply had to sign whatever papers he brought.'

'Did he like being King?'

'I think he liked to sit on the throne, wearing his crown. But he hated Domenco. He wanted to reign by himself, without that Domenco instruct him. I felt sorry for him, for I too disliked Domenco now, but no one could be friends with Marco. Everyone was waiting until he die.'

'How long did he last?'

'He died in 1617, nearly two years after his father. Domenco was planning his coronation at that time, but Marco died before it happened. His mother accused the physicians. She said that they had hastened his death. I know not. But now my Laurencio was King. He was only four, so I became Queen Regent. But, of course, Domenco still did everything.'

'And did *his* coronation take place quickly?'

'Yes, a date had been set for Marco's coronation. Invitations had been sent. Everything went as planned, except a different king was crowned. Domenco said that kingship is not about the individual. What is important is the continuity of the crown, not who wears it. But for Domenco, the person *did* matter. It had to be someone he could control.

'The day of the coronation was strange for me. I was dressed in a black mourning gown, with a veil. I was meant to be grieving for a husband I had disliked rather than celebrating the crowning of a son I adored.'

'Laurencio and I joined the procession led by the Cardinal Archbishop (the Holy Father had granted him his red hat a few months before). I felt jealous of the foreign princesses. Their bodices glistened with diamonds, rubies, emeralds, pearls. Their robes were embroidered with gold thread and edged with ermine, while I wore black.

'But I was proud of Laurencio as he walked beside me, dressed in violet. He understood the solemnity of the day. Despite their finery, the princes behind him were not greater than he.

'We entered the abbey, led by fifty gentlemen of the king's household, all dressed in red gowns with gold buttons. Heralds, carrying gold maces, greeted us. Then the Cardinal led Laurencio to the High Altar. He knelt and kissed the reliquary. He sat on the ancient, stone throne. The Cardinal anointed his head with oil from St Adriano's olive tree—the tree in the garden of the monastery he had founded. He placed a crown on his head—a heavy, gold crown, but Laurencio did not flinch. I never wanted that he be King, but I was proud of him that day.'

'Why didn't you want him to be King?'

'I hated it all by that time—the power, the bowing courtiers, never knowing whom I might trust. Once, when I had trusted Domenco, I accepted that I must be Queen, but now it was different. I hated that he was my son's father and I knew that he cared only about power for himself.'

'He was as bad as that?'

'Perhaps not. I think he believed in the monarchy and its continuance. He truly thought he was doing God's work, even if this meant fathering the future king. And the work was never complete. It was not enough that his son was on the throne. He knew that there were plots against him. The queen, my mother-in-law, was still alive and still hated me. There was a group of ministers who were her favourites. Domenco feared that they plotted against us. But there was no obvious rival to my Laurencio and the church was on our side—at that time. Domenco did not attempt to dismiss these ministers from the Council. Instead, he gave me papers to sign so that he could increase the size of the Council—and increase the number of his supporters on it.

'Laurencio and I were popular with ordinary people, who had not liked Marco or his father or grandfather. Domenco wanted that we be better known outside Montello. We travelled to Torrago, the country's second largest city, and processed in triumph to the gate, where a wooden arch had been built for the occasion, with images of the sun and moon engraved above the words *Pax et Justitia*—peace and justice. There the mayor and aldermen greeted us and a girl, dressed as a nymph, gave Laurencio the silver keys of the city on a red, silk cushion, while an older woman, dressed as the goddess Ceres, presented me with a cornucopia, overflowing with corn and fruit. The crowd applauded. Then twenty sick people approached us, with ugly swellings on their necks and faces. They had the King's Evil. If the king touched them, they would be healed—or so they believed. He touched them all—one by one. I heard no more about them.

'I hoped that we go to other cities too, but Domenco decided that the visits were too expensive. After that, I saw ordinary people rarely, except on Sundays when Laurencio and I joined a procession of courtiers from the palace to the cathedral for the celebration of Mass. We walked slowly, because Domenco wanted that people should be able to present petitions to us. There were few at that time—mostly disputes about land.

'On other days, I stayed in the palace. Sometimes Domenco brought me documents to sign; sometimes I had to address meetings of the Council. But usually, I had not much to do. I felt lonely again, because I saw Laurencio little, except when we attended Council meetings or ceremonial banquets. Domenco was organising his education by now: languages, statecraft, fencing…'

'And natural philosophy?'

'Yes—and natural philosophy. Orostel was old now, but still he loved his potions. "Drink this," he said to me. "It is *aurum potabile*—drinkable gold. If mixed equally, it will grant you *vitam perpetuam, vitam sempiternam*, life everlasting." I still thought he talked nonsense, but he was harmless. His study was on the top floor of the palace. It was cold at night, because he kept open his window and stared at the sky through a telescope he had acquired in Italy. He said new stars had appeared in Cygnus—the Swan. The constellation was sacred to Favonia and the stars foretold great change.

'Quorino painted another portrait of my Laurencio. He was sitting on his pony and he looked so happy. Did you see it in the gallery? He painted me too.

I cared not to see my portrait, but I liked to talk to Quorino. He was very serious, but kindly. We used to look together at the paintings and frescoes in the gallery. There was a portrait by Titian of my father on a horse. He was a young man, but already he had the deep lines on his brow that I remember. I fear he was never a happy man. There was also a painting of him at the Battle of Lepanto. He was in a group of kings on the *Real*, the flagship of Don Juon of Austria. I had felt proud of him when I first saw the picture as a child. I learnt later that he was never at Lepanto.'

'Then why was it painted?'

'I know not. Favonia was part of the Holy League. I suppose the picture showed the strength of Christendom, united against the Ottomans.

'Another picture was by Semyarto. It showed King Solomon welcoming the Queen of Sheba. He had painted them with the features of my parents. It is the only picture I saw of my mother. She was beautiful. I know not how good was the likeness, but I stared at her a long time. Quorino admired the construction of the picture: how Solomon's back, as he bowed in greeting, formed a diagonal line with a camel's hump. The line stretched up to the sun in the top corner of the canvas. I listened, but I looked always at her face—her long dark hair, her blue eyes.

'Then two things happened. Domenco received news from Italy—I knew not what. But he sent Quorino to Rome. He told me that he was going to buy more paintings for the palace. It was part of Laurencio's education that he should learn to appreciate the grand masters of Europe. But I knew that Quorino was going as Domenco's agent.'

'You mean he was a spy?'

'If Domenco sent anyone anywhere, he had to keep his eyes and ears open… But I missed Quorino. I still went to the gallery, but I went alone. I stared long at the three Archangel tapestries. My father had brought these from Flanders. They were woven with silk and wool with gold and silver thread and they depicted Raphael as he accompanied Tobias on his journey; Gabriel bringing the good news to Our Lady; and Michael slaying the devil.

'On warm days, I would stroll in the palace grounds with Rosamaria. The square terrace was bordered with an avenue of yew hedges. At each corner was a statue: Justice, Prudence, Fortitude, Temperance. In the centre was a round pond, circled with flowerbeds where grew many exotic plants. Three more statues stood here: Faith with a cross and chalice; Hope, holding her anchor;

Charity, leading a child. And in the middle of the pond was the Swan of Favonia, water gushing out of its two beaks. I preferred to leave the terrace and walk down the dark lane, lined with cypress trees, which led to a waterfall and a hidden grotto: the Cave of Eternal Wisdom. Inside was a statue of Minerva.

'On cooler days, I read in the library. My father had assembled many books by persuading priests and nobles to bequeath their collections. Some were Catholic books, but others were humanist and also there were Islamic manuscripts. Some of them were condemned by the Inquisition, although no one said anything at that time.'

'You said two things happened. What was the other one?'

'The other thing was war. To placate the Holy Father, Domenco sent a battalion of 2,000 men under General Flirenzo to join the Habsburg forces in fighting the Protestant Bohemians. I was sad. Our soldiers were fighting Federico, the Elector of Palatine—he was the brother-in-law of my Prince Henry. How different everything might have been. And I felt so powerless. I was Queen Regent, but I could decide nothing. Domenco gave me a speech to read out to Council: "No kingdom is more averse to war than Favonia, but we must fight to preserve the true faith."

'But I believed not what I said.' She paused, looking mournful. Alex prompted her to continue.

'And what happened to Quorino?'

'He was away for more than a year. Domenco had given him money and letters of introduction to the Vatican and the Italian court. He had seen many paintings and had painted copies of many. His style changed after that. He became more interested in landscape. He also bought several canvases for the palace: a Tintoretto and a Correggio. Also, two paintings of Prince Laurencio of Favonia.'

'What? By Konrad Brassens?'

'One was. But it was not the painting you know. They were both pictures of a boy—about the same age as my Laurencio, but he looked very different. One was by Brassens, the other by Rubens.'

'But who was he? The prince, I mean.'

'According to Quorino, he was the son of Marco and Mathilde—the Huguenot woman whose marriage was annulled because it had not been consummated.'

'So, it must have been consummated after all?'

'I think not. But somewhere there was a boy claiming to be their son. Imagine Domenco's anger. He burnt the two paintings himself. Quorino was furious. No one should destroy paintings, he said—especially not one by Rubens. Domenco let it be known that the paintings had been lost at sea on the journey home. He hoped that he hear no more of the false Laurencio.

'Meanwhile, news was received that the Habsburg army had won a great victory at the Battle of White Mountain. Few soldiers had died on the winning side. There was great rejoicing and a service of thanksgiving was held in the cathedral. We all sang the *Te Deum*. Afterwards there were celebrations in the courtyard of this palace. There was a tournament with jousting and quintain in the afternoon and a masque with shepherds and nymphs dancing and playing panpipes in the evening. It was meant to show the triumph of peace over war. Domenco arranged everything and he was praised by many, although there were murmurings about the expense.'

'And were the soldiers treated as heroes?'

'They had not returned home yet. They had begun the long journey back through Italy, but then the General received a message to turn back to help the Spanish crush the Bohemian Revolt. I think Domenco wanted that they come home, but the church overruled him. He had seemed so powerful when he returned after the old Cardinal's death, but now he had to do what the church said. Those three men—the Nuncio, the Cardinal Archbishop and the Inquisitor General—held the power now. But wars cost money and Domenco had to raise it.'

'How did he do that?'

'By taxes. He introduced taxes on flour, ale and salt. Everyone had to pay, but few could afford it. Many were locked up for debt. Many beggars were on the city streets and I started to receive petitions as I processed to Mass. Peasants told me how they already had to pay tithes to the church and rents to their landlords. Now they had to pay tax on their food as well. If they could not pay, their landlords could not afford their own contributions.'

'What happened to the petitions?'

'Nothing. Domenco stopped the processions. I had to go to Mass by carriage. I liked it not. When I walked, I felt that I could share in the grief of my petitioners. But the carriage was a barrier between us. Now no one could talk to me and some threw stones. I was scared. Protesters were arrested and hanged.

'So Domenco increased discontent, but he raised little money. Then he made a big mistake: he started to tax the clergy. Suddenly the church was his friend no longer and plotters against Domenco saw their chance. Noblemen who had been ministers in the old Council and favourites of the queen were meeting bishops and telling them of their suspicions about Domenco: how he had been prepared that I convert to Protestantism in order to marry Henry; how the library contained books on the Index; how his grandmother had been Jewish. I feared lest they spread rumours that he was the father of my Laurencio, but they dared not criticise royalty. Many came to see me—the Condo of Somewhere, the Duquo of Somewhere Else... They all swore allegiance to me, but urged that I dismiss Domenco. I was angry. I hated Domenco now. He had betrayed me. How could I not hate him? But he was still my Laurencio's father. And I saw what he had achieved. He had done that which was impossible: for a few years, he had united the church and the nobility. Now that he was in difficulty, all the nobles were opposing him. They said that they wanted what was best for Favonia; I knew they just wanted power for themselves.

'Domenco published broadsides, celebrating a further victory at the Battle of Wimpfen, but no one cared about Wimpfen. No one had heard of the place. And other pamphlets appeared, which condemned Spain and the Habsburgs—they said they were becoming too powerful in Europe and we ought not to support them. They also criticised the cost of the war and demanded that the soldiers come home. Some even argued that we should support the Elector. They published handbills showing the wheel of fortune, with the Favonian swan and the Palatine lion perched on the top, while the Habsburg eagle lay crushed beneath the wheel. So, there were still practising Protestants in Favonia. I remember one handbill which said, "Hell reigns where there is no peace with God."

'Then the first soldiers *did* return—those not fit enough to fight at Wimpfen. It was true that few Catholic soldiers had died at White Mountain, but many were wounded. They came home in carts. Some had lost a leg or an arm; others were covered in bandages. Many others had died on the way home—from their injuries or from fever. Still others had been killed for looting. No one was rejoicing now.

'Now the plots against Domenco were increasing. He cancelled the clergy tax, but he was too late—the damage had been done. And still he needed money.

The soldiers were deserting or joining other armies—armies which could pay them.

'But no one predicted the events of St John's Eve, 1622. Always bonfires are lit on that evening. Women bring bunches of herbs—St John's Wort, fennel, rosemary—to the cathedral, so that they be blessed. Then a man, dressed only in camel skins like the saint, leads the priests and monks in a procession to the city square. The priests swing their censers and all carry lighted tapers, which they use to light a bonfire in the square. Young men take their sweethearts' hands and jump through the flames to affirm their engagement. Effigies of witches are burnt.

'But that year it was different. There was another effigy on the bonfire: Domenco's. As it burnt, the crowd cheered. Then some apprentices, who had spent the holy day drinking ale, grabbed flaming branches from the fire and ran through the town, setting fences alight and cursing Domenco. Several houses were burnt and the gates of the palace. Then the palace guard rode out and struck the rioters with their swords. Many died. Others were arrested.

'Domenco immediately wrote a proclamation which heralds read throughout the city. He wrote that rioters would be killed on sight, that assemblies of more than three people would be illegal, that now was the time for a strong leader.

'Many people agreed with him, but he was no longer that leader. Members of the Council were opposing him, even some of those whom he had appointed himself. They came to Laurencio and me. They swore their loyalty to the Crown and begged that we support their faction. I despised them all.

'But power was still with the church. Its leaders were no longer supporting Domenco and he made another mistake. He realised that the war was unpopular and expensive. He declared a ceasefire and ordered General Flirenzo to bring his battalion—or what remained of it—home. He wrote a pamphlet in which he attacked the Christian doctrine of a "just war". He quoted Erasmus to justify his opinion.

'But he misjudged. The common people wanted an end to the war, but they cared not about Erasmus—even if they could read. And the Catholic leaders were furious. For them, the war was a holy crusade against Protestantism. They condemned Erasmus, whose books were on the Index.

'Now Domenco's enemies were everywhere. Opponents of the war and its expense hated him. Catholic supporters of the war hated him. From the Vatican, the Holy Father was criticising him for withdrawing from the Catholic League against Protestantism. From Madrid, the Condo-Duquo Olivares—King Filippo's First Minister—sent a deputation, begging that he continue fighting. From Paris, the Cardinal Richelieu urged him against supporting Spain.

'Then the Council came to him as a group. They told him that they were going to denounce him to the Inquisition. He chose the better option: self-exile. The next day, he and his wife quietly left the palace in an unmarked carriage and drove away. I never saw him again.'

'Did you feel sorry for him?'

'A little. He had been part of my life for as long as I remembered. Suddenly he was gone. And his replacements were no better. These councillors who were advising me now were as hungry for power as he was. But Laurencio was a little older by now. I thought perhaps we could rule together and ignore the Council as much as possible.'

'You wanted absolute monarchy?'

'Perhaps. But we were forgetting the church. The Cardinal, the Nuncio and the Inquisitor General decided everything. So, the war continued, although we sent few soldiers. We could not afford them, but we had to keep happy the Pope.'

'And were *you* happy?'

'I lived for my Laurencio. Soon we accepted that we had little power. We let the Council and the church argue amongst themselves. We did as we were told. We had to save money. The palace where I lived after my father's death was pulled down and the building materials sold. We dismissed many staff. But we were still Queen Regent and King. If we stayed distant from the arguments of church and Council, we stayed distant from people's dislike of them. Laurencio and I were popular again. We processed to Mass once more and received people's petitions. And as Laurencio grew older, he began to enjoy life. He took mistresses. I approved not, but everyone tolerated his actions. And then he married—Teresa, the niece of the Duquo of Savoy.'

'And did you hear any more about Domenco?'

'We heard many rumours—often he was at battles or other important events. We had news from him at the coronation of Carlo (my Henry's brother), at the surrender of Breda, at the Treaty of Monzón, at the Battle of Nördlingen. And usually, we heard that the other Laurencio was with him.'

'Really? So, he was a threat to your son?'

'I feared that he be. I think Domenco was plotting. Always he plotted. Perhaps he wanted that the other Laurencio be king in exile. Perhaps he wanted at last that they invade Favonia. But he was getting old by now. I think he was no danger. And then the news stopped. After Nördlingen, there was nothing. I heard not of Domenco or the other Laurencio. My own Laurencio was safe at last.'

She stood up. 'It is time I leave. Thank you for listening to my story.'

'Thank you for telling it to me. By the way, what happened to Orostel, the alchemist? Was he dismissed with the other staff?'

'No, that was one time when the three Catholic leaders disagreed. In 1623, the Holy Father issued 'Omnipotentis Dei'—a declaration against magicians and witches. The Inquisitor General said Orostel must die, but the Nuncio said No— the Pope had ruled that the death penalty be necessary only if a person entered into a compact with the devil. No one could think that of Orostel. So, he stayed in the palace, mixing potions. "Drink this," he said to me again. "Here is life everlasting."'

She shook Alex's hand. He watched as she walked towards the door of the café and waved as she turned to smile at him one last time.

***

'Hi Alex. How was your week off? Did you go away?'

'Hi Kath. Yes, I was in Exeter—staying with my parents. Didn't do much. Just relaxed.'

'Back to Mum's cooking? Oh, by the way, do you remember that painting by Brassens? The one that was meant to be of King Laurence? Well, I met the curator of the exhibition and she agreed to look into it. I've just heard from her. It turns out that there was a mix-up in an old catalogue which had never been corrected. Brassens never painted Laurence at all.'

'So, who was it in the picture?'

'I don't think it was anyone in particular. The painting was called *A Vision.* That's all I know…'

Appendix 1

The Favonian Royal Family

Marco II m Francesca of Savoy
1489-1562   *1491-1521*

Fernando II m Cristiana of Denmark   Alphonso m Erica of Austria   Eduardo III m Marian of Navarre
1510-1556   *1515-1556*   *1515-1556*   *1533-1602*   *1518-1601*   *1527-1596*

Marco III m Thérèse of Valois   Sophia   m   **Laurencio I**   Federico
1530-1599   *1569-1592*   *b 1553*   *1545-1615*   *1550-1611*

Juliana   Marco IV
b 1592   *b 1590*

Appendix 2

The Stuart Dynasty

James VI of Scotland (James I of England) m Anne of Denmark

1566-1625   *1574-1619*

Henry Frederick   Charles I m Henrietta Maria of France   Elizabeth m Frederick V, Elector Palatine

1594-1612   *1600-1649*   *1609-1669*   *1596-1662*   *1596-1632*

On the Thames

The event was not intended for people on their own. Barbara realised this as she stepped off the Thames path, just outside the walls of the Tower of London, and walked down the gangway. She was surrounded by couples. A steward helped her to board the boat; another checked her name on the list and led her to a seat next to the window, through which she could see across the river to the old warship—'HMS Belfast,' she read.

Stephen would have loved a river cruise. What a shame that they hadn't organised one earlier—as soon as they had both retired. But he could never be bothered to do anything. If only she had taken the initiative before his stroke put an end to any possibility of joint outings.

Still, it was good of Joe and Sheila to buy the ticket for her and to look after Stephen for an afternoon. She was determined to enjoy herself.

A man was shown to the empty seat opposite her. So, she was to have a companion after all. She said, 'Hello,' and he echoed her. Would he say anything else? Did she want him to say anything else? He looked a little older than she was, tall, balding, a little stooped, but still good looking. Although it was a warm, dry day, he kept on his long raincoat. She had a sudden fear that he might be a flasher. Then she immediately felt ashamed: how likely was he to expose himself in front of all these people?

Stewards were bringing around plates of sandwiches and cakes, pots of tea and coffee. Barbara and her new companion both chose tea. She added milk and passed him the jug.

'Plenty to eat,' she said.

'Yes,' he replied, 'but I have to be careful.'

She thought of saying, 'Why? You're not overweight.' But she decided not to. It might have sounded too flattering. She wasn't chatting him up. She had a sick husband at home. She helped herself to a salmon sandwich.

The boat was moving now. They were travelling downstream, away from the Tower on the north bank, away from the Shard, which dwarfed all the buildings on the south bank. They went under Tower Bridge. Stephen would have loved to see that; he would have explained the mechanism to raise and lower it.

The tide was low. Below Butler's Wharf was an exposed beach. It was like the seaside. Barbara thought of trips to Brighton 60 years ago: the sand, the sea, the piers.

They were now passing some grassland on the south bank.

'That's the site of Edward III's manor house, that is,' said the man in the raincoat. 'Built about 1350. And that's the Angel pub—1830s, I think.'

'You're very knowledgeable,' said Barbara.

'Oh, I used to live near here as a boy. Look at the wooden pillars supporting the Angel. You wouldn't see them at high tide.'

Barbara couldn't think of an answer, so she just smiled, as she started to eat an egg and cress sandwich. She looked through the window on the other side of the boat, over the heads of the other passengers. The buildings on Canary Wharf dominated the Isle of Dogs. They had seemed so massive, so modern when constructed. Now the city skyline was punctuated with towering office blocks.

'I remember that area before the new buildings,' said the man. 'When ordinary people used to live there. Before the office workers took over. There was poverty—yes—but there was community, there was atmosphere.'

This sounded like a prepared speech. Barbara didn't know how to respond. 'I wish I'd seen it,' she said.

A steward re-filled her teacup. She sat in silence for several minutes, drinking, enjoying the motion, looking at the bank without focusing on anything.

'This is Greenwich Reach,' said her companion. Barbara wasn't sure what a reach was, but she had been to Greenwich. She remembered the park, although it was not visible behind the riverside buildings.

'There's the Cutty Sark.' She looked at the tea-clipper, surrounded by tourists.

'And that building with the round walls—that's the end of the foot-tunnel. I used to go through there as a boy. I remember running through it the first time. I was so out of breath. Couldn't think why, because I was fit in those days. It was the lack of oxygen underground, you see. It's all different now. I get out of breath whenever I walk anywhere now.'

Stephen had got breathless quickly for several years. She should have made him go to the doctor.

The boat was turning around now, moving towards the bank of the Isle of Dogs, before beginning the return journey.

'Mudchute Park,' said the man.

'You're an excellent tour guide. Would you like one of these cakes?' They had finished the sandwiches.

'Better not,' he replied.

She helped herself to a small profiterole, looking around at the other passengers, who all seemed to be demolishing their cakes greedily.

'It's rather hot, isn't it?' he said.

'I don't mind if you take your coat off,' said Barbara, nervously. Was she inviting him to expose himself to her?

Cautiously, he undid two of the buttons.

'It's tricky, you see. I'm all wired up.' The gaps revealed a large wire hanging around his neck.

Barbara looked concerned, while feeling guilty about her earlier fears.

'It's all right. It's only a blood pressure monitor. My GP texted me to say I need to have it checked—it's because of the tablets I'm on. I saw the practice nurse today. I thought she'd just take a single reading, but she said I'd got to wear all this apparatus for 24 hours.'

'Oh, don't worry. It's much better to have it monitored throughout the day,' Barbara replied, feigning an expertise she didn't possess. 'A single reading isn't always reliable.' Why hadn't she told Stephen to have his blood pressure checked? She was silent again. She drank some more tea.

'We're going past Wapping now. That's the Prospect of Whitby pub.' He pointed to a building overlooking the north bank.

'I suppose you've been drinking there as well?'

'Of course—long ago, mind you. I'm careful these days.'

'It looks a nice pub. There must be a good view over the river.'

'Yes. The staff are friendly too.' He looked wistful. Surely he could still go into a pub, even if he didn't want to drink alcohol anymore?

The tea was almost cold now, but Barbara drained her cup. She didn't eat any more cakes. They sat in silence.

Soon they were going under Tower Bridge again and returning to the landing stage. As the men on the quayside moored the boat, the staff inside all lined up by the exit, with collection plates on display.

'They make it a bit obvious, don't they,' said the man. 'I'll put something in for both of us.'

'Thank you,' replied Barbara. She felt he was being too presumptuous. She would have liked to determine how much of a tip she wanted to give. They weren't a couple. It was not for him to decide the amount. However, it would have been cruel of her to give some money after his offer. Instead, she simply thanked the staff, as one of them helped her on to the landing stage.

'I'm going to Tower Hill tube now,' said the man in the raincoat. 'How about you?'

Tower Hill would have been good for her, but she pondered for a minute. Ought she to invite him to go somewhere with her—a pub or a café? But they had both drunk too much tea and he had implied that he didn't drink alcohol now. Besides, she wanted to get back to Stephen, wanted to relieve Joe and Sheila.

'I think I'd better go to London Bridge,' she said. 'I enjoyed our little chat.' This was true, although the conversation had been one-sided: he had asked her nothing about herself. 'My name's Barbara, by the way.'

'It was nice talking to you, Barbara. I'm Ernie.'

'Well, goodbye then, Ernie.' She waved and began to walk along the Thames path towards London Bridge.

Slowly Through the Wood and Darkly

They noticed him as soon as they sat down. He was at the far end of the café, staring at them. At first, Lauren felt affronted. How dare he stare at her like that, the old lecher? But the stare, though intense, was not lecherous. It was a long time since anyone had looked at her with so much interest, she thought, glancing briefly at Adam beside her. She relaxed, opened her book and began to read.

Adam was wondering how he ought to react to the man. Should he stand up and challenge him? He knew he would only make a fool of himself. He too opened his book, but he found it difficult to concentrate. He had an unpleasant morning ahead of him. These few minutes with Lauren in the café on a Monday morning normally felt part of the weekend, even its culmination. Today they couldn't obliterate the problems to come. He had a meeting with his boss at 10 o'clock to discuss the departmental budget: James would be expecting to see a spreadsheet, clearly setting out this year's and next year's figures, showing at least a 10% saving. Despite the early hour, Adam should have been at the office already, collating the figures.

Lauren was also anticipating a busy morning, but *her* boss was away on a business trip, so she would have control of her workload, could set her own priorities. She was enjoying the last few pages of her novel, pausing only to sip her coffee.

Adam's eyes refused to focus on the text in front of him. The book—a study of marriage and the family in eighteenth century England—had absorbed him the evening before, but now he wished that he had brought something lighter, something to distract him from those ominous budget figures. He looked up. The man was still staring at them. Lauren, having finished her book, looked up as well. She smiled at the stranger.

He had stood up now and was approaching them. A tall, bearded, weather-beaten man of middle age. He was smiling in a friendly manner.

'Excuse me.' The accent was American. 'I was just wondering if you had ever read *Slowly through the wood and darkly*?'

'No,' said Lauren. 'Who's it by?'

'It's by Omero Martinez.'

'Is it a novel?' asked Adam.

'Sure, it's a novel. I recommend it to you—to both of you.'

It was still early when Lauren arrived at the office. Having checked her emails to make sure there was nothing urgent, she logged on to Amazon and searched for *Slowly through the wood and darkly*. It was there, available in print or digitally. She ordered the digital version, entered her credit card details and downloaded it to her Caterpillar. The book was hers in just two minutes. For a few moments, she felt a wistful regret. She used to enjoy the excitement of going into a bookshop, often failing to find the book she was looking for, yet leaving with one still more enticing because of its unexpectedness. But who had time for bookshops these days? She settled down to her work.

Adam's morning was as stressful as he had feared. He managed to type all the figures on to the budget spreadsheet, but he didn't have time to check them. He felt sure that James would point out some mistakes. Sure enough, he asked Adam to justify two numbers in the next year's column and Adam's response was unconvincing. He was dismissed after an hour, with instructions to submit the budget again by noon. Although he was able to meet this new deadline, his other work suffered. By 12.40, he had had enough. He left the office, walking briskly for ten minutes, stamping out the frustrations of the morning. Then he reached the public library, a favourite lunchtime refuge.

He went straight to the fiction shelves, to the letter M. To his delight, the book was there: *Slowly through the wood and darkly* by Omero Martinez. He ignored the design on the front cover; he didn't read the summary on the back. He wanted nothing to pre-empt his response to this book which he had been urged to read. Having borrowed it, he left the library and entered the café next door. At precisely 1.08, a panini in front of him, he began to read.

He had mixed feelings about the book. Although he enjoyed historical fiction, he wanted it to be properly researched, so that it could add to his understanding of the period. This one was full of mannered archaisms: "Forsooth", "Gadzooks", "Prithee, Sir Knight". He doubted if courtiers would have been speaking English at all at that time. Nevertheless, he liked the atmosphere: the description of the horses and dogs being prepared for the hunting expedition in the forest was exciting. He could almost smell the animals' breath as they panted in anticipation of the chase. He liked too the character of Piers, the young squire—a reluctant member of the party—even if his concerns about animal cruelty and his sense of alienation seemed anachronistic: would anyone in the Middle Ages really have thought like that?

Lauren had had a productive morning. By one o'clock, she was ready for lunch. Hurrying down to the staff restaurant, she bought a sandwich and took it back to her desk. Eight minutes later, having switched on her Caterpillar, she began to read the digital book she had bought.

She was quickly engrossed in the story, even though the subject was unoriginal: a women-only society, trying to live in harmony with nature, deep in a forest. She questioned the viability of the smallholding they had established, with just a few hens, a vegetable garden and some fruit trees. However, she liked the characters: Octavia, attempting to espouse the anarchist principles of the commune, though inevitably becoming its leader; Zenobia, who, as the daughter of a gamekeeper, knew every inch of the forest, while lacking the self-conviction to challenge Octavia effectively; Francesca, who had opted out of conventional city life in order to join the women of the forest, but who now found herself yearning to escape from this society too. Francesca was Lauren's favourite character.

When Adam arrived home that evening, Lauren was already cooking supper. The pasta was simmering in the pan while she stirred the final ingredients into the sauce. Adam started to prepare a salad, describing the meeting with James as he worked. Lauren listened sympathetically, but not uncritically—she would have handled James very differently. Neither mentioned the book which both had started reading. They felt that the American's recommendation, although explicitly addressed to them both, had been intended for one person only and did not concern the other.

They ate the meal while watching a documentary about deforestation and the growth of cities. Afterwards, without discussing the programme, Lauren went to the room they used as their study, saying she needed to complete some work. Adam washed up, before lying down on the bed to resume reading *Slowly through the wood and darkly*.

Piers and Adam were both disgusted by the climax of the hunt, as the hounds brought the stag crashing to the ground and Sir Robert Fitzhugh, leaping from his horse, cut the deer's throat. Then there was rejoicing over the body while the courtiers passed around a flagon of wine. Piers ignored the revelry and escaped into the density of the forest, walking so far that he could no longer hear the shouting and singing. At last, he heard the winding of the horn, signalling that the hunt was about to resume. He began to hurry back, forcing his way under branches, scrambling through vicious brambles. He had no idea which way he had come and was hoping to hear the horn once again, but all was silence. He continued walking without any sense of where he was going. He was lost.

Adam was wandering, deep in the wood. He kept finding small paths which petered out just as he thought they were leading somewhere. Then he woke in a panic, still stretched out fully dressed on his bed. He staggered up and went to the bathroom to brush his teeth. On his way back to bed, he opened the study door.

'You're not still working, are you?' he asked.

Lauren looked up from her Caterpillar.

'No, just reading. I'll come to bed soon.'

In the forest, Jocasta was ill. She sat all day in her tent, coughing loudly and incessantly. Loretta administered medicines regularly: a potion made of St John's wort and comfrey, a balm of rosemary oil for her chest. A herbal candle flickered. Nothing seemed to do any good. Octavia convened a meeting.

'The question is,' she said, 'do we continue with natural remedies or do we need to go back to the city to get some conventional medicine?'

'I think we've got to get some other medicine,' said Zenobia. 'Loretta's treatment isn't working.'

'That's because I don't have the right ingredients,' replied Loretta. She hated anyone questioning her expertise. 'I need ginger, aniseed, turmeric.'

'Well, we'll still have to go to the city for those.'

'Are you sure we shouldn't let nature just take its course?' asked Alicia. 'If the natural remedies don't work, perhaps it's because it's Jocasta's time to die.'

Francesca was furious. 'Of course, we've got to do what we can to help her. We've got to go to the city—to the health stores or the chemist. I don't know which. Probably both.'

'Are you prepared to go, then?' asked Octavia.

'Yes, if everyone else is too scared.'

'I'll lead you through the forest,' said Zenobia. 'You'll be lost otherwise.'

They left the next morning. There was no path, but Zenobia didn't need one. To her, every tree was different, each an infallible signpost. She ducked under branches, crawled through undergrowth, jumped over streams, Francesca struggling to keep up with her. They spoke little, intent only on the journey. At last, after more than three hours, they reached the end of the forest and stared out at the plain. Rising above it were the office blocks, cranes and high-rise flats of the city.

'You're on your own now,' said Zenobia. 'I'll wait for you here at sundown.'

Having switched off her Caterpillar, Lauren got ready for bed. When she squeezed under the duvet, Adam was already asleep.

Adam left home early the next morning. It was not that he was anxious to arrive at work in good time; he wanted to ensure that he would have a seat on the train so that he could continue reading uninterrupted.

Piers wandered anxiously through the forest. He couldn't decide whether he should be searching for his colleagues or trying to find a way out of the wood. He hoped that by continuing to walk, he would succeed in one or other aim. However, he couldn't be sure that he wasn't walking around in circles: every tree, every clearing looked the same.

But at last, he saw daylight through the branches. Hurrying towards it, he found himself at the edge of the wood, with a plain stretching out in front of him. Above the plain was a hill, covered with buildings. But they were not the buildings of Sir Robert's castle, nor the hovels of one of the nearby hamlets. These buildings formed a large city, although a very different one from Winchester, which Piers had visited once. Lofty towers, consisting mainly of glass, reflected the afternoon sun. Several roads led into the city, with strange, metallic, horseless vehicles racing along in both directions.

Adam was surprised. He hadn't expected this juxtaposition of a medieval forest and a 21st century city. He wasn't convinced that it was successful, although he had to admire the author's skill in evoking the two contradictory worlds. He shared Piers' awe and dismay as he stared out at the unfamiliar scene.

Lauren left later. The tube was crowded; there was no room to read. She stood, squashed between a large man and a massive suitcase; its owner was trying to look as though it had nothing to do with him. Lauren shut her eyes and thought about the conference which she had been asked to attend in her boss's absence. It would certainly be boring; would it be unbearably so?

Soon she was sitting at the back of the lecture hall, her Caterpillar on her knee. She had extended the gadget so that two screens were visible. From time to time, she would type a few of the speaker's words on to the right screen, making it appear that she was paying attention: "Leveraging the synergies", "Embracing fungibility", "Upskill or outsource". Later she would write a report for her boss, a separate bullet point for each phrase. She could picture him nodding in agreement with each piece of meaningless gobbledegook. If only Adam could realise how easy it was to please a boss.

In between typing, she was secretly reading the text on the left-hand screen.

Francesca ran across the plain until she reached the first main road. The noise of the traffic was overpowering as she walked along the narrow pavement into the city. She was feeling nervous. After nearly three years away, she wasn't sure if she could cope with city life again: the speed, the crowds, the oppressive buildings. But at the same time, she felt excited. Life in the forest, which had once seemed so radical, so unconventional, had long ago become boring. She had developed no close friendships with the other women. She respected Zenobia for her woodcraft, but there was no warmth between them, while she despised Octavia for her bossiness. In the city, anything could happen; she might meet anybody.

As she stepped on to the escalator leading up to the shopping centre, she began to change her mind. She felt hatred towards the crowds of people ascending and descending in mindless anonymity. At the top, she quickly located a chemist's shop, but she lingered a few minutes before entering. She felt nervous about the transaction. Although Octavia had given her some money, she had no credit card. Technology had been changing so quickly at the time she entered the forest; would anyone still use cash?

Lauren was urging Francesca on. At last, remembering that Jocasta's health might be dependent on her successful expedition, she entered the shop. Quickly she found various cough treatments and chose two of them. At the check-out, she experienced a momentary panic as the assistant directed her to the self-service queue. Ignoring this, she was soon served by a live person, who, despite looking shocked at Francesca's dirty clothes, accepted her money without question.

The health food shop was on the same level of the centre. Francesca found the ingredients which Loretta had requested and paid for them. There were still three hours to sundown. What should she do until then? She saw a coffee shop and felt an instant craving. She had drunk enough chicory and nettle tea to last a lifetime. Sitting near the entrance, she sipped her cappuccino and gazed at the people walking past, wondering whether she wanted to be part of their world again.

Adam had an undisturbed morning. He worked hard and felt that he deserved his lunch break. In the café, he opened his book again.

Piers walked tentatively across the plain towards the city. The only way into it seemed to be by one of the roads with their terrifying metal and glass vehicles rushing interminably to and fro. He stood on the pavement, deafened by the noise. Then he walked nervously until he arrived at the city.

There were more vehicles, but there were also people, moving around in ones and twos. He had never seen so many people, all of them dressed oddly. He almost screamed when he saw dozens of them rising up a magic, metal staircase. He watched as others set foot on it and eventually, he did the same, worried that this might be the last step he ever took. To his surprise, he found the experience pleasurable: the staircase moved slowly, allowing him to look around at all the people and vehicles on the streets below, at the large glass buildings towering above him. He tripped as he stepped off the staircase. Now he had to walk again, but at least there were no vehicles up here. He felt relatively safe.

What were all these people doing? They were walking in and out of a series of glass-fronted rooms. How they loved glass in this city. A few people talked to each other, a few had young children, but most seemed to be on their own. They carried heavy bags and when they emerged from the rooms, they were carrying even more. Was this a market? If so, what was everyone buying? Piers was feeling lost—more lost than he had felt in the depths of the forest.

Then he saw another room, glass-fronted like the others, but for once the people inside were not rushing. Instead, they were sitting around tables, eating and drinking, some of them talking, some reading, some holding strange devices, busily pressing buttons with their fingers.

Just next to the door, a young woman was sitting alone, an empty seat next to her. She was dressed as strangely as all the others, but he found himself attracted to her and wondered if she were of gentle birth. Her clothes were torn and muddy, suggesting that she was a peasant, but she seemed to be living a life of ease, sitting there, drinking from a steaming chalice. Approaching her, he removed his hat and, bowing, addressed her:

'Prithee, beauteous damsel, wilt thou grant me the honour of sitting at thy fair right hand?'

Adam frowned. These false archaisms didn't work. They were inconsistent: the author conveyed Piers' thoughts in modern English; it was only in his utterances that he used this antique phraseology. How would the woman respond?

After the lecture, the delegates split into small discussion groups. Lauren put away her Caterpillar and tried to look interested. She even made a few comments—some obvious points, but profundity was not expected nor, she guessed, would it have been welcomed. The discussion was followed by a "networking buffet lunch". Lauren didn't network, on principle. She took some sandwiches into one of the break-out rooms and continued reading, an imaginary "Do not disturb" sign positioned clearly beside her.

As she gazed at the people hurrying past, Francesca saw a young man in fancy-dress approaching her. He wore a long green coat (very dirty), a large, plumed hat, black leggings and pointed, muddy shoes. What was he doing here? Maybe he was a student collecting for Rag Week. Well, she wasn't going to give him anything. She lowered her head, determined not to look at him, but she was too late. He swept off his hat, made a flamboyant bow and spoke to her.

'Prithee, beauteous damsel, wilt thou grant me the honour of sitting at thy fair right hand?'

She scowled. 'Sit down if you must,' she said. She wished she had something to read, something to show unequivocally that she didn't want to talk. Remembering the medicines she had bought, she opened one of the boxes and began studying the information leaflet, feigning an interest in side-effects and contra-indications.

Lauren wondered what the author was planning. She had thought that the book was contrasting an idealistic life in the forest with the turbulence of a city existence. What was the significance of this interloper?

Adam looked at his watch. He ought to be leaving now if he were to be back at work on time, but he had so nearly finished the book that it was a shame to be interrupted. He hoped no one would notice if he were a few minutes late.

Piers heard the woman answer him: 'Sit down if you must.' Her scowl did not encourage him to speak again immediately. Instead, he took a piece of rolled-up parchment from his pack. It was a sonnet he had written for Sir Robert's niece. He read it to himself, wondering if he dared read it aloud:

At dusk I heard the tuneful nightingale
And thought my lady sang a serenade,
Deep in the forest, in some secret glade,
Beneath the moon, mysterious and pale.
I woke at dawn to hear, above the vale,
The laverock singing, clear and unafraid,
And thought it was my dearest love who played
A sweet aubade, which told a sweeter tale.
And now at noon-time nobly shines the sun,
His beams enlightening all the pasture green,
While I from out the casement stand and stare.
But where art thou, my own, my only one?
No trace of thy pure beauty can be seen,
No vestige of thy wondrous, golden hair.

He would have to change the reference to "golden", he thought as he glanced at the dark-haired woman beside him; otherwise, she might like it.

'You can't read her that,' thought Adam. 'She'll kill you.'

It was nearly 2 o'clock. He should have been back at his desk by now. Meanwhile, Lauren noticed that her fellow-delegates, still enthusiastically networking, were filing into the lecture hall for the final, plenary session. Adam and Lauren continued reading—reading about Piers who was rehearsing his poem, reading about Francesca who was studying the leaflet.

A voice interrupted them. To Piers, the accent was strange, but no stranger than any of the others in this strange city. Francesca recognised it as American.

'Excuse me. I was just wondering if you had ever read *Slowly through the wood and darkly*?'

Alan's Tower

Alan had come upon the garden fête by chance. It was for a good cause and he was happy to spend more than his 50p entrance fee, but, as he strolled across the damp grass, he could see nothing very attractive. He felt tempted by the sideshows and gazed wistfully at the coconut shy. However, he was thirty years older than the boys who were monopolising the synthetic coconuts. He turned to the stalls, where he was a relative youngster.

The clothes stall was impossible. It was surrounded by jumble sale aficionados, elbows splayed to prevent anyone from beating them to a bargain. The plant stall was calmer, but Alan had no space for any more plants. Next to that was "Grandma's Attic", a trellis table, sparsely covered with a few candlesticks, a copper kettle, a garish toby jug and a pair of white spats.

That left the book stall. Surely there would be something there to interest him?

At first, he was disappointed. He glanced along the rows of romances, the outdated school textbooks, the car maintenance manuals for models which should have been in transport museums. Underneath the table, there were boxes of magazines and pamphlets which were apparently thought too dreary to display: a set of "Reader's Digests", some religious tracts and a collection marked "Travel: 3 for 10p". Evidently, the organisers had little hope of selling these. As Alan leafed through them, he could understand why: they included travel supplements from newspapers and brochures from ferry companies. But there were also some guidebooks. He picked out a leaflet about the San Marco in Venice and a more substantial book about the church in Lymington—he had visited it once while on a walking holiday in the New Forest. He would take those two and he might as well choose a third—just to gain his 10p's worth. He thumbed through the remainder of the box and was about to pick one item at random when he saw a booklet which almost made him drop the two he was holding: "Blackthorn Heights: a National Trust guide".

It was published in 1996—five years earlier and twenty-five years since he had last been there. He skimmed through the opening pages, glancing at the photographs—it all looked much tidier and better-maintained than he remembered. Still, he had to buy it. Having paid the stallholder, he walked to the refreshments tent, where he bought a scone and a cup of tea. Then he sat down and opened the guidebook.

He started to look at the pictures in more detail. There was one of the heath in winter, snow covering the trees and children tobogganing down the slope. Another was a Victorian photograph of a group of whiskered men in hats, who had been hare-coursing on the Heights. A third showed the tower—Alan's tower.

Of course, the tower didn't really belong to Alan. How could it have done? Yet in all the times he had visited it during his adolescence, he had met only one other person there. He could still remember his indignation at seeing that intruder; he felt the same sensation now. The book, in depicting the tower, was making it publicly available. It even gave it a name—Dilston's Folly—and a history. It had been built by Lord Dilston in 1784, at a point where it could be seen, dominating the hillside, from the windows of his hall in the valley. Alan had never wanted to know the reason for the tower's existence. It was simply there—that had been enough.

He had always known that other people must have been aware of its presence. It was so near the popular parts of the Heights—no more than half a mile from the car park and picnic area where Grandad had taken him so often as a child. They would stand at the viewing point on the edge of the hill and Grandad would point to the town where he lived in the valley and to the higher hills beyond. Then they would walk past the picnickers and the boys playing football, and into the wood. Alan was scared the first time they went along those tree-lined tracks. Everything seemed so dark after the bright sunshine on the open heathland. But there was no cause for alarm—they met plenty of other walkers before returning to the car park, where Grandad bought them each an ice-cream.

After that, Alan insisted on going to Blackthorn Heights every time he visited Grandad. Then, one summer day, when he was twelve, he was allowed to go there by himself.

At first, he felt lonely. He missed Grandad's chatter—his reminiscences about his boyhood on the heath: the tree where he had attached a rope and swung precariously over the edge of the hill; the slope which he had raced down with his school friends. But once he entered the wood, Alan started to enjoy the solitude, seeing and hearing things with his own senses, rather than relying on another's experiences, another's responses. How often, he wondered, had he walked past that small grass path without noticing it?

He would have missed it that time too if he had not heard the sudden crack of a broken twig in the undergrowth. There, on the track in front of him, was a hare. It stood, motionless, for a few seconds. Then, with a long sideways leap, it started running along that path. He watched it, its long ears erect, its massive hind legs driving it along and out of sight.

Alan followed, though with no hope of catching up with it. The path led out of the dark wood into the open, sunny air. No longer were there huge beech and oak trees on either side of him, but small hawthorns and rowans. There were flowers too: willow herb and meadowsweet. But Alan felt uneasy. He had grown accustomed to the dark, woodland tracks. Here he felt exposed, vulnerable. Certainly, other people had walked here before him, but not recently—the grass was long and untrampled.

Then he saw the tower.

It stood on a ridge: a tall, square, flint tower, with a parapet, slightly ruined. Tentatively, Alan approached it. Despite a sensation that he was being watched, he forced himself to walk around the structure. It had no door, but there was a large, arched window, three feet off the ground. Through this, he could see a pine tree growing up through the centre of the tower, its topmost branches protruding above the parapet. Alan was too frightened to go close to the window. He crept around the tower, sure that someone was about to leap out on him. Suddenly, there was a movement under his feet. He jumped backwards, just as the hare bounded away in front of him, before disappearing into a clump of bracken.

Still scared, Alan hurried back to the main track, where, to his relief, he saw a young couple, arms around each other, walking towards the picnic area. He followed them, trying to look unconcerned, but anxious not to lose sight of them until he reached the more populated areas of the heath.

He had not intended the tower to be a secret. Usually, he told Grandad everything. It was one of the pleasures of visiting him, for he always had time to listen. But Alan's parents were staying there too; they complicated everything. Dad, though in his forties, still behaved as if Grandad were a tyrannical father. He seemed scared of him and they could never hold a normal, relaxed conversation. Mum was different: she treated him as an old man, speaking loudly and slowly to him, although his hearing was still good.

In this atmosphere, a discussion of the tower was out of the question. After that, maintaining its secrecy became a habit. No one else would understand its significance, because no one else could experience it in his imagination.

So, Alan had claimed the tower as his own. There it stood, fixed in his memory, a beacon defining his adolescence. How many times had he seen it during those years?

Yes, how many times? He took another sip of tea and counted. Six times perhaps—seven at the most. Had he exaggerated its importance? Had that last, momentous adventure shaped his experience of previous visits? He tried to think of his life as a teenager: at home, at school, with friends in the park, on holiday. The tower seemed to dominate each recalled vignette. It was as though he were looking at a photograph album and each photo contained a superimposed image of the tower. But had he stamped that image only after his final visit?

Alan used to stay with Grandad for a week each year—usually in the summer. And so, during each visit, Grandad would continue to drive to the top of the Heights and park there. He didn't walk as much as he used to, but he was happy to sit in his folding chair, a handkerchief over his head, gazing out over the valley. This left Alan free to go on his pilgrimage alone. He would stride through the woodland and then, checking to make sure no one was looking, would disappear down the grassy track. Always he would be in a state of anxiety—supposing the tower had been knocked down, supposing children were playing in it? But each time he was lucky. The tower stood in stately solitude. Alan stared at it in homage for a few seconds, before hurrying back to Grandad.

He was fifteen when Grandad sold his car—he was too old to drive, he said. But he was always happy for Alan to spend an afternoon by himself, so the pilgrimages continued. It was on one of these occasions that Alan changed the ritual. Having stood in front of the tower for a few minutes, he impulsively strode towards the window, hauled himself up on to the crumbled ledge and squeezed down to the ground between the inside of the wall and the trunk of the tree, which was almost filling the space.

Immediately, there was a crackling sound in the branches above him. He looked up and saw the highest boughs swaying in the windless sky. Through the window, he saw a white form dropping from the top of the tower. Before it touched the ground, two large wings began to beat in a slow, silent rhythm. It was a barn owl. Alan watched it fly over the undergrowth and disappear into the wood.

Clumsily, almost guiltily, he clambered out of the tower. He felt privileged to have shared it with the owl, but he resolved never to climb into it again. He acknowledged the owl as the rightful owner.

His next visit, unusually, was in late February. It was a cold afternoon when he made his trip to the Heights. There had been a snowfall overnight and white patches still flecked the landscape. As he looked over a hedge, he saw two hares in a field. They were chasing each other across the hard ground, running fast and changing direction at speed. Sometimes one would come to a sudden halt, rise on its hind legs and box the other. Next it would leap up on all fours, before charging across the field again.

Alan watched them for ten minutes, his teeth chattering. Then he went up the hill, through the woods to the tower. He stood on the crisp, frozen leaf-mould, gazing up at the building as it dominated the countryside. After that, he hurried back to the warmth of Grandad's house.

And so, he came to his final visit. He suspected at the time that it would be his last. He was seventeen and about to start his last year at school. Grandad would come to stay at Christmas as usual, but he didn't know what would happen after that. Where would he be next summer? Working? Waiting to go to university? Unemployed? He hadn't made any decisions. Indeed, he had pretended that no decision needed to be made. He had wanted to live in eternal adolescence, with long visits to Grandad and the tower. Of course, he knew that this would not happen.

He didn't make the journey to the tower immediately. Instead, he spent most of the week with Grandad. They worked in the garden together; they strolled into town, where they ate egg and chips in the café; they stayed at home, playing cards. Then, after lunch on the last day, he set out on the expedition.

It was a hot afternoon. By the time he reached the top of the Heights, he was sweating and he looked longingly at the ice-cream van in its usual place in the car park. But that was for later. After he had looked once more at the tower, he would celebrate with an ice-cream, in honour of the tower itself and of Grandad, who had introduced him to the tradition. He entered the wood, his excitement rising in expectation. To his annoyance, there were other people around. He was forced to loiter, to stop to tie up his shoelaces, for nobody was allowed to see him approach the tower. At last, he was alone and safe. He turned into the small, grassy path and instantly stopped. There, in front of him, was the hare. It looked at Alan for a few seconds with its honey-coloured eyes. Then it raced away along the track, its short tail stretched out behind, dark on top, white underneath.

Alan followed apprehensively. He remembered how once he had encountered the hare again at the tower. Would the same happen today?

It was the season of berries. The hedgerows were red with hawthorn and rowan. And, of course, there was blackthorn, with each branch bent down by the clumps of sloes, blue with a purple sheen glinting in the sunlight. Grandad used them for sloe gin: Alan had seen the jars on the pantry windowsill, the berries— sunk to the bottom—suffusing the liquid with red.

Through this blazon of colour, Alan walked until, turning a corner, he saw the tower—and someone standing next to it.

Alan stopped in dismay. The intruder was a boy of about his own age, dressed in an old-fashioned way in brown corduroy trousers and a green cloth shirt. He stared at Alan, a little nervously, but with an air of defiance, as though he were saying, 'This is my tower.'

Alan continued walking, never taking his eyes off the boy. He passed him without speaking; he passed the tower without looking at it. He continued walking down the track, where he had never been before.

The track wound down the hill to a small road, which eventually brought him back to the town. He walked in silent fury. He had meant his visit to be a valedictory ceremony. Instead, he hadn't even looked at the tower, nor had he eaten the celebratory ice-cream. He arrived at Grandad's, sweating and angry.

He couldn't leave it like that. He must make one more visit to the tower. As he sat with Grandad at the kitchen table, eating bread and jam and drinking tea, he was trying to pluck up courage to speak. He felt his legs swinging violently, uncontrollably. He was going to say something unkind; he was going to desert Grandad on their last night together.

He stood up, carried his plate and cup to the sink, cleared his throat and spoke, trying to disguise the urgency of his request.

'Er, do you mind if I go out for a short time? I fancy a little walk as it's my last evening?'

'Yes, of course, Alan. But remember, you're still underage. No heavy drinking now.'

Alan felt shocked, but also relieved. Grandad's suspicion was so far removed from the truth.

'Don't look so worried,' said Grandad, laughing. 'You won't be the first seventeen-year-old to have a drink in this town. But you be sensible, mind. And don't be late back.'

Spared of any need for further explanation, Alan quickly finished the washing-up and prepared to go out. As he opened the front door, Grandad called after him, 'The White Hart's a nice pub.'

It was still light as Alan walked up to the picnic place. The wood, however, was darker than earlier and completely deserted. He felt nervous and was pleased when the familiar track led him back into the open. Anxiously, he approached the tower: would that too be deserted or would the boy still be guarding it?

There was nobody there. He walked up to it, touching it where the intruder had stood, as though to reclaim his own territory. At his feet were pinecones from the tree inside the tower and some strange lozenge-shaped objects which he guessed were owl pellets. He touched one with his shoe—it seemed to be composed of fur and bone.

He wondered what to do next. Should he simply stand and stare at the tower for a few minutes as usual? If this were really his last visit, surely he should mark it in some way. Yes, he would go inside again, despite his earlier promise.

He pulled himself up on to the ledge and dropped, as before, to the ground between the tree and the wall. This time, there was no sound from the branches above. He gazed through the opening at a still, silent world. As the sky darkened, he felt scared, immured in his sequestered tower. The ritual was over: it was time to go. Pulling himself up with his arms, he swung one leg on to the ledge, glancing upwards as he did so.

There, framed by the parapet of the tower, shining through the branches of the tree, was the crescent moon.

He stared at it. Then, still in the same clumsy position—one leg bent, the other straight—he suddenly felt the strangest sensation: he was being drawn upwards, up, up through the tower. He opened his mouth to shriek, before landing heavily on one of the branches. Perched incongruously, he looked down at his feet: sharp, pink, lethal talons at the end of thin, scaly legs. Above there was a mass of pale, mottled feathers.

Before he had time to feel amazement, his owl-self took over.

At the base of the tower, Alan had felt scared by the silence; now there were sounds everywhere. Insects were buzzing, leaves were rustling, the footsteps of tiny animals were pattering through the undergrowth. By turning his head, he could focus on a single sound: he knew the exact route which an unseen shrew was taking. He could distinguish when it was running over grass or leaves or twigs. His sight was acute too: he saw a flock of minute gnats hovering by a tree in the distance, while protruding from a leaf of bracken was the twitching foot of a field mouse.

The owl was hungry. But there was something else he could see. It was too large for food, yet the sight aroused in him a primal bloodlust. It was the hare, sitting upright and alert on the path to the wood. As it saw the owl, it thumped the ground with its hind legs.

The owl launched himself from the treetop.

At once, the hare turned and ran, its ears laid flat over its back, its tail horizontal. The long, thin back arched and lengthened, arched and lengthened.

Behind it flew the owl, with slow-beating, silent wings. Then he emitted a shriek. The hare turned, rose on its hind legs and, with superb balance, punched the air with its forelegs. The owl's head went back, his wings closed over them, his feet stretched forwards, the talons open. They scored into the hare's neck as both creatures crashed to the ground.

Alan stood up. He realised that he was grasping the shoulder of the boy he had seen that afternoon. A thin trickle of blood was oozing from the boy's neck.

'Who are you?' Alan stammered.

The other boy recoiled from his grip.

'Randall,' he said. Then he turned and ran towards the wood. Once he stopped to look back, before disappearing into the darkness.

Alan was scared of the dark wood. He turned, walking briskly past the tower, without even glancing at it. Then he continued down the hill to the road he had walked on earlier in the day.

'So how was the White Hart, then?'

Alan felt himself blushing, but Grandad only laughed.

'Don't worry. You're home early and you're sober. That's all that matters. Come and take the weight off your feet.'

Alan hadn't meant to go to the pub as he walked nervously back into town. It was a cold evening, as he remembered it, though probably his memory was false. It was still summer, after all, but he had been shivering—shivering with fear. The pub looked warm and cheerful. Recalling Grandad's recommendation, he couldn't resist going in.

The visit was not a success. He had expected to see a few elderly, country locals. Instead, the customers were young and middle class. Their superficial similarity to himself made him feel all the more conspicuous. Although not crowded, the pub was noisy, with a jukebox turned up loud.

He sat self-consciously at a table on his own, sipping half a pint of bitter. Then, in an effort to look nonchalant, he strolled casually to the jukebox, where he pretended to study the choice of music, while really working out how to operate the machine. At last, inserting the money, he chose his three records.

The walk back to his table seemed very long. Was everyone staring at him? Two young women laughed.

'Dig your trousers!' said one.

He looked down. A green stripe stretched up his jeans the length of his thigh—moss from the inside of the tower, he realised to his embarrassment.

'He's got good taste, though,' said the other woman. 'I like this record.'

Despite their mockery, they seemed friendly. Perhaps they would have been happy for him to sit and talk to them. However, he returned to his table, finished his beer quickly and left.

As he crossed the carpark, his first record had still not been played on the jukebox.

'Well, how about a nightcap, as you're still sober?'

As they sat, drinking sloe gin and eating biscuits, Grandad started talking and his first topic was the Heights. Had he known all the time, Alan wondered, that he had just been up there? Some of Grandad's stories he had heard before, but others were new. He talked of walking on the top in a gale with his fiancée, the grandmother Alan had never known. That was before the First World War. They were up there again, staring at the sunset, after he was demobbed. He described a beacon lit there twenty-five years later to celebrate the end of the Second World War.

How well Grandad knew the Heights. As he listened, Alan realised with a shock that Grandad must have been aware of the tower. It was impossible that he had not come across it—maybe he knew it well. Alan was about to mention it, hoping that Grandad would say something that would make sense of the evening. But then the subject changed.

'So, what are you going to do when you leave school, Alan?'

'I'm not sure yet. I'll probably apply for university, but I don't think I'll get in.'

'I'm sure you will if you want to.' Grandad paused. 'Your father always thought I was disappointed that he didn't go to university. But that wasn't it.' He paused again. 'You see, what worried me about your father was that he couldn't spend time on his own. He didn't have what they call an "inner life". He would never have gone up to the Heights on his own as you've just done, this afternoon.' (Did Alan imagine a hiatus before "this afternoon"? Again, he wondered if Grandad knew where he had been that evening.)

An inner life. Alan had been hoping to edge the conversation back to the Heights, allowing him the opportunity to mention the tower. Now he felt that he was being instructed not to divulge his secret. He felt proud that Grandad was praising him at the expense of his own son. To broach the subject of the tower now would have been to betray Grandad's confidence in him.

Thirty years later, a half-drunk cup of tea in front of him, Alan was pondering if Grandad had been wrong. Surely he ought to have reached out to his son, acknowledged their differences and even welcomed them. The awkward formality between father and grandfather might then have been averted.

But these were the thoughts of the middle-aged adult. To the teenager, Grandad could do no wrong. Alan had sat back, wallowing in the praise. Briefly, the bewildering events of the day faded. As Grandad talked, Alan felt more and more relaxed. Warmed by the fruity, alcoholic drink, he began to doze. Later, half asleep, he struggled upstairs to bed.

They slept late the next morning and were still washing up after breakfast when Alan's parents arrived to take him home. The goodbyes were difficult. Alan wanted to throw his arms around Grandad; instead, they didn't even shake hands.

Mum and Dad were cheerful on the drive home. They brought Alan up to date on the next-door family, who were DIY enthusiasts (although no one used those initials at that time). Having taken off their front door, they had been unable to replace it, because they couldn't find the bracket. Mum and Dad, with other neighbours, had been out at midnight, hunting by torchlight.

Alan enjoyed the stories. They were a distraction from his preoccupation with the tower and the events of the night before. But all the time, he knew it was only a temporary distraction. The memories were too close, too intense to be obliterated by such mundane events. As he listened to his parents, he realised the impossibility of mentioning the tower to them, but the urge to discuss it with someone was stronger than ever. He had resolved the night before not to talk about it to Grandad. How stupid of him. Grandad was the only person who could take his story seriously. At the very least, he would have listened sympathetically; perhaps he would have been able to offer an explanation. Alan decided that he would tell Grandad at Christmas. It might even be easier to talk in his own home, with the Heights a hundred miles away.

Grandad died in October.

Alan was too devastated to concentrate at the funeral. He could remember little about it, except that, after the service, while he was sitting in the car, waiting to be driven to the crematorium, he saw a familiar figure emerging from the church with the other mourners—it was Randall. As the car started, the boys' eyes met in brief acknowledgment.

Randall didn't go the crematorium, nor was he among the guests who went back to Grandad's house afterwards, where Mum had prepared refreshments. Alan loitered disconsolately in the kitchen. It was his first funeral. He hated all the talking and laughing. Later he would learn to appreciate the custom as a necessary part of mourning, but at that time, he found it distasteful. He was glad when all the guests had left and Mum was ready to drive him home, leaving Dad to deal with the morbid rituals involving lawyers and estate agents.

As they drove out of the town, Alan caught his last sight of the Heights—a black, lowering presence silhouetted against the evening sky.

He finished his tea. During his daydream, the guidebook had closed. Idly, he opened it at the first page, which he hadn't looked at before. There was a map of the Heights, showing all the footpaths. He pinpointed the picnic area (now the site of a National Trust shop), then traced the track through the wood. Diverging from it was the small path which led to Dilston's Folly and on down to the road. It was all so simple. How could there be any mystery to the tower?

He glanced at the top of the page, where a previous owner of the guidebook had signed his name: "Randall Cartwright". Alan stared in amazement at the signature. Could it be the same person? Randall was not a common name. Still, it had to be a coincidence. Perhaps he could locate this Randall Cartwright through the internet, but he didn't think that he could be bothered. Could he cope with the disappointment of finding that it was a different person?

He stood up and dropped his polystyrene cup and plate into the litter bin. Then, impulsively, he threw all three guidebooks into the bin as well. He could always find better books about the San Marco and, as for Lymington, most of the church was no older than the eighteenth century.

He walked across the grass, passing the sideshows, where the attendant had given up trying to collect money from the boys, who were now hurling coconuts at each other. They looked the same age as Alan on his last visit to the tower. Why was there no tower to complicate their lives?

As he reached the exit, he understood why he didn't want to try to contact Randall Cartwright. It wasn't the fear that he might not be the person he had encountered all those years before; it was the conviction that he certainly was. For he didn't want to know Randall's connection with Grandad; he didn't want to learn of his involvement with the tower; he didn't want to revive the memories of that night.

The Church on the Hill

The setting sun leaves a flickering trail of gold across the sea, bisecting the wash of the ferry as it begins the crossing to the mainland. From the deck, I look back at the town, rising above the harbour on the low hill. At the peak is the Church of Sanzo Miquele, its tall spire stretching up into the darkening sky. From here, it looks so close, so accessible: just a short, gentle climb to the top of the hill.

I had arrived early that morning. Alighting from the ferry, I chose a café and sat outside in the sunlight, overlooking the water. The waiter seemed amused by my accent: although I had studied the old tongue, I was unfamiliar with the contemporary vernacular. However, I think he welcomed my efforts and soon I was enjoying my coffee, while reading the guidebook to the church that I was planning to visit.

Of course, I had read it before, but now that I was so near, there was an immediacy, an urgency to the words and photographs. A church had stood on the hill since the seventh century; the present building dated mostly from the eleventh. Round arches adorned the exterior on two levels; inside, I would see more arches in the nave, lit by the sun's rays streaming through the glass in the clerestory. The great west window was more recent—a huge gothic frame reaching up to heaven. There had been several towers in medieval times, each one a casualty of the winter gales. A new one was built in the seventeenth century: a small dome, buttressed by four Ionic pillars. On top of this was the spire, dwarfing the other buildings on the hill.

I couldn't wait to see this edifice. Having paid for my breakfast, I set off up the hill. I didn't need directions. I simply had to climb to the top and I would be there.

I was walking beside a busy road, leading through an industrial estate. Huge lorries were stopping in front of warehouses, where they were loaded or unloaded. Boxes were being piled on to one of them, while metal girders were lowered on to another from a crane. Men in hard hats were shouting commands and warnings. It was a noisy, unattractive scene, but I reminded myself that this was a working town, with none of the artificiality of some historical sites, which have surrendered their essence to the commercialism of the tourist industry.

Unconvinced by my reasoning, I continued walking, surprised by the distance. Glancing behind, I saw the sea, glistening in the sunlight far beneath me. To my left, some crumbling factory chimneys were being demolished by a wrecking ball. The noise was deafening, the dust stifling. Then, in front of me, at the top of the hill, appeared three wind turbines, their sails rotating gently in the breeze.

Where was the church?

It was nearby, on another hill, slightly higher than this one. A deep valley separated me from it. I felt irritated: I hadn't realised that there were two hills. But I was also awe-struck. From this vantage point, the church looked even more impressive, with the west window and the door beneath it, the relief sculpture of St Michael, sword upraised, carved under the chevron border of the arch. I began my descent, walking quickly past some office blocks, a school, a housing estate. At the bottom was the town square—the guild hall and corn exchange at one end, a covered market at the other. A road led uphill from the market stalls.

This route looked more promising. I passed large houses with massive gardens. Black squirrels were running across the lawns and leaping from branch to branch of the trees. Again, I was surprised at how far I was walking, but I was sure I was going the right way. Soon I was passing ruined flint walls— presumably the remains of the monastic buildings which had surrounded the church before the religious wars. I could even glimpse the church tower between some trees above me.

I reached the trees—three old oaks, their massive, interlocking branches spreading out to form a leafy net over the hill-top. But the church was not there. It was above me, on the summit of yet another hill. Once again, I had to walk down into the next valley before approaching it.

I was feeling angry by now, but at least it was a pleasant walk, down a long country lane, with lambs bleating in the meadows beside me. At the bottom, I set out on the path up the next hill. A few flat fields of wheat and barley gave way to more sheep as I began the ascent. I was walking on a farm track, leading into a dense forest. Was this the right way? At a tavern—the only building in sight— I stopped for a glass of beer and some bread and cheese. I was the only customer. When I asked the barman the way to the church, he laughed. Was it my accent and my old-fashioned vocabulary again? But he seemed friendly. Leading me to the window, he pointed to the track I had been following.

Feeling slightly reassured, I entered the forest. Beech and silver birch trees grew thickly either side of the path, interspersed with impenetrable hawthorn and brambles. Only a thin streak of sky was visible; all else was darkness.

I seemed to be walking a long way, but at least I was going upwards. Surely every step must be leading me closer to the church?

At last, I emerged from the forest.

I was on a mountain path. My route led me between sharp, rocky escarpments, along narrow ledges, over rickety bridges. I couldn't see the summit; I couldn't see the church. Above me was a wild and angry sky: dark, swirling clouds, pierced with shafts of flaming light.

I walked and walked. I should have given up and turned back, for I no longer cared about the church, but some compulsion drove me ever upwards. I walked through day and night, through summer and winter, through youth and age. I saw no one, no living being, except for a solitary eagle, soaring high above me.

When at last I saw the church, I felt no relief. I was an old man now. I continued towards it, gasping for breath, my aching back stooped, my hands withered, my feet numb with cold.

I arrived at the mountain top with no sense of triumph. No cairn or beacon marked the apex: just bare rock, smoothed flat by the wind. And on the next mountain, high above me, stood the church, balanced precariously on the peak, its walls covered with snow, its spire lost in the clouds. Between the two mountains was a deep, seemingly bottomless ravine.

I turned around and began the descent. I knew now that I would never see the inside of that church; I doubted that I would ever return to the valley. Probably I would die on the bleak mountainside. In a trance, I walked down the path which I had struggled up.

From time to time, I thought I could glimpse the forest ahead of me, but it might have been a mirage. I didn't care. I would never reach it.

It really was the forest and I did reach it, although I felt no solace. Perhaps I should just curl up under some leaves and sleep forever.

There was a pool beside the path, just before it disappeared beneath the trees. I hadn't noticed it on the outward journey. In the centre, a stream of water gushed out of the open mouth of a stone fish. I waded out to the fountain, drank deeply and bathed my face and arms in the cool water. Instantly, I felt strength returning to my tired limbs. With renewed energy, I strode through the forest, emerging into the open countryside after only a few minutes. I passed the tavern and was soon at the bottom of the hill. Ignoring the other hills, I continued down the gentle slope until I was among the cafés and gift shops which had greeted me when I disembarked from the ferry.

It was early evening. A glance at a newspaper in a shop window showed me that it was still the day of my arrival. The ascent and descent had lasted no longer than an afternoon stroll. I walked to the ferry terminal, joining the long queue of passengers. Where had they been during the day? Why had I seen no tourists on my travels? I showed my ticket at the ticket office, boarded the ferry and climbed up to the deck…

And so, I look back at the town on the low hill. The church at the top seems so near. In the gathering darkness, the tall spire mocks my thwarted efforts.

By Time Eclipsed

'Indeed, it is hard for a scholar to lose his sight. And yet, I have still much to be thankful for. I, who have been counsellor to three Regicks and Tutor to two Fitzregs, am now, in the very twilight of my years, invited to instruct you also. It is an honour and a privilege.'

'But you've deserved it, haven't you? Father says there has been no greater servant of the realm than you.'

'He is so kind. Always he has been so kind to me. Unlike your grandsire—in his early years, I mean. He died a fine statesman—the best ruler we have ever had. Except for your own father, of course.'

'Tell me about my grandfather. I've heard so much about him from other people, but never from you. And you must have known him better than anyone.'

'Your noble father has asked me to instil in you the wisdom needed to govern our people. I should not be wasting time in idle gossip.'

'But don't you see how important it is that I know about my ancestors. After all, if my grandfather really made such mistakes, I need to be sure that I don't do the same.'

'Ah, you have conquered! But do you look to the hourglass. Ere the sands have run through, we must start your much-delayed Rhetoric class.

'Know then, that as a young man, I was summoned from the Monasterium to advise Guilhelm IV, your great grandsire, on a matter of diplomacy. There was the threat of war with Albacota, a nation whose history and culture I had studied. The Regix was pleased to value my counsel and war was averted. I had thought to return to the Monasterium, but he detained me and announced my appointment as High Counsellor. He was a great man, but of little learning. He was almost unlettered; of arithmetic he knew nothing. But he was ever determined that his son should not suffer such disadvantage, so when the Fitzreg had enjoyed his first seven summers, my duties extended to instructing him in those arts and sciences with which I was acquainted.

'He was an able boy, but he wanted dedication. The arts with which he was enamoured were hunting, sword-fighting and archery, not the dull divinity, history and state governance which he studied under my tutelage. Often, he would absent himself from his lessons. Often, he would be found with the Cavalry General, practising his equine swordsmanship. And indeed, even I, who know nothing of martial arts, was amazed at his agility on horseback and the speed and artistry of his thrust and parry.

'He was only seventeen when his father died. Had he been a little older, he would, perchance, have lost that headstrong ardour, that contempt for study and contemplation. I had thought that he, as Regix, would not require my services any longer. Yet it pleased him to retain me as counsellor and, indeed, he even heeded my advice on many affairs of state, particularly financial matters, for, despite the opportunities I had given him, he was nearly as deficient in arithmetic as his father. However, in the border skirmishes with Galleria, he steadfastly refused to listen to me, and many lives were needlessly lost.

'Yet he never bore me a grudge. Though scorning my want of adventure, he would always listen to my counsel, even while mocking it. Until one day he deemed that I had gone too far. "Sire," I addressed him. "Hast thou thought whether we need to act in regard to the eclipse?"

'"The what, Francillicus?" The familiar, taunting gleam danced in his eyes.

'"In just three months, Sire, there will be a total eclipse of the sun. The moon will block it out for two minutes. A darkness will descend upon the earth in the middle of the day; birds will cease to sing. My concern is that your subjects, ignorant of what is foretold, will panic. They may fear the wrath of the gods. Some may go mad; some may even kill themselves; some may go blind from gazing at the heavens. All I advise, Sire, is a Regical Proclamation, assuring the people that the darkness will be short-lived and that there is no reason for alarm."

'"How now, Francillicus? Thou hast surely o'erreached thyself. Canst thou command the celestial bodies to conjoin at thy whim?"

'"Sire, those celestial bodies obey laws of a higher power than mine own. My task has been merely to study these laws. They are immutable: that which I have foretold cannot fail to come to pass. Indeed, hadst thou not neglected thy studies in astronomy, thou, too, wouldst know what is to come."

'"Enough!" He rose from his throne, his eyes blazing with fury. "Thou dost forget thyself. Thou art no longer our tutor but our counsellor—a position from which thou canst speedily be relieved." He paused. Then, sitting down again, he smiled. "Come, Francillicus. Let us not quarrel. Speak no more of this eclipse. It will not—nay, it cannot—occur. Now, let us turn to the preparations for the visit of the Filreg Sassamornia."

'I left it there. How could I do otherwise? Yet I was still worried. The eclipse would take place, howsoever the Regix denied it. Thus, two months later, I approached him again. The visit of the Filreg had passed off successfully. He had been charmed by her beauty and their betrothal had just been formally announced.'

'So that was my grandmother?'

'Yes, indeed. She who yet lives in the Grey Turret. It was a good match, and his happiness would, I hoped, make him susceptible to my renewed pleas. "Sire," I said, "hast thou thought again of those events which are to come to pass?"

'I saw at once that I had misjudged his mood. His face grew red with rage. "Speak not of such things, Francillicus, if thou dost value thy life."

'"Sire, all I ask is for a Regical Proclamation. Just to say…"

'"Here is our Regical Proclamation. Thou, Francillicus, art condemned to the dungeons, there to spend the rest of thy days, chained, with bread and water for thy only fodder. Guards, take him away!"'

'He said that? My grandfather said that?'

'He was not a bad man. 'Ere the guards had fastened the chains in the dungeon, the master steward arrived and bade them release me. He then conducted me to a chamber in the west wing. My door was locked, but inside, I had all that I could desire. A comfortable bed, chairs, a table, bookshelves. Food and wine were brought me, tubs of hot water, clean raiment and, better than all these, books. I had only to request a volume from the library and it would be brought. Parchment, quills and ink also. What more could a scholar wish for? There was a casement too, o'erlooking the courtyard, but I could not see the sky.'

'So, you never saw the eclipse?'

'Alas, no. But I spoke greatly about it to the servants who brought me my provender. From them, I learnt that no proclamation had been issued, but it mattered not greatly. I explained to them what was to come to pass and they told friends and colleagues. Soon the news was spreading throughout the city. Of course, those who dwelt in the depths of the forests and the slopes of the mountains far beyond the city walls learnt nothing of this from us. Yet I feared little for them. They were wise in the lore of the heavens. Their seers had perchance foreseen the eclipse long ago, and panic was alien to them. No, it was the city-dwellers who concerned me—they who had lost their native wisdom, but who lacked any book-learning to recompense them.'

'And what about my grandfather? What was he doing?'

'Alas! Hubris, hubris. He refused to accept the reality of the eclipse. While at first he vented his rage on me for daring to foretell the event, he later turned his wrath on the thing itself. I believe now that he knew its appearance was inevitable, but he was furious that a celestial perturbation should demonstrate the paltriness of his own earthly power. When the great day came, the servants told me that he had had his horse saddled at dawn and had galloped out of the city on his own.

'As for me, I was concentrating on my work—my treatise on *The initiation rites of the endogamous Ombraginians*. You will find it in the library. I doubt anyone has looked at it, but scholarship was ever its own reward.'

'So, the eclipse passed you by?'

'By no means. As I mentioned, there was a casement to my room, and as Totalitas approached, so I perceived a darkness descending. I hastened to look down at the courtyard, where a throng had assembled. It pleased me to observe that all had heeded my counsel and were refraining from looking directly at the sun. But on the floor of the yard, there was a wondrous sight: a multitude of tiny crescents mirroring the form of the sun above. Then, total darkness, total silence—not a bird sang. Until gradually, the darkness lifted, the crowd dispersed and I returned to my study.'

'And what about my grandfather?'

'His horse trotted home, riderless, during the afternoon. Men were sent to scour the country, far and wide, in search of the Regix. Throughout the evening and the night, they sought him, and the next morning, at first light, his mangled body was discovered, some five leagues from the city. They bore him back and the physician attended him, under whose wise and healing hands, the fractured bones were set, the searing pain eased. There could be no complete cure: one leg remained shorter than its pair, and so the Regix could never regain his erstwhile agility. Yet what he had lost in strength, he had gained in wisdom. Thereafter, he was a changed man.'

'Did he release you?'

'Instantly. Even while sick and in the physician's care, he released me with full pardon. Once he was strong enough, he summoned me for an audience with him. Thus, I learnt of his adventure: how he had ridden, madly and defiantly, amongst the rocks and hills, daring the darkness to descend as foretold. Then, as the moon began to pass in front of its fiery rival, he stared at it, shouting furious oaths, until his steed, terrified, reared on her hinder legs so that her master, fine rider though he was, was flung to the ground.

'On hearing how he had essayed to outstare the sun, I feared the worst, and indeed, my fears were all too quickly realised. His sight was damaged and all the balms and unction which the physician applied could not cure him. Within a twelve month, he was blind.'

'Was he married by then?'

'Indeed, yes. Your grandmother was both a comfort and a support to him. She loved him dearly and ministered to his every need. More than that, she encouraged his new-found maturity, suppressing any hints of his youthful arrogance.

'For it was maturity and tolerance which characterised the remainder of his reign. He would listen to everyone: to those who tilled the soil, to those who baked the bread, to those who built the dwellings. Many were the decrees he issued, improving the lot of the common people. The realm thrived and all partook of its riches.

'And he would listen to me. Yea, the blind Regix harkened to the words of his counsellor whose own eyes were dimming fast, though through no fault of the eclipse. Only time is to blame for my sightlessness—time and too much study by candlelight.'

'Was my father born by this time?'

'He first saw the light of day some two summers after his parents' nuptials. The Regix was eager that his son should not repeat his own contempt for learning, and he was sedulous in reminding him not to neglect his books. Yet no reminder was needed. Your father was an ardent and able scholar. Seldom was he found far from a learned tome.'

'Did he read your treatise on the Ombraginians?'

'Mock me not, youngling! He read what was needed for the wise Regix he was to become. He ascended the Regical Throne ere even he had attained his majority. But it mattered nought. He reigned fairly and wisely from the day of his coronation. Me thought he might have no more need of me, and I began to think of my retirement. Indeed, he granted me a generous pension, but insisted that I should be ever at his disposal, should his need be great. It has pleased him to ask my counsel on a few occasions. And then, last week, he desired that I should aid him in yet one more instance of his wisdom.'

'What was that?'

'Why, child, to instruct you. When the gods decreed that he should not sire a male heir, I had not thought that my tutelage would be required, for no Filreg has ever received instruction ere now. Yet he resolved that his daughter should have as good a preparation as himself.

'Alas, though, I fear lest I betray his expectations. We have delayed too long. Let us commence forthwith our class in Rhetoric.'

Shadows in the Wine Bar

Despite the cold, I hesitate outside the wine bar before feeling confident enough to enter. Inside are about thirty people, none of whom I recognise. Then a woman approaches, smiling, her hand outstretched.

'Kathryn! So glad you could come.'

This must be Sheila, who rang me at work to invite me to the reunion. My first thought was to decline. Did I really want to see those students again after thirty years? Then curiosity overcame my doubts—curiosity less about what the others were doing than about how I had progressed from their world to my current existence.

So, apprehensively, I made the long train journey north from Euston.

'Sheila! Lovely to see you! You haven't changed at all.'

This isn't a complete lie. As a student, she was attractive, stylish and frightening. She is still attractive in middle age, but cosier, more maternal. She no longer scares me.

'Sorry I wasn't more communicative when you rang. I was so taken aback by your call.'

She roars with laughter as if I have said something funny. The Sheila I recall was too self-composed even to smile.

We chat about jobs. Then she motions me towards the others.

'Do you recognise everyone?'

Suddenly I realise that I do.

'Hello Rob. How are you?' His bald head and glasses prove only a superficial disguise. With him are seven others from our year—evidently all close friends, still living locally, still meeting regularly. I envy the continuity of their lives.

I am not conscious of moving around the bar, but I find myself at different places throughout the evening. It is as if the room is spinning around, randomly depositing everyone opposite a new partner. Now I am reminiscing with Nadine, now engrossed in conversation with Laura. We must have said more to each other in these ten minutes than in the three years we studied together. Why hadn't I got to know my fellow students better?

Then there is Duncan, who once asked me out. I liked him, but we were both too shy to say much and we parted after just one drink. He is still shy: he asks me in detail about my work, but doesn't allude to my private life. Similarly, I learn nothing about him.

Suddenly it is midnight and the bar is emptying. I am among the last to leave. As we step out into the cold, the others all turn away from the city centre. It seems I have no part in their lives outside the confines of the bar.

I hurry, thoughtfully, to my hotel. I am glad I came, but I feel disturbed rather than overjoyed. I have seen too many paths that I might have taken. Will this evening change anything? Having re-established contact, we could easily repeat the event, but we could never recapture the intensity of this night—the memories, desires, regrets, all enclosed in a single room.

I have travelled far today—two hundred miles and thirty years.

Revelations of Death and Revolt

'Can I come in? Can I come in?'

The loud, drunken voice shattered the silence. A woman stood up and disappeared into the church. I heard her telling the intruder that he could come in as long as he kept quiet. Following her into the cell, he threw himself prostrate on to the floor, beside the central candle.

Silence resumed.

I had wandered into the medieval church, just to pass the time until my appointment. As I walked up the nave, admiring the large east window, a woman looked out from a room off the south aisle.

'Would you like to join us? We're just starting a Dame Alis meeting.'

I didn't want to go to a meeting, but I followed her anyway into a bare room, built of the same flint as the rest of the church. There was just one narrow window, but by the light of a few small candles on a ledge by the door, I could see eight people sitting on wooden benches around the sides of the room. A man edged closer to his neighbour, allowing me to sit down next to him.

The woman spoke again.

'We were just doing the introductions. Would you like to say something about yourself?'

'Well, my name's Ellen. I live in London, but I've come here because someone I know has just died. I'm his executor, so I've got to sort out his affairs.'

There were sympathetic grunts from the others. One of them said, 'Would you like me to light a candle for him?'

As she was striking a match, another woman spoke for the first time, 'I think we ought to get started now. Some of you haven't been here before, so perhaps I should say a few words first…

'We are meeting here in the cell where the anchoress, known as Dame Alis of St Martin's, lived for over thirty years in the fourteenth century. She lived almost in silence, writing, praying, working. And we meet in that same spirit of silent prayer and contemplation. Silence is so rare in our modern world. It is a chance to listen rather than ask. We shall sit for about half an hour, but anyone can leave at any time.'

Another woman said a short prayer and the silence began.

'Why am I here?' I thought. 'I don't go to church. I'm not even a Christian. What am I meant to be thinking about? Should I leave now?'

I stayed. I stopped worrying about motivation and let the silence enfold me. The speaker was right. We so rarely experience silence. I would be going to see the solicitor soon, but I didn't need to worry about that now. I didn't need to worry about anything.

'Can I come in? Can I come in?'

As the man lay on the floor in front of us, it was difficult to recover that sense of peace. He lay still and quiet, except for a few noises which sounded, appropriately, like incantations.

'A revel! True Commons. Bocking. Questermongers. Savoy. A revel!'

These were some of the words he uttered. I didn't know what any of them meant. I sat, trying again to retreat into the silence.

'Our Father, which art in heaven…'

A man led us in prayer and the session ended. As we stood up, the woman who had invited me into the cell asked me if I would like to say a prayer in memory of my friend. She led me into the church, to the front of the nave, where we sat down. I felt embarrassed—I didn't believe in prayer, but I followed her unquestioningly.

'Would you like to tell me a little about your friend?'

I paused. Did I want to divulge my relationship? Then I surrendered.

'Well, he was my ex-husband, you see. We separated nine years ago—should have done long before that.' I looked at her to see if she disapproved. She nodded, encouragingly. 'Some people might think, "Why am I bothered if we split up so long ago?" But it's not that simple. We had such a good marriage at first—even though it didn't last. He's still a part of me. That sounds silly, I know. I could never have lived with him again, but I couldn't just turn my back on him. And now I find I'm his executor, so I don't even have any choice.'

'What was his name?' she asked.

'Gavin.'

'Dear God, we thank you for the marriage of Ellen and Gavin. We remember before you the happy years they spent together. We know that there were problems on the way, but we pray that now, at the end, there may be a reconciliation. We commend them both to your undying love. Amen.'

We sat in silence for a few minutes. Then I thanked her and made my way to the west door. The strange man was on his feet, talking to the others, who all seemed undisturbed by his odd behaviour. I nodded in passing to them as I left the building.

At breakfast in the guest house the next morning, I nibbled at some toast. I was too upset by my visit to the flat the day before to be hungry. The solicitor, Russell, had been very sympathetic and friendly, but he was all too obviously wanting my business. He stressed the dangers of acting as executor on my own: I would be liable if anything went wrong. Why not let the experts do everything? Didn't I have enough to worry about already? I resented the pressure, particularly as Gavin's affairs seemed to be in good order. He had always been organised. He owed no money on his credit card; his utility bills were all paid by direct debit; his mortgage repayments were up to date. He didn't appear to have saved much money, so even with the value of the flat, inheritance tax would not be payable. Why did I need a solicitor to advise me? However, he was insistent and eventually I signed a contract for him to do the work. At least it meant that he would organise the sale of the flat—something I had not been looking forward to from such a distance. I insisted on retaining control of the funeral arrangements: these were too personal for me to hand over to a third party.

Once I had signed, Russell instantly became more conciliatory. He said I could spend as long as I wanted in the flat on my own and I could remove any personal papers that did not involve finance (so long as I signed for them). At last, he left me, having asked me to drop the keys at his office the next day.

I stood in Gavin's bedroom, remembering, imagining. How long had we been happy together? Four years? No, less than that—I had felt secure for a long time, but not happy. Even when I found out about Linda, I didn't feel threatened. He would never have set up home with her. After all, where was she now? Why wasn't she the executor?

Should I have tried harder to maintain the relationship? But what relationship was there at that time? Should I have been satisfied with security? Many people would have yearned for a secure marriage.

These speculations were getting me nowhere. I needed to get out of the flat and leave everything for Russell to deal with. I would just take a quick look at the desk. I had already seen the bank statements and other financial documents, but there were some letters too. I picked up a bundle in familiar handwriting, all neatly tied up in order. So, he had kept all my letters to him, some of them over twenty years old. There were other letters too, including a large wad from his mother and an even larger one from Linda. I checked the dates. The oldest was dated 1979—nine years before I had met Gavin. When I had first discovered one, she had already been writing to him for fifteen years. I remembered my reaction at the time: it wasn't shock as much as relief. I had felt that I could leave him without feeling guilty, although I had never felt comfortable with our separation.

The last letter from her was from 2008—two years after I had left him. What had gone wrong?

I put all three bundles in my bag, wrote down the details on the headed notepaper Russell had given me and left the flat.

The direct route from the guest house to the solicitor's office did not go near the church, but a short diversion brought me there. I was thinking about the funeral. Could I hold it at St Martin's? As far as I knew, Gavin had had no connection with any church. The easy option would have been to hold a quick service at the chapel in the cemetery, but I felt he deserved more than this. I had a relationship with St Martin's now. Perhaps I could meet the vicar or maybe someone I had seen the day before, just to discuss the possibilities.

The church had no graveyard now. The west door opened on to the pavement of a busy road. There would be nowhere for him to be buried. Perhaps I should just forget the idea.

A man crossed the road in front of me, running towards the church, looking furtively behind him. He was dressed strangely in a short brown tunic and black woollen hose held up with a rope belt. A black hood was pushed back from his head and dangled down his back. He wore leather, calf-length boots. Despite his odd appearance, he looked familiar.

Reaching the church door, he grasped the knocker and shouted, 'Can I come in? Can I come in?'

At once, I recognised him as the man who had intruded on the silence the day before. Not wishing to see him again, I turned down a side-street running parallel to the church nave. A small extension jutted out from the building, with a window, through which I could see the face of a woman, topped by what looked like a nun's veil.

She smiled at me.

I had a busy morning. After leaving the keys at the solicitor's office (and signing another form), I had a brief meeting with the funeral director to discuss options. Then I went to Gavin's doctor's surgery to collect the death certificate. This I took to the town hall, where I had an appointment with the Registrar of Deaths.

Afterwards, exhausted, I returned to the church.

As I opened the door, I was surprised how different the interior appeared. It was in darkness, except for a few candles, but it was still light enough to see the brightly coloured murals. Had these been covered up yesterday? On the wall beside me was a huge depiction of a man carrying a child across a river—St Christopher presumably. The chancel arch showed an assortment of people climbing up the left side, while on the right many were falling into the jaws of greedy devils. God sat at the top of the arch, welcoming with one hand and expelling with the other. I noticed how the damned included several grandly dressed men, even one who looked like a bishop, his mitre tumbling down in front of him. Beneath the arch was a carved, wooden screen, separating the nave from the chancel.

The church was noisy: children were running around, shouting, while a baby was crying in its mother's arms. Two men seemed to be conducting some business in a pew; one of them was signing a long piece of parchment with a quill pen. Everyone wore old-fashioned clothes.

I walked across the church to where the meeting had been held the day before. A door blocked my entrance, although a window was open. As I approached, I heard footsteps behind me and turned to see the man with the hood and leggings hurrying towards the same door. I moved out of his way, sitting down on a nearby pew, pretending to be absorbed in prayer while I looked at him through the gaps between my fingers.

'Can I come in? Can I come in?'

The woman in black habit and veil appeared at the window and spoke calmly to him.

'God save you, Brother. You are welcome.'

'I am troubled and need help.'

'Speak, my brother.'

'I have sought sanctuary in this church. Men are pursuing me, for I have sinned.'

'Aye, I saw you from my world window. But fear not. God forgives all sins. The greater the sin, the greater his compassion for the sinner.'

'But the priest would not absolve me. He said I lacked penitence.'

'Do you not repent of your sins?'

'I repent that I slew a man. I repent with all my heart. I see now. He was not my enemy. He was just a Fleming. Others said that he must die, that he was stealing work from us. I was weak. I killed him, but he was only another labourer. He was not my enemy.'

'Who then is your enemy?'

'The noblemen, the lawyers, the bishops. I killed none of them, but my comrades did. I repent not their deaths. Had he they call John of Gaunt been at the Savoy Palace, gladly would I have slain him. Nor do I care that the archbishop met his death in the chapel in the Tower. No place may be a sanctuary for a tyrant.'

'And yet you seek sanctuary for yourself.'

'Aye, but surely God is with me. When we gathered at Bocking, John Ball was preaching to us. He is a parson, a man of God. He said it was a Christian's duty to overthrow our oppressors and oppose their unjust taxes. "Render unto Caesar…" he said.'

'Christ is on the side of the oppressed. That is true. Any cruelty inflicted on them is inflicted on Christ. But think not therefore that we should kill the oppressors. Every time a murder is committed, then Christ is murdered too. But fear not. He came to earth to be murdered; he has already forgiven his murderers: "Father, forgive them; they know not what they do." He wants to suffer more, so that he can forgive more. Such is his love.'

'I desire not that our Lord should suffer, but I want evil men to suffer.'

'We see things as good or evil, but God sees them not so. Everything that is done is God's doing, so everything is good. Sin has no substance; it can be known only by the pain it causes. It makes us know ourselves and plead for mercy.'

'So, what must I do now?'

'You must needs pray, as Holy Church teaches. Prayer unites the soul to God; it proclaims that the soul should will what God wills.'

'But what of Despenser's men who pursue me? What if the priest should admit them?'

'Prayer is still the answer. Through prayer you shall know yourself in the fullness of eternal joy.'

'I thank you, Dame. I shall pray.'

He knelt in the next pew to mine. I stood up, wondering what to do next. I had hoped to speak to the vicar about Gavin's funeral, but how did that relate to the fugitive's troubles? I saw a priest, crossing the church. As he bowed before the altar, I noticed his black habit, his tonsured head, the crucifixes and rosaries dangling from his girdle. I could not speak to him.

Quietly I tiptoed out of the church.

I leaned dizzily against the church wall. Where was I? When was I? I looked along the street. It was almost deserted, but then a car drove fast towards me, so fast that it almost ran over a pedestrian who was absent-mindedly crossing the road, his ears muffled by headphones, his eyes focused on the mobile device he held in front of him. Yes, it was 2015 after all, but what had been happening in the church?

I wished I hadn't agreed to arrange the funeral. I could have been back in London by now, in my flat with the reassuringly irritating music booming from next door, the constant sound of traffic from outside. This street, now that the speeding car had disappeared, was quiet again.

Although I had eaten only a sandwich at lunchtime, I couldn't face a restaurant that evening. There was a kettle in my room in the guest house, so I went back there, made some tea, opened a packet of biscuits and turned on the television. I didn't want to watch anything, but I was nervous of the silence. Then I laid out the letters from Gavin's desk.

I looked first at the ones I had sent him. These dated mostly from 1989 and 1990. I had met him the year before, when I was a naive eighteen-year-old undergraduate and he—twelve years older—was studying for his Master's. How I had worshipped him: his wisdom, his maturity, his unpatronizing indulgence of my youthful ignorance. In the two years after he had returned to work and I was still a student, I was planning everything we would do together—the holidays, the films, the restaurants. It was only after we were living together that I realised that he didn't want to do anything. He preferred to stay in every night, reading and studying. I couldn't even persuade him to come out for a pizza. He didn't see the need, particularly as he was such a good cook.

Gradually, the age difference, which had made him exciting and mysterious at university, had become a barrier. Why should I, at twenty-three, have wanted to be confined in the flat? I had started going out for the evening—sometimes to the cinema on my own, sometimes to the pub with friends from work. I had missed him at first, hoping my absences would encourage him to go out with me again, but they had no effect. He would ask me if I had enjoyed myself, but nothing else. Soon I was looking forward to an evening without him, taking time to put on make-up as if I were going out on a date.

I turned to his mother's letters. I had liked her. According to the solicitor, she and his father were still alive, although old (too old, presumably, to be executors). I would meet them at the funeral. That might be difficult.

Her letters, which started in 1977, were long and friendly, but she didn't seem to have lived a very active life either. She wrote about her job and the weather; in her later letters, after her retirement, she wrote about the garden and the weather. Gavin must have inherited her lack of adventure.

Then I looked at Linda's letters. These were completely different. They were written quickly and described holidays, tennis matches, days out, visits to friends. What did she have in common with Gavin? Presumably they had met when he was an undergraduate, but what sort of relationship had they had? I don't think they had been lovers; certainly, they weren't lovers when I first heard about her. She was no threat. I had used her as a scapegoat—an excuse to escape from a marriage which had no future because it had no past, except in my early dreams. And yet Linda was important because Gavin hadn't mentioned her. They had shared a secret life even if he never saw her. Of course, he was allowed a secret life, but shouldn't his wife have known about its existence, even if she were unable to share it with him?

During the 1980s, her letters became more political. She raged against the Conservative government and wrote in detail about all the demonstrations she had been on. What had Gavin thought about those? He used to have an academic, not an active, interest in politics. I couldn't imagine his taking the trouble to join a demonstration. However, this hadn't stopped her from describing marches about nuclear weapons, the miners, local government. I turned the pages without reading them, anxious to find how the series of letters ended and why she had stopped writing. Then some familiar words caught my eye.

They appeared in a letter dated April 1990 and were part of a description of the anti-poll tax march.

'Of course, you'll have read about the march in the papers. My god—how the media love a bit of rioting. Needless to say, that was only part of the story. We were marching with our banner near the head of the demo and everything was peaceful—no trouble at all. When we got to Trafalgar Square, we didn't hang around for the speeches. We went off to Islington for a curry. I didn't hear about the rioting until I got home later that evening.

'Mind you, I wasn't surprised. Things were pretty hectic at the start in Kennington Park. The march was very late getting under way and a lot of people had gone to the pub to pass the time. I went to the White Bear myself—not for a drink, just to use the loo (always a problem on a demo). Some people were already quite drunk, so any police provocation was bound to cause trouble later. A strange thing happened in the pub. As I was pushing through the crowd on my way out, I heard a shout from outside: "Can I come in? Can I come in?" A man, dressed rather old-fashioned in a cloth shirt and corduroys, entered. I stood aside to try to give him a gangway. He thanked me and then said something like: "I killed a man, but I wish I hadn't—he was innocent. Choose carefully who you kill today." The words sent a shudder down my spine as I escaped from the pub to re-join my friends. I bet that man got caught up in the rioting later. He's probably in prison now.'

I had read enough. I couldn't escape from this man. He was haunting me. Of course, I told myself that any resemblance between him and the man in the church was entirely coincidental, but my denial was unconvincing.

I put the letters back in my bag, boiled the kettle and tried to settle down to watch television.

I checked out of the hotel the next morning. I couldn't delay my return to London any longer. I had to focus on arranging the funeral and then catch the train home. Strangely, my experiences at the church hadn't dissuaded me from wanting to hold the funeral there; instead, the events had conspired to convince me that it was the essential location. However, I wasn't prepared to waste any more time. If I encountered any problems there, I would go back to the funeral director and organise a straightforward funeral at the cemetery chapel.

Everything looked normal as I approached St Martin's, but then I heard marching feet behind me. Turning, I saw a troop of men in helmets and chain mail. To get out of their way, I hurried across the road, noticing that it had become little more than a mud track. A chicken squawked in fear and raced away from under the soldiers' feet. A man pushing a handcart, laden with meat around which a horde of flies was hovering, paused and stared angrily at the troop.

They ignored everything. Reaching the church door, their leader hammered on it and shouted, 'Open in the name of the king!'

They didn't wait for an answer. Breaking the door down with their spears, they disappeared inside.

They were gone only a few minutes. Then they re-appeared, dragging the stranger behind them, ignoring his cries and curses. They manhandled him along the road and turned down the lane beside the south wall of the church. I followed at a safe distance. The anchoress was standing calmly at her window. She called out kindly to the captive:

'Farewell, my friend. Never fear the wrath of men. Remember always the love of Christ. Know yourself, my brother.'

As they vanished from sight, I leaned in bewilderment against the church railings.

'Hello, it's Ellen, isn't it?'

The woman who had prayed with me was coming out of the church.

'Are you managing to get things sorted out? There's so much to do, isn't there?'

'Yes, I think I'm getting there. There's just the funeral to organise still. I was wondering... Would it be possible? I don't know...'

'Would you like to hold it at St Martin's?'

'Well, it's rather impertinent of me to ask. I doubt if Gavin ever set foot in the church. It's just that after our meeting the other day, I feel I'm sort of a part of this church now.'

'I think it's lovely that you feel like that. Yes, I'm sure it will be possible. But I should warn you that it will probably work out more expensive than a simple service at the cemetery chapel. And you might have to wait a bit of time. I don't know what your diary's like?'

'No, that's fine. There's no hurry. So, what do I need to do? Should I contact the vicar?'

'Shall I see when he's available?' She took her mobile out of her bag. 'Let me give him a ring... Hello Richard. It's Jean...'

'I am the Resurrection and the Life,' saith the Lord.

I had ordered forty service sheets to be printed, but only a quarter of them were needed. Gavin's parents had greeted me with hugs and kisses and no recriminations. If they felt that I had let him down, they didn't show it. Two of his other relatives were there too—I had a vague memory of meeting them once. There were three men I didn't recognise—perhaps they were work colleagues.

Then there was a woman of about Gavin's age. Could she be Linda? I had written to her at the address on the last letter, but I didn't know if she had received it. And Jean, my new friend from the church, was there. How lovely of her to come and support me. She had greeted me at the church door, with a gentle touch of my arm.

The vicar was giving the tribute now, summarising the details of Gavin's life which I had described to him. In his words, Gavin had become such a loving and considerate man. Were the congregation silently condemning me for my neglect of him? I buried my head in shame, shutting out the face of the kindly young vicar as I thought of what might have happened if I had stayed with Gavin. I had never been particularly happy on my own. What had he felt about the separation?

As a bell tolled, I raised my eyes. What was I looking at? Richard had vanished; in his place stood the priest I had seen before in the church, the crucifixes and rosaries hanging from the girdle around his black habit. He kissed a board embellished with a sacred painting of the crucifixion. Then, as the bell tolled again, he raised the chalice and the holy loaf. The congregation was silent.

I gazed, perplexed, at the priest, when suddenly there was a loud beating at the door. A man shouted, 'Can I come in? Can I come in?'

Laughing and Grief

The classical master taught Laughing and Grief.
Spoken by the mock turtle in *"Alice's Adventures in Wonderland"* by
Lewis Carroll

It was only 9.30 when I finished bringing my diary up to date. After the pressure of the ever-lengthening record of unwritten experience, the rapid completion came as an anti-climax. Had it been necessary to decline the invitation to an after-work drink, to create that imaginary meeting with a friend, so as to mask the reason for my enforced absence? Perhaps, for if I had gone out tonight, my anxiety would have been still greater: one more evening to commit to memory. How long before I would have had time to release it on to the page, giving it leave to be remembered or forgotten as it saw fit? And so, I had rejected the possibility (albeit unlikely) of a worthwhile experience in order to record previous unexceptional ones.

For as I glanced at the newly scribbled entries for the last fifteen days, I wondered why I had bothered. What was there here so important that it had to be set down above the high tide of oblivion? The account of my weekend in Chester was worth noting—I might read that again in the future—but the other entries merely testified to a rather dull, uneventful life. Apart from the description of a film I had seen, a typical day consisted of: 'Home after work—ironed shirt—read a little.' The entry for tonight was: 'Home after work—quick snack—brought diary up to date.' So, I was writing a journal about writing my journal. Occasionally I had described a meal I had cooked, but not often enough for it to be a record of my eating habits. Work was almost taboo, so the diary could not serve as a study of changing work patterns in the office. To do that, I would have had to complete an essay every evening, thus reducing still further the time available for any spontaneous living. Yet by excluding work, I had created an unreal reflection of my life. I had omitted all mention of skills I had learnt, of office politics, of relationships developing over several years. An interesting discussion with a colleague would be ignored because it happened at work, while the gossip overheard at the hairdresser's might be recorded almost verbatim.

I looked scornfully at the accumulating files of diary entries and wondered again: why did I bother? Why waste so much time, cause myself so much pressure, for such paltry results? It was partly because the discipline of writing an entry for each day ensured that unexpected encounters—in café or street— were not ignored. However, even these could not always be retrieved. I recalled a strange dialogue with two people as I walked home from the station one evening, but I couldn't say when it occurred—six years ago, eight years ago? How could I find the entry now? I had once contemplated converting the diary to electronic, searchable form, but had quickly dismissed the idea—it would have been too time-consuming.

So, useless though most of them were, I had diary entries for every day for the last fourteen years.

Except for Saturday 19th October 2002

This omission was not premeditated. I had made some quick notes as I sat on the train that evening on the journey home. But the next day, when I tried to translate these notes into a coherent narrative, I found the exercise too difficult. For it was not just the events of twelve hours which I needed to transcribe, but the memories these events evoked, memories stretching back forty years.

I shut my eyes. trying to relive the history of that day…

I am sitting on a train, travelling north from Euston. From the age of 28, I used to take this route to Denbridge once or twice every year, until Lewis and his family moved to London last summer. I was apprehensive on the early visits, having to get to know you—my oldest friend—in your new roles as a fiancé, a husband and finally a father, but I soon adjusted and I used to look forward to meeting you again.

The journey evokes few memories from my earlier days in Denbridge. My parents drove me there when I moved in with my uncle and aunt; if I returned home for the occasional weekend, I always travelled by bus. There was just one daytrip by train to meet some of my sixth form friends for a reunion in a London pub. I had anticipated an Athenian symposium: an impassioned mixture of drinking and intellectual discussion. There was drinking, certainly, but as the only one of the eight who was not yet a student, I felt an outsider from the conversation. While the others were boasting about their first six months at university, their new-found freedom, their encounters with girls, I could offer only another term at school and six weeks in a conventional job at my uncle's insurance company. They all congratulated me perfunctorily for passing my Cambridge entrance exam, but it would be seven months before I started my degree. My current respectability seemed to them a bourgeois betrayal; they laughed when I admitted that I wore a suit to work. How I missed you, Lewis, my one true friend. You would have despised the others' superficial responses, but you were away in Israel, putting your ideals into practice on a kibbutz.

There was a proposal to spend the afternoon in a café until the pubs re-opened in the evening, but I made my excuses and walked—cold and miserable—back to Euston. Why had I let myself be excluded? Why hadn't I dispelled my inhibitions, surrendered to Dionysus and, briefly, conquered the constraints of time? Instead, I had sat gloomily, aloof from the drunken frivolity. It was a wretched journey back to Denbridge, but I cheered myself up with a hot, comforting bowl of tomato soup in the dimly lit station buffet. As I alight from the train today and pass through the barriers, I look at the bright café which stands there now. (Is it on the same site? I can't be sure.) There is no soup for sale— just the usual choice of different coffees and pastries. Would they have dissipated my disappointment in the same way? I remember walking home, preparing to tell my aunt how much I had enjoyed the day, when really it was only that bowl of soup; the pub lunch I had already forgotten, submerged in the alcohol and inane conversation.

Today is the first time since then that I am leaving the station alone, for later there was always someone to meet me. Sometimes Lewis or Esther would be driving into the car park just as I arrived; sometimes the whole family would be waiting for me at the ticket barrier. I remember, Lewis, arriving soon after the birth of your son. We had not seen each other since your marriage three years before, though we had written to each other frequently. I was even wondering if I would recognise you, but your familiar smile and wave from the car window quickly obliterated any signs of aging.

I am crossing the car park now, walking past the Railway Tavern, where we had a drink together earlier. It was in 1981—the first time I saw you in Denbridge—when you had invited me for the day to meet your fiancée. Lunch with Esther and her parents had been tense and difficult: snatches of formal conversation, punctuated by long silences. Afterwards you and I walked back to the station and, arriving early, we stopped for a drink. Gradually, the tension lifted. We talked and drank beer. I missed one train. I was tempted to miss the next one as well, but I needed to be up early the following day. You told me about Esther, about her job at the estate agent's, about the tragic death of her elder sister. We discussed whether this was the cause of the uncomfortable atmosphere at lunchtime.

Then we reminisced: how we had met twenty years before and how our friendship had endured so long. Was I thinking of my trip to London and of that other group of old school friends? I am in contact with none of them now. Perhaps it is only hindsight which juxtaposes the two days, because of their shared location of Denbridge Station.

A short road leads from the station to the high street. To my right is the town centre, with the town hall and the parish church adjoining the main square. That is the scene depicted in the guidebooks, but I turn left. It is unfamiliar territory: Lewis and Esther always used to drive me in the other direction, avoiding the traffic and the busy shops. Strangely, the street doesn't figure in my earlier memories either. I had little need for shopping. I had brought two suits and other clothes from home, while I ate either at work or with my aunt and uncle. But surely I must have walked down here occasionally? I look at the shops: the names are familiar from every high street in the land, but they conjure up no recollections from Denbridge.

I stroll down the road, looking desperately for something familiar, something to validate my early life. At last, I find W. H. Smith's. I bought a few books there once and, obsessively, I walk in now. But there is nothing of interest—the same magazines and paperbacks that I could find in any other branch.

It is the traffic lights which signal the way back to my youth. The road to my right leads to my old office. I can reach my former home by going straight on or turning left. I choose left and quickly come to one of the buildings that unite the two worlds of my past: St Mark's Church, where my aunt used to worship every Sunday morning and where she had hoped that I would accompany her. I did occasionally, although I had not been brought up as a churchgoer, while my classical education had instilled in me a fatalism tempered by Epicureanism, a belief that the greatest good was the absence of pain and disturbance. The equanimity I sought seemed at the time far removed from conventional Christianity with its emphasis on suffering. My uncle, though very much in favour of the Church of England and its traditions, was seldom dressed in time for the service and I usually followed his example. I regret my laziness now; it gave my aunt such pleasure to show off her nephew. But the formality of church-going thirty years ago was too oppressive for me. After wearing a suit to work, I found the expectation of dressing up still further, to match my aunt with her flamboyant hat and ornate brooch, too restrictive.

Across the road from the church is a row of shops, including a café. There had been a café somewhere near here when I was living in Denbridge. One Saturday, my aunt and uncle had gone out for the evening. They had left food for me, but I had preferred to go out on my own and furtively find my own place to eat. The café was dark, dingy and almost deserted. I ordered egg and chips and sat in a long, narrow room, looking towards the kitchen, where I could see the chef preparing my meal, a cigarette dangling from his mouth, the ash hanging precariously over the pan. I watched with horrified fascination to see if any would fall. The food arrived untainted: it was one of the best meals I ever ate.

The café I enter today is clean and bright. I sit facing the window, from where the church is still visible. It was there that Lewis and Esther were married, where I officiated as best man. It was only when I received the formal invitation from Esther's parents that I learnt their surname and suddenly suspected that the elder daughter, who had died so tragically, was someone I had known. Once again, I wonder if I had been at all responsible for her death and, once again, I try to convince myself that it was impossible. I met her only twice; she killed herself nearly a year later. How could I have had anything to do with it?

A woman in her early twenties walks into the café. I start to stand up and greet her: 'Hello Charlotte,' I nearly say. Then I realise that Charlotte would be over fifty by now. Perhaps this is her daughter, but when I look at her again, I realise that the resemblance is not very marked—this girl has darker hair, her eyes are brown instead of blue, she is shorter. It is my memory which has created the similarity by association, because it was through Charlotte that I met Denise, Esther's sister.

Charlotte was a secretary at the insurance firm where I was working; she and I were the only clerical staff in our department of seven; she was the only woman. I cringe as I recall how superior I had felt towards her at first: though we were on the same grade, I was about to go to Cambridge, whereas she would probably never rise above a secretary. I hope that she didn't recognise my snobbishness. I was also very shy and I like to think that she would have assumed this to be the only reason for my reserve. I owed so much to her patient explanations of my various duties, which, despite my supposed academic potential, I would have struggled to master without her guidance. Gradually, we became friendly and it was she who organised my farewell drinks.

As the young woman leaves the café with a take-away coffee, I exchange glances with her and see that she is totally unlike Charlotte. A few minutes later, I too leave, taking a last look at the church. It was probably there that Denise's funeral had taken place. Were the family regular worshippers there, I wonder. Had I even seen them on one of my occasional visits with my aunt?

A little further along the road there is a secondary school. It is a comprehensive now, but it was the one Esther attended as a grammar school student. She must have been there while I was working in Denbridge, as she is four years younger than I and five years younger than her late sister. Fortunately, my two meetings with Denise would not have registered with Esther, although I was lucky that her friendship with Charlotte also seemed to have left no trace, for she might have made a connection with me through Charlotte.

The school is much smaller than the grammar school I attended with Lewis. I think about our friendship there. We had outgrown the intense inseparability of our early years at junior school, when we would be sitting together in class, messing about together every playtime and walking home together after school. We remained close, but the formalities of grammar school created a distance. The individual desks, where pupils sat in alphabetical order, kept us apart in class; there was no afternoon "playtime", while the morning break was different in more than the change of name. Most boys stood around talking, except for a few who played football or cricket with a seriousness totally alien to the spontaneity of junior school games. I think both of us felt excluded from these groups, but we didn't always gravitate towards each other. I remember long lunch hours spent walking alone around the massive playing fields. What were you doing at those times, Lewis? Why don't I know?

But we remained friends. We still often walked home from school together; sometimes we would help each other with our homework. Then, as we progressed through the school, we gradually became more studious. Setting ourselves apart from our peers, we found ourselves drawn back together—at first through the absence of other close friends, but slowly through a renewed amity, dependent on the closeness of those early years and the endless supply of memories.

I think it was the school trip to Paris, when we were fifteen, which re-established our close friendship. We shared a room at the cheap hotel and, between the organised visits to Notre Dame and the Louvre, we spent most of our free time together, wandering around back-streets, travelling on the metro and sitting in cafés. We also discovered the book the other was secretly reading. I first noticed a corner of John Stewart Mill's "On Liberty" sticking out from under your pillow. To assuage your embarrassment, I revealed my own, equally pretentious text: the "Philoctetes" of Sophocles—in English, although I had already decided that I would shortly be able to read it in Greek. We discussed our plans and, for the rest of our school life, we shared and encouraged each other's studies, despite our different aspirations. I loved the classics as literature—the plays and poems rooted in mythology. Your reading was directed to social change: the hours you spent poring over Paine, Owen, Marx or Kropotkin were never an end in themselves. But our interests overlapped. You read Plato, Aristotle and Cicero in translation and we talked about those authors at length. Without your encouragement, I would have studied them from duty only, while always longing to return to Homer and Aeschylus, Horace and Catullus. Once, unable to find an English version of the funeral oration of Pericles, as written by Thucydides, you asked me to translate it from the original. It was a poor effort, but the spontaneity, the mistakes, the corrections, the protracted pauses while I consulted a dictionary gave the exercise an excitement which would have been missing from a published translation. We discussed the text throughout the afternoon.

And so, we entered the third year sixth together, each preparing for the entrance examination and each succeeding—you in Politics, Philosophy and Economics; I in Classics. I was slightly jealous that you won a scholarship, but I was more disappointed that we were going to different universities—you to Oxford, I to Cambridge. If only we had been together as students, perhaps sharing digs. But maybe it was better that we separated—our later reunion was all the stronger.

Just past the school in Denbridge is a narrow alley leading to the park. This was a great discovery for me. After a few days of walking to and from work along the busy main road, I found that instead I could stroll across the park. Those ten minutes of greenery, away from the traffic, gave a new rhythm to my day. It was also a secret: my uncle and aunt had given me detailed instructions about how to get to work. I don't think they would have liked the thought of my walking along this alley at night.

Of course, it was not always night, but those dark, winter evenings— immediately after my discovery—stand out in my memory. There was just one streetlamp in the alley. I remember two men, magnified by the light, giving me a flicker of fear as I approached them, although they grunted an acknowledgment as they passed. I wondered, as I walked under the lamp myself, if I too would be magnified to a passer-by, but there was no one to see me and I walked on alone into the park.

Although I didn't find the alley at once, I discovered the park on my very first afternoon in Denbridge, when, unable to endure my new home with my uncle and aunt for a minute longer, I made my excuses and found myself here almost at once. I stood for some minutes, staring at the grass, feeling home-sick and youth-sick. Why had I agreed to come? The next eight and a half months stretched out interminably in front of me, living in a house which was not my home. And once this time was over, there would be no return to my own home; though I would still be living there in the holidays, it would be only a temporary residence—no longer the secure, boring, irritating home of a seemingly endless childhood. I stared enviously at a group of young boys kicking a football around. An asphalt path surrounded their pitch and I began walking around this, trying to appear uninterested in the game. Every few minutes, one of the boys would accidentally kick the ball towards the path and would run to collect it. I longed for it to career in my direction, so that I could retrieve it and share, momentarily, not in their game—I have no interest in football—but in their youth, their innocence. I don't know if they noticed my repeated circuits, but on my fifth lap, the ball finally arrived in my vicinity and I kicked it back. Hearing their shouts of thanks, I experienced a temporary consolation and was able to walk to my new home with a modicum of contentment.

On my return from work, I would often repeat this circuit, letting the tensions of the day evaporate, deferring for a short time the different tensions of the forthcoming evening with my uncle and aunt. Once, in summer, as I was enjoying the "breathable light of heaven", I saw the silhouette of a man sitting on a tree stump in a small thicket at one corner of the park, holding to his lips something which glinted in the sun. From a distance, he looked like Pan, playing his pipes in a sacred grove, though when I approached, I saw that he was a down-and-out, drinking from a can. However, he shouted a cheerful, if incoherent, greeting to me, so the vision was not annihilated.

Nearly twenty years later, I came here with Lewis and Esther. Their children were racing their tiny bikes around this same asphalt path towards the swings and see-saws at the far end of the park which I am now approaching. It was here that Esther lagged behind, gazing at the playing area. I stopped chasing the young cyclists and turned back to ask her what was wrong.

'We came here once—Denise and me. I suppose I was about six, so she must have been eleven. I remember her pushing me on the swing. I'd never been so high. I was terrified.'

But it was not her fear that she was remembering. This was the first time I had heard her talk about her sister. I knew that I should encourage her to say more, although I was afraid that my own knowledge would become apparent. We were silent for a short time. Then I resolved to be brave.

'Do you want to talk about what happened?'

'Oh, it didn't last long. Once she stopped pushing me, I soon came to rest.'

This wasn't what I had meant, but I was grateful for her misunderstanding, whether it had been deliberate or not. I changed the subject and talked about how fast Rob and Sally were cycling. Not for the first time, I wished that I had told Esther that I had known her sister. My memory of a happy, confident young woman would have been a comfort to her. But guilt at my sense of culpability had prevented me and now it was too late.

A road marks the end of the path. As I approach it, I can't decide whether to turn left to my uncle's and aunt's home or right to Lewis's. I toss an imaginary coin, trying to leave the decision to the gods, and turn left. After two right turns, I am standing outside my former home. The house is still there, though it looks very different. The garage has been extended to the pavement, while a single plate-glass window stretches across the ground floor at the front of the house, revealing that the two rooms I remember have been combined, with a massive dining table filling most of the new space. I liked the two small rooms: the cosy sitting room, where I watched television with my aunt, and my uncle's austere study. I wonder if the large kitchen at the back has changed too. It was there that we ate our meals, including that first Sunday lunch, when my parents had driven me here and the five of us sat rather awkwardly over a roast joint. The families had never been close: although my aunt was my father's sister, she was eleven years older and her husband was six years older still. I was wishing my own brother and sister were there to ease the tension. I remember longing for the meal to end, but at the same time dreading my parents' departure. Once they had left,

95

I went upstairs to my bedroom to unpack. It took me a long time: I kept stopping to stare miserably out of the window, looking to where I am standing now. Then, realising that I had been upstairs too long, I returned to the kitchen and cheerfully told my aunt that I would like to go for a short walk, feeling the need for exercise after the long car journey. She looked surprised, but acquiesced on condition that I were back in time for tea. It was dark when I eventually returned, after my visit to the park and my single kick of the football, but I wasn't too late.

We had "low tea" on Sundays: bread and butter, with home-made jam and cakes. My aunt was a good cook, though I didn't feel much like eating on that first evening, after the large lunch and my perturbed state of mind. My aunt kept fussing, continually asking if I wanted more cake or another cup of tea. I felt ready to scream at her to shut up and leave me to nurse my anguish in silence, but I managed to control myself, recognising, even then, how hard she was trying to make me feel comfortable. After tea, I offered to wash up and I felt more relaxed, my hands in the hot water, as I answered my aunt's questions about my brother and sister. Then my uncle spoke to me:

'Would you mind stepping into my study for a few minutes, please.'

I didn't realise at the time how privileged I was. Never again in the eight months I lived there was I to set foot in his sanctum. Even my aunt only ever went in to clean it in the mornings.

It was lit by a single standard lamp next to the desk and, despite the cold winter evening, the window was open to allow the cigar smoke to escape—this was the only room in the house where my aunt permitted him to smoke. He poured me a whisky and I sat, shivering in the darkness, listening to his monologue.

How long was I in that room? Thirty years later, it seems that I was there for several hours, but maybe it was no longer than twenty minutes. I can't remember much of the speech, but I still recall the rhythm and cadences—a quiet, but forceful diction, with a hint of a north country accent. Odd phrases and sentences recur to me, while most of what he said in the ensuing months has vaporised.

'I joined Citadel Life when I was demobbed as a nineteen-year-old lad after the Great War. Fifty-two years later, I still go into the office every day…'

'Citadel Life expects hard work, dedication and total, absolute loyalty…'

'Nothing is more important than insurance: putting your affairs in order against the possible and the inevitable…'

'It's not just a job; it's not just a career. Citadel Life has been my family. Citadel Life is life itself…'

I was scared and bewildered. How could I cope with a job predicated upon such uncompromising commitment? And did I really need to subscribe to such exacting values when I would be working there for so short a time? An insurance office did not figure in the academic aspirations I was embracing. I inwardly rebelled against his pomposity, although later I thought of the performance as melancholic. As I contemplated his childless marriage, his uneventful domestic life, I could understand why he should take such exaggerated value from his job.

At last, I was released, to be welcomed by my aunt, who, in a much homelier manner, was making cocoa.

'Has he told you all about your work? You can go in tomorrow with a head-start now.'

I agreed, although nothing my uncle had said had given me any insight into what my job would be.

'You'll go in together tomorrow, won't you? So Colin knows where to go?'

I tried to suppress a look of horror. I remembered holding my mother's hand as she led me to infant school on my first day. But I was nineteen now.

'Oh, I don't think the lad wants his old uncle to take him to work.'

I smiled gratefully. I felt that he was showing a sensitivity that I had not previously recognised. Perhaps I was partially correct, although I soon realised that my uncle had another motive in saying these words. While he was being truthful when he said that he still went to work every day, he rarely arrived before 11 o'clock. Meetings with the few clients he still saw were all scheduled for the late morning, while the main activity of his day was lunch in the Executive Dining Room. He wouldn't have wanted to disrupt this routine, even for my first day.

We sat, drinking cocoa, while my aunt talked amiably about the neighbours and some of her friends from church. Soon I went to bed.

I quickly adapted to the order of home life: a fried breakfast every working day to "set me up", then high tea punctually at 6.30—scrambled eggs, kippers, kidneys… After that, my uncle would retire to his study, with some business files, the Financial Times and his detective novels. He would spend the evening there, smoking cigars and drinking slightly too much whisky. Meanwhile, my aunt and I would take our second cup of tea into the sitting room, where we would sit in front of the television, while she talked about the people she had met that day.

It was often 8 o'clock before I felt I could go up to my room to study. Then, two hours later, she would call me down again for a bedtime drink. It was not meant to be like this. I had imagined a rarefied atmosphere of intense, uninterrupted study from 7 o'clock to midnight. Instead, with so little time and without the incentive of any academic assignments, I idled away the evening, my books in front of me, but my eyes not focusing on them. I usually managed to read a little Latin; sometimes I would even write a few, derivative lines of Latin poetry. (I cringe as I remember a verse declaiming that "the same perpetual night awaits the lover, the poet, the tradesman and the emperor.") These probably helped me to do tolerably well in Latin at Cambridge. However, I neglected my Greek and my 2:2 was my eventual reward—not good enough for the academic career I had so confidently predicted. O Nemesis, you know the way to smother a man's boasting.

In retrospect, I wonder why I bothered to study at all at that time. Why didn't I go out and meet people or stay in and read novels in English? Yet I enjoyed my evenings: the cosy atmosphere of daydreaming in front of my books, with the prospect of a friendly cup of cocoa afterwards. I didn't then realise that it was the enjoyment of a lotus eater. I was unaware of the problems that would inevitably follow.

I never went back to the house after my work ended. Two years later, my uncle finally retired altogether and the couple moved away from Denbridge. I look resentfully at the house. After my miserable start there, I was happy in my lazy manner. I look at the "improvements" which have impeded the memory. What had the household gods—the Lares and Penates—thought of those?

The house is very near Lewis's old home, but I have never walked from one to the other. I take turnings to the right and left, only to find myself in a cul-de-sac. I return to my uncle's and aunt's house and continue back into the park. Then I leave by a different exit, which leads me past the Park Tavern. I had lunch there a few years ago, with Lewis and his family. We sat in the garden, looking out over the parkland. It seemed very different from how I remembered it twenty-five years before—a small bar, the customers squeezed between converging walls. I used to go there occasionally on my way home from work, treasuring a few minutes of a different, more Bohemian, existence than the neat order of my aunt's regime to which I was about to return. As I watched other customers arriving, talking to each other, preparing—perhaps—for a night of heavy drinking, I could glimpse another world—one I had no wish to inhabit, but one which thrilled me with a frisson of excitement.

How often did I go to this pub? Three times—maybe four. I would drink a single glass of bitter lemon, except once. One wintry day in February, I bought a glass of wine and imagined myself looking out into the snowy landscape of one of my favourite poems—Horace's Soracte ode. I liked to think it summed up my philosophy on that cold evening:

Dissolve the cold, generously piling up wood in the fireplace and, Thaliarchus, kindly bring out the four-year-old wine from the Sabine wine jar. Leave the rest to the gods…

There was no log fire in the pub and there was a degree of affectation about the experience, but I left happy, as I walked home to my aunt's tea.

This pub, where I once drank with Lewis, leads my memory back to The White Lion in my hometown, where I would occasionally spend an evening with you during the university vacations. We were a little shy of each other at first, after our protracted separation, and would talk formally about our courses: the essays we had written, the exams we had sat. Gradually, the discussion would move to current affairs. I never shared your passion for politics, but on those evenings in the mid-70s, I felt engaged in a way I had never been before or since. You would ask me my opinion of some item of news—the miners' strike, the three-day week, Ireland—and I would reply in a conventional, often bigoted, manner. Then you would ask further questions, playfully demonstrating the contradictions in my argument. In the late 1990s when the House of Lords was being reformed, I recalled one of those sessions because we had discussed this topic all those years before.

'Do you support the House of Lords?' you asked me one night.

'Yes, I think so. It puts a check on the power of the Commons.'

'Would you consider yourself a democrat?'

'Yes, of course.'

'And do you agree that the House of Commons has at least a modicum of democratic accountability?'

'Yes, a modicum. We vote for the MPs.'

'And what democratic accountability do the Lords have?'

'Well, none really. They vote in the chamber, but no one votes for them.'

'So, in order to safeguard our democracy, you believe that an elected body should be regulated by people who owe their position to inheritance or patronage?'

I felt aggrieved, for I knew what you were doing: unlike you, I had read some of Plato's dialogues in the original Greek; I had studied the elenchus as a debating technique. But you always disarmed me with the breadth of your reading and understanding and by your humour. I remember howling with laughter several times in that pub. How could Socratic dialogue have been so funny?

For you, these discussions were not merely a rhetorical game. You had an evangelical fervour, but you always seemed genuinely interested in my thoughts. I knew that your ideas were rooted in activism as much as theory—you attended the demonstrations, organised public meetings, wrote campaigning leaflets—but you differed from the other students I knew who did the same. With you, there was no aggression, no empty sloganizing: you espoused an idealistic belief that right would prevail by the ineluctable force of rational argument. Perhaps you were right: after listening to you, I always felt that I had developed an understanding of issues which I could never glean from a newspaper or broadcast.

Later, when we had both left university and you were studying for your teaching diploma, we would discuss educational theory. Your conversation would encompass the thoughts of Rousseau, Locke, Montessori and Piaget, but always it seemed to return to Plato. You decried his authoritarianism and elitism, were sceptical about his metaphysics, but adored his methods of argument. You loved the importance he gave to education and used to quote his dictum that teaching is not like putting sight into blind eyes, but should develop the understanding that is already there.

By that time, I was working in an office again. I had abandoned academia and the beloved Greek and Latin texts which for so long had been my mental companions, even when my laziness had left the physical volumes unopened. But after our meeting, I felt temporarily inspired: for a few days, I would read passages in both languages and dream of reviving my interest. Then the mundanities of my job would overwhelm the dreams.

The Park Tavern is behind me now. I take two left turns and am standing outside Number 32, Lewis's old home. It is only eighteen months since I last saw it, but it is a sorry sight now. A property developer has taken it over and gutted it. The formerly neat front garden is covered with piles of bricks and a cement-mixer. The fence is down.

I try to count the number of times I have been to the house. I did not see it on that visit to Lewis and his future in-laws, so my first sight must have been the day before the wedding. I arrived in mid-afternoon; we discussed the plans for the next day and then went to the pub with a few friends. It was a very sober stag night and we returned early. The house was full, with various relatives staying. I slept downstairs on the sofa. I have never set foot upstairs.

My regular visits began three years later, after Rob's birth. There was no baptism, but you made it clear that you would like me to assume the role of quasi-godfather and I realised that this was intended to be a serious commitment. So, I visited you at least once a year—usually twice; in those eighteen years, I must have come here nearly thirty times before your move to London on your appointment as headteacher of a failing school in Tower Hamlets.

It is only now that I am struck by the extraordinary coincidence of your move to Denbridge. When you arrived as Head of History at the new comprehensive, it was already six years since I had left and the memories of those eight and a half months with my uncle and aunt were dissipating. Colleagues from school and university had scattered across the country; it seemed hardly surprising that your destination should have been here rather than any other provincial town. But now, another twenty years later, it appears increasingly odd: no one else I know has moved here; most of my acquaintances have never even passed through the town. It has become a secret domain I share with Lewis, a domain existing in memory and imagination as much as in reality. For you were with me in those early days, though physically you were far away. So often, it was you I was talking to as I walked alone through the park, you whose approval I sought when I expressed an opinion on anything in public. Those distant, fading recollections underpin the more recent memories of my visits to you: the different periods intermingle, so that I am sometimes unable to recall whether a Denbridge experience belongs to my late adolescence or my middle age. Yet, while we share this world in my imagination, I know that for you my eight and a half months here have no resonance. Physically, you never inhabited that part of the world, while the events from that time which impinged on your family I have kept from you—a secret within our secret world.

My visits followed a familiar pattern. I would arrive at about 10.30 on a Saturday morning: Lewis or Esther would drive me to their home; I would play with the children when they were young and chat to them when they were older; we would have lunch at home or in a pub or restaurant. Then we would go for a walk and return home for a cup of tea before I was driven back to the station.

It was only gradually that I noticed a difference in you. Those early visits were so focused on the young children and their needs that there was little chance for any serious conversation with you. Later, though, I realised that that kind of conversation no longer had the same appeal for you. If I asked you a question about your school—about the national curriculum, for instance, or special needs education—you would answer readily enough, but you seemed interested only in the practicalities of the issues. They were policies which had to be implemented; they didn't elicit the omnivorous hunger for ideas which I was used to. You were clearly a good teacher: you had been recruited as head of department after just two years at a school in Birmingham. Then, three years later, you had been promoted to Deputy Head. I was surprised at how readily you had accepted promotion—I had never thought of you as personally ambitious. Thereafter, although you didn't underestimate or try to conceal the difficulties—there had been incidents involving both drugs and knives at your school—they were just more problems to be solved; you didn't seem to question their relation to society.

Your knowledge was still there. I noticed it on my later visits when Rob was studying for his A levels and showing off his political awareness to Sally. You didn't participate, except to correct any factual inaccuracies: 'No, the Equal Pay Act was passed in 1970, but it didn't come into force until 1975'; or 'No, the 1870 Act set up board schools only in those districts where voluntary schools didn't exist.' When discussing 19th-century education as a student, your talk would encompass demographics, the needs of industrialisation, the influence of Protestantism, the French philosophers, the fears of revolution and the rise of trade unions. Now, you could spare only a single, factual sentence.

Why had you changed? Did you remember what Pericles had said in that passage we had read together all that time before: that a man not engaged in politics is useless? Was it simply that you had grown up? Was your idealism incompatible with the day-to-day reality of school life? Or, lacking the energy for further activism, did the theorising seem futile, self-indulgent? Perhaps the change was all for the best. Could I, in my middle-aged slothfulness, have coped with the pious energy of a left-wing saint? But it was that saint whom I had idolised in my adolescence—not a staid teacher, focused on his own career.

Was Esther responsible for the change? She is highly intelligent, but is no academic and never went to university. Despite the easy compatibility between the two of you, she is not the person I would have expected you to choose as a partner. Wouldn't her sister have been more suitable for you? I experience a sudden gush of jealousy, imagining you married to the woman you had never met.

I dismiss these thoughts. Esther is perfect for you. She encourages you and takes a deep interest in your work. I have enjoyed talking to her. She would tell me all about her job at the estate agent's: about her colleagues, her boss, the IT problems. I didn't expect an analysis of housing policy from her, so why should I have yearned for your thoughts on education? At least you are pursuing a career for which your studies prepared you, whereas I have abandoned all interest in the classics. However, I was only a mediocre scholar, whereas I had thought of you as "the gods' rival in wisdom". But how wise were the gods?

Some words of Vergil come to mind: *omnes fert aetas*. I feel pleased that I can remember them after so many years, although they are not very profound: 'Time carries everything away.' Then, suddenly, I recall the next two words: *animum quoque*. What does that phrase mean? I must have read it without translating it. If I had needed to find the English equivalent, I would probably have chosen "even the soul", but "soul" has a Christian connotation, which gives the wrong impression. "Individuality" or "essence" might be better—perhaps even "life force". Is that what you have lost? I shudder at the thought.

Instead of politics, we would talk—you and I—of the distant past, diving deep beneath the apparently taboo years of our studious adolescence and re-surfacing in the pre-intellectual innocence of our childhood. For me, this introduced an egalitarianism into our friendship. You had been a bright child even then, but you had not been so obviously my superior. We reminisced about walking home from school together. We used to play in a disused allotment (now part of a housing estate), where we built a den in the undergrowth, fortified by the remains of a chicken coop; in heavy rainstorms, we raced matches along the fast-flowing torrents in road-side gutters; we threw our school caps to each other from ever-increasing distances, only to see yours drift over a high wall into a garden. The secret mission to rescue it ended in laughter.

Always there would be laughter when we recalled these events. We would sit doubled-up around the table while the rest of the family looked on in bemusement, for there was nothing intrinsically funny about the memories. It was just that they were *our* memories; they had helped create the people we had become, although the routes were unrecognisable. For me, at least, the humour lay partly in two irreconcilable images of the same person, separated by nearly forty years.

I walk away slowly, resisting the temptation to turn back one last time. My mood is elegiac, but my threnody is very different from the one I was humming so recently as I left the house of my long-dead aunt and uncle. I still see Lewis and his family; I shall continue to see them; our friendship is assured. But our conversations, no longer rooted in this soil, develop differently. Removed from the crucible of those earlier memories (which you didn't share), they have lost an intensity, a specificity and are dissipated in a welter of mundanities.

I reach the main road. This is the route I took on the first few days of my life at my uncle's and aunt's, before I discovered my secret way through the park. Clad in a suit—the first time I had ever worn one—I found my costume as alien as my surroundings. I tried to disguise my appearance with my old school mac, which I wore with collar buttoned up. I didn't want any passers-by to think I was the sort of person who went to work in a suit—as if anyone would have been interested.

On that first day, I turned to wish a school crossing man a good morning. In my mood of nervous apprehension, I welcomed his friendly greeting in return. I thought I detected an Italian accent and, though I have never studied modern Italian, I felt we shared a Latin link—conspirators against the powers of besuited finance in which I was about to be engulfed.

The school is still there—it is where Rob and Sally were pupils. Schools seem to surround me oppressively, forcing their memories of childhood upon me. How miserable I had been at my own junior school in the early months, sitting next to a boy I never spoke to. Then Lewis had moved to the school. Was it inspiration or expediency that had induced the teacher to seat us together, giving me the responsibility of making you feel at ease? I don't think I was very successful. At first, I spoke to you no more than to your predecessor. Then, suddenly, we were talking incessantly. Often we would be told off for speaking in class—yes, I, who had previously been too scared to open my mouth.

How long did that intensity of feeling last? It was not just the move to grammar school which changed us; there had already been a slight separation, for I had other friends by that time. There was Adrian, whom you knew well, but also Kelvin, who was never close to you. Sometimes I went to his house on a Saturday without you. Was I betraying our friendship or had we tacitly agreed on a mutual rejection of an exclusiveness which couldn't extend into adolescence?

Yet ours was the friendship which survived. Kelvin, a casualty of the 11+, I never saw again and, until today, I have rarely thought about him. Had the exam results been different, perhaps it would have been Kelvin who would remain my long-term friend, although I feel no emotional attachment to his memory. Denbridge would be a different place. Even if you had come to live here, your move would not have concerned me as we would not have remained in contact. That Denbridge which I know—the locus of the complex mingling of memories—would not exist and I should not be standing here today.

But of course, you did pass the 11+. Your intelligence meant that the result was never in doubt, so perhaps the Fates had decided long before that our paths would meet again in this town.

On my first day here, this route seemed an endless trudge, but today I am at the traffic lights by the church in a few minutes. Then, instead of retracing my steps to the High Road, I turn left into Regent Street. When I first walked here, I knew little of London and the name had no metropolitan resonance. I remember thinking only that the buildings were not Regency, but at least a hundred years more recent. They are residential houses at first; then, as the road veers right to join the town square, the houses give way to older offices. I pass an estate agent's—was this where Esther had worked? It is the right area, though I never bothered to establish the exact location. This is another link, which I had not appreciated, for my old office is just two doors further along.

It is still recognisable in the upper storeys. The neo-Gothic arches and turrets, the copper dome remain—symbols of Victorian dependability. But the ground floor is different: the façade is entirely glass, with, emblazoned above the massive door, the name of the multinational financial services company which took over Citadel Life fifteen years ago. The reception area is enormous, the desk flanked by a fountain and a rotating metallic sculpture. I remember the revolving doors in the brick wall which admitted me into the building on my first day. A uniformed security guard escorted me to the desk in the small reception area, where the receptionist rang for Mr Armitage and invited me to sit in one of the two armchairs. I waited nervously, glancing at the portraits of earlier, elderly insurance dignitaries, men imbued with the same values as my uncle. I thought of the Roman virtues—pietas, gravitas, constantia. The men portrayed here would all have embraced those same qualities: each of them would have made the same speech as my uncle, instilling absolute loyalty to the firm. I pictured my new boss as a similar man, slightly younger, but with the identical outlook. I was anxious to impress him and not to let down my uncle, but, at the same time, I was desperate to avoid any charge of favouritism. Would Mr Armitage resent my arrival, the nepotism which had dropped me into the job without even an interview? I mused pedantically on the word: "nepos" was the Latin for "grandson", so I could justifiably absolve myself from any such accusation. However, "nephew" derived from the same Latin root.

My etymological ruminations were interrupted by the arrival of a young woman—the same whose likeness I would think I was seeing thirty years later.

'Are you Colin?' she asked. 'My name's Charlotte.'

It had not occurred to me that women would be working here. I had imagined the office peopled with elderly, besuited men like my uncle—the seniors attended by male confidential clerks—all speaking in whispers. There was no room for women in that world. As we travelled up to the fourth floor in the lift, I began to realise how wrong I was.

'What were you doing before you came here?' asked Charlotte.

'Oh, I've only just arrived. I just walked here.'

'No, I mean where were you working before?'

I had thought that everyone would know all about me. I was the nephew of an important director; I had passed my Cambridge entrance exam. I was both pleased and upset to find that I was nobody of significance.

Leaving the lift, we crossed the corridor to a large office, with a smaller one adjoining it. Charlotte led me into this and introduced me to Mr Armitage.

'David, this is Colin.'

A young man stood up, smiling. His hair and sideboards were a little longer than I had expected; the trousers of his suit were slightly flared. On his desk was a small, framed photograph of his wife and daughter. As I look back on that encounter and think of the differences between office life then and now—the open-plan rooms, the computers on every desk—I think that the differences between David's career and those of my uncle and the sombre figures who adorned Reception were even greater. Those older men would never have made concessions to modernity; they would never have allowed any testimony of their family life to impinge on their office personas.

'Glad to see you, Colin. I hope you'll enjoy your time with us. I'm sure Charlotte will look after you, but if you ever need to talk to me, don't hesitate to come into my office.'

So began my eight months at Citadel Life. I quickly adjusted to the new routines: opening envelopes; photocopying, stamping and filing documents; taking letters to the post room for franking; more filing. So much of the work would be mechanised now, but I don't remember it as particularly antiquated. I even used a Telex machine to contact other branches: twenty years before email was widespread, I was already typing messages and sending them electronically.

I had no intrinsic interest in insurance, especially in the work of Surrender Values where I was based. However, without ever trying to, I absorbed much about the subject. Sometimes I was given documents to proof-read; sometimes I would work briefly in other departments; sometimes I would find myself sitting next to more senior staff in the canteen and I would learn a little about their jobs. My uncle too would talk about the work of the office over our evening meal, before retiring to his smoke-filled study. Thus it was that, three years after my departure, having gained a degree too mediocre to allow me the academic career which I had aspired to, I found myself being interviewed for a job in an accountancy firm. I can recall the interviewer glancing at my CV. He never mentioned my classics degree, but quizzed me on my work at Citadel Life. I was able to answer satisfactorily, despite despising the work and despising myself for the ease with which I had acquired my expertise, while my classical education, at which I had worked so hard, had failed me. And the vindictive gods laughed, mocking my lazy aspirations.

I worked closely with Charlotte at Citadel Life. We shared the outer office, she concentrating on the typing and I doing most of the other clerical jobs. After overcoming my snobbish feeling of superiority, I quickly learnt to respect her own advanced office skills. We never took our lunch break together, as one of us needed to be available to answer the telephone, but we chatted a little at our desks. She talked about films, holidays, last night's television, so my evenings with my aunt were not entirely wasted. If I had rigorously maintained my projected programme of evening study, I would have had less to say in the office the next day.

David was always friendly, though he didn't chat much. He would leave his office to give us instructions, thank us appreciatively and return to his work.

At lunchtime, after a quick meal in the canteen, I would usually leave the building to go for a walk. There was never any pressure to be back early at my desk and I was able to walk some distance. Often I would make my way into the square, as I do today. It looks very different.

A steady, but not excessive, stream of traffic used to flow both ways around the square; now two sides are pedestrianized, while the cars on the other sides are trapped in a one-way system as their drivers attempt to escape across the bridge. I have seen the square only once since I worked here: Lewis drove me past here with the family for an afternoon in the country on one of my visits. Esther casually pointed towards the office and remarked, 'That's where you used to work, isn't it, Colin? My office isn't far off either.'

I wanted to shout out, 'Stop the car. This is my heritage.' But Lewis was already driving across the bridge. I resolved to say something on our way back, only to find that Esther, who was driving by that time, took us in a different direction to avoid the one-way system.

I walked around the square during my first lunchtime in the job—past the town hall, the clock-tower, the church, a small theatre. Not yet used to the distance, I then hurried back to the office, fearing that I would be late. I was at my desk twenty minutes before I needed to be.

I didn't notice the pub on that first day, but it must have been there, because this was where I had my leaving drinks on a Friday in September. It was called the King's Head then, though as I enter it now, I see that it has become The Bald Monkey. It had been a narrow, unobtrusive pub, easy to overlook from the square. The sign now allows no one to miss it. Inside, it is similar—as far as I can remember—though not as dark. I buy half a pint of bitter and a cheese sandwich. I came in here on my last day, with David and a few other colleagues. On our arrival, I was disconcerted to see my uncle, ensconced in a corner. However, he showed great sensitivity—shook my hand, shook David's hand, bought all of us drinks and then left, ready for more whisky later in the evening, in the safety of his study.

David also behaved impeccably. He chatted about his days at university, reassured me that I would do well, thanked me for my hard work and then left, but not before buying me another beer and telling me to enjoy myself.

I was left with two men in their mid-twenties from another department, neither of whom I knew well. Now is the time for drinking, said Horace, and they both seemed intent on getting drunk. I felt uncomfortable and was anxious to leave, but as I emptied my glass, they both insisted that I should have another. Two unstarted pints were now in front of me and I saw that they were determined to make me even drunker than themselves. I don't remember the conversation; I think it was just about drinking. I started gulping down one of the pints, resolved to leave after finishing it. After all, I would never see the men again.

Then two young women walked into the bar.

'Hello Colin,' said Charlotte, greeting me with a kiss (the first and last time she ever did this). 'Sorry I'm late. This is Denise.'

What did she look like? I know how she appeared three years before, because there was a photograph of her on the mantelpiece at Lewis's home in Denbridge; it's still there in your new London house. This image of a seventeen-year-old girl is what I remember, although I can barely assimilate it with the person I met that night. The photograph shows a pale, sad, vulnerable girl, very different from the sun-tanned, energetic, self-confident woman who greeted me. Perhaps it is simply the repeated sightings of that photograph—furtive glances when her sister and brother-in-law were out of the room (I didn't want to draw their attention to my fascination)—that makes this image prevail over the other. But perhaps it is because subsequent events seem to confirm the earlier image as the true self—the later one merely a false persona.

I'm still surprised that she liked me. What could she have seen in a drunken, immature office worker? Maybe it was just the contrast with my two colleagues, who were more drunk and—I believe—more immature: they had pounced on Charlotte and were regaling her with their puerile banter. Or maybe it was just that Denise could get on with anyone. She asked me about my degree course and was the first person since I left school to seem genuinely interested.

'Oh, I wish I knew Latin and Greek—just a little, at any rate. I'm reading English and it would be so useful. You know, when you're reading Keats or Milton—they're so steeped in the classics; if I knew a little, I'd know what they were on about.'

English had been my third subject at A Level and we talked for some time about literature. I realised how much I had missed academic discussion since Lewis's departure. Then she changed the subject.

'But at least I've been to Greece and seen some of the places.'

It was my turn to be impressed. Foreign travel was still a rarity at that time and my school trip to Paris could not compete with a holiday in Greece. I felt jealous as she talked about the buildings on the Acropolis. I had written an essay on Greek architecture, but had never imagined travelling there. My family holidays had always been a fortnight on the south coast of England; I had no idea how one would organise a trip to Greece.

'Did you go on your own?' I asked. 'Or in a group?'

'No, I went with my boyfriend. Former boyfriend, I should say—I dumped him soon after.'

I didn't know how to respond to that, so I asked, 'And have you been to Italy too?'

'No, I went to Spain this year—with my new boyfriend. I haven't dumped him.' She gave me a playful punch in the stomach. 'Not yet, anyway.'

Embarrassed, I changed the subject, 'How do you know Charlotte?'

'Oh, we were at school together. We don't see much of each other these days, with me being away at university. But I think it's important to keep up with old friendships. They're a part of you, aren't they?'

I agreed and talked about my friendship with Lewis and how I had missed you while you were in Israel. She listened sympathetically, asking a few questions about you. I had never known anyone take such an interest in our life together.

As I sip my drink today, I seem to recall much of this conversation verbatim, but I know that I am deluding myself. I have re-enacted the dialogue so often—with embellishments and suppressions—and what I am remembering are those re-enactments rather than the original interchange. Other topics I talked about with Denise that evening have vanished from my memory, drowned in Lethe's unredeeming waters. Had those other words been too painful to remember or merely too boring? Either way, we must have talked for two hours that evening.

Suddenly, it was closing time. Charlotte had extricated herself from the two men, who were pleading with the barman to sell them another drink. I felt guilty about having left her with them while I was enjoying myself with Denise. The three of us stood in the doorway for a few minutes, breathing the fresh, smoke-free air. Denise asked when I would be leaving Denbridge.

'Sunday,' I said.

'Me too. Let's meet up one last time tomorrow—the three of us.'

We weren't in a fit state to make many decisions, so we agreed to meet here, in the same pub, at 6 o'clock and then decide what to do.

I felt queasy all the next day, wishing I had drunk less and hoping that I wouldn't be expected to do the same that night. I was the first to arrive here and I bought a glass of bitter lemon. Denise came a little later, on her own. I was pleased, even though I had grown fond of Charlotte. But then her words disappointed me:

'Hello Colin. Sorry I can't stay long tonight. I'm catching the early train for Sheffield tomorrow and I still haven't packed.'

It seemed a poor excuse, but at least she was here. I offered her a drink and she asked for a gin and tonic. We sat, sipping from our glasses; the easy conversation of the night before had vanished. Then she suggested that we exchange addresses and she took out pen and paper.

'We must write to each other,' she said.

But we didn't. I remember those early days at Cambridge, when I longed to write to her, but somehow never did. I was too miserable, too ashamed. How she would have despised my self-pitying words, she who seemed so much at ease in student life. It was only too late that I realised she had not been happy. Perhaps we could have shared our sadness; perhaps everything would have been different if we had. With me to confide in, maybe she would still be alive today. Had I killed her through my neglect? Or am I endowing my young self with too much maturity? Would I have exacerbated rather than mollified her depression?

As it was, I endured my misery in solitude, never supposing that her thoughts might have been similar. For how could they have been? Wasn't she studying with her equals? Unlike me, alienated by the formality of my life: the gowns, the rules, the snobbery (much of which I was imagining). Most of my fellow Classics students came from public schools and I felt that they were looking down on me, that they were better than I was. (Most of them *were* better, but I don't now think that they looked down on me.) I missed my old classics teacher at school. As the only boy studying Greek, I had come to know him better than any of the other staff, better, perhaps, than any other adults apart from my parents. Retiring at the same time as I left school, he was proud to have guided one last classics student to university—the first for three years. I had expected to be taught by similar tutors at Cambridge: elderly, academic, unworldly. Instead, they were much younger—one used to drive a Harley-Davidson at great speed around the streets. None of them took the fatherly interest in me that I had found so encouraging at school. I was left to my own misery: too unhappy to study much in those first few weeks, too shy even to set foot in the library.

After I had settled down at last, it seemed too late to write to Denise—after all, she hadn't written to me. I would have sent her a Christmas card, but I didn't have her Denbridge address. I sent one to Charlotte instead—a proxy card for Denise. Perhaps Charlotte understood, for it was she who wrote to me later to inform me of Denise's death.

No, I never wrote to Denise, but I remember writing my address in this pub and whispering a pretentious prayer to myself as I finished my drink: 'May the winged heels of Hermes bear you safely on the train to Sheffield.' But Hermes, I recalled later, was a psychopomp, guiding souls through the gateway of Death.

What I said audibly was:

'I hope you have a safe journey to Sheffield.'

She laughed. 'Thanks. But we don't have to part just yet. Do you want another drink or shall we go for a short walk?'

And so, we left the pub and walked on to the bridge as I do now. This was the corner where, forty minutes later, we separated for the second and last time. I can't remember what we said. I know we didn't kiss, although I had wanted to so desperately. I seem to recall describing a semi-circle on the pavement with my right foot as I muttered a few valedictory platitudes, but that is a mannerism of mine which, perhaps, I have used to plug the oblivion. When at last I walked away, I didn't look back—afraid to see that she was not doing the same.

I am now standing at the centre of the bridge. This was my destination during my second lunch-hour at Citadel Life. I stood looking downstream at the neat, tarmac paths on either side of the river, sheltered by well-tended trees. Then I crossed the road to look upstream. The view here was wilder. A canal joined the river just before the bridge; a muddy, overgrown towpath ran along one side of it. It was a tempting prospect, but not one compatible with my suit and polished shoes. I often used to stroll along the paths downstream in my lunch hours, but as Denise and I descended the steps to the canal, it was only the third time I had been there. Now, thirty years later, I begin my fourth descent.

I am excited. I thought that the path had vanished amidst the disruption caused by the building of the ring road a few years after my departure, but it is still here, though slightly different from how I remember it. It is not so wild; the path has been cleared of undergrowth; the trees, whose branches used to stretch across the water, have been pruned. A narrow boat is moored by the bank;

evidently the canal is navigable again. A few people are walking along the towpath. It is a pleasant setting, although I miss the wildness of those earlier expeditions. I first came there in early summer and felt, after only a few minutes, that I was far away from civilisation, as I walked through a swathe of waist-high meadowsweet and cow-parsley.

The next time was more frightening. It was that evening when my aunt and uncle were away. After my meal in the café, I walked a little way along here. A slight mist was oozing out from the banks; ducks were roosting along the lower branches of trees. I felt scared—would I meet some stranger, preying on innocent victims? I tried to sing quietly to myself, recalling that Horace, journeying far into the woodland from his Sabine farm, had been singing of his Lalage, so that a huge wolf, mollified by his innocence, had turned away, leaving him unharmed.

I sensed an elegiac tone to my third trip even at the time. It was my last evening in Denbridge, my last evening—for the time being, at least—with Denise. Her subsequent death has altered my memory of the walk, endowing it with an added poignancy. I think we walked for about twenty minutes in each direction, although I can't remember enough conversation to fill that period. She spoke of an English professor, William Empson, who lectured occasionally on her course and was also a published poet and critic. She recited a few obscure, esoteric lines of his and laughed at my look of bewilderment.

'Yes, I know, but never mind. It's your turn now. Let's hear some Latin poetry.'

I have re-enacted that scene so often, always choosing a different poem. Should I have recited some erotic lines of Catullus?

Let us live, my Lesbia, and let us love,
And value at one farthing
All the censures of old kill-joys!
Suns may set and rise again:
For us, when once our short light has set,
There is one everlasting night to be slept.
Give me a thousand kisses, then a hundred,
Then another thousand, then a second hundred...

That might have established a different, less formal foundation to our relationship. The rest of the walk would have changed. Maybe later events would have been affected. But how could I have quelled my embarrassment sufficiently to declaim the lines with the necessary bravura? And how would I have felt if events had not changed and I had been left with the memory of having predicted "everlasting night".

Something more pastoral might have been better to accord with the riverbank on which we were walking:

I found a stream, running without an eddy, without a murmur, clear to the earth below; from above, every pebble could be counted; you would scarcely think that the water moved. Silvery willows and a poplar, nourished by the water, gave a natural shade to the sloping banks…

I could have stopped there. There was no need to continue Ovid's narrative of the naked nymph, bathing in the river until pursued by the lustful river god.

But why, instead, did I choose Horace's ode "To Pyrrha"? Was it because—consciously or unconsciously—I thought it appropriate for her? Was it because I had already been thinking of Horace and Lalage? Was it simply that I remembered it almost perfectly—a short poem from an A level set book? In my re-enactments, I was not constrained by the limits of my memory; the texts lay open in front of me.

'That sounds good,' said Denise, impressed, as I finished the Latin recitation. 'Now let's hear the translation.'

Perhaps I should have made up some anodyne words on a different subject. She wouldn't have known. But I wasn't quick-witted enough. Perhaps I even wanted to challenge her, to test her response.

What slender boy, besprinkled with liquid perfumes, makes urgent love to you, Pyrrha, amid many a rose in your pleasing cave? For whom do you bind back your golden hair, artless in your elegance? Alas, how often will he bewail the fickleness of faith and fortune and, in his inexperience, look amazed at the seas stirred up with black winds: he who, too trustful, enjoys you now in your golden prime and who, ignorant of the breeze's treachery, hopes that you will always be free from any other, always worthy of affection. Wretched ones, who look on your beauty without having experienced what you are. As for me, the temple wall with its votive tablet shows that I have hung out my sodden garments to the god who is lord of the sea.

She giggled with embarrassment. 'Is that what you think about me?'

'No, no, it's just a poem.'

'Well, what's all that about wet clothes on the temple walls?'

'It's what the Romans used to do after surviving a shipwreck. A ritual thank-offering to Neptune.'

'So, I cause shipwrecks, do I?' She was silent for a minute and it was my turn to be embarrassed. Then she smiled again.

'OK, how about something in Greek instead?'

I was careful this time. Eventually, I recited some lines from Sophocles. I don't know how accurate either the original or the translation was, but it was the best I could do. They were lines I had studied with Lewis: my sole contribution to a discussion on civil disobedience, when you had ranged effortlessly over Thoreau and Tolstoy, Ghandi and Luther King. You had admired the lines as an expression of an individual's conscience against the power of the state; I had felt proud to have introduced you to them. Now I felt that they were bringing a little of you into my relationship with Denise, consolidating it with vicarious wisdom.

That edict did not come from Zeus. These are not the laws ordained by Justice, who dwells below with the gods of the dead. Nor did I think that your decrees were strong enough to override these unwritten, immutable statutes of heaven. For they are not of yesterday or today, but eternal, though none can tell when they came into being...

'I like that. What is it?'

'It's Sophocles. From "Antigone".'

'I thought so. We read that on our course—part of the history of tragedy.'

We talked about the play for a few minutes. Was she still thinking about it ten months later, while she was cramming those pills into her mouth? Although I had no foreboding, my choice of Greek text was as inappropriate as the Latin one: a play where two brothers have slain each other; where their sister hangs herself after being entombed alive; where her fiancé and his mother both kill themselves in consequence. Five deaths, three of them suicide.

I like to think that happier memories might have outweighed these scenes, for she suddenly grabbed my arm:

'Look, a kingfisher!'

We stared, enraptured at the flash of blue and orange, disappearing into the foliage across the water. Then I destroyed the moment by showing off my classical learning.

'Do you know the story of Halcyon? She was the daughter of Aeolus, the god of the winds, and her husband was killed in a shipwreck. She mourned for him so much that the gods took pity on her and turned her and her husband into sea birds. She builds her nest on the waters and her father keeps the winds still and tranquil while she's on the nest, so that nothing can disturb the eggs. That's where we get the phrase "Halcyon Days".'

'But what's that got to do with anything?'

I felt awkward. I had missed the point of the story.

'"Halcyon" comes from the Latin for kingfisher,' I said, tamely.

'Oh, I see.' She wasn't as impressed as I had intended. 'You like shipwrecks, don't you? They're almost an obsession for you.'

We were silent again as we approached the canal lock where I am standing now. It was a depressing place in those days, with barbed wire blocking the lock and the footbridge to the boarded-up, dilapidated lockkeeper's cottage. Today the canal is in use again; the cottage has been renovated. If the scene had been like this all those years ago, would I now find it so dispiriting? Or was it only Denise's subsequent death which has affected me in this way?

We stood for a few minutes, looking over the barbed wire to the other bank. Could she already see the twin-oared boat coming to fetch her, the ferryman leaning on his pole? Had Death already severed a single lock of her fair hair? Or was she still carefree, mindless of the imminent ordeals?

I can remember nothing of the walk back, from that inaccessible footbridge to the busy road bridge in town. I seem to see us trudging along, as if I am high above us, looking down, too remote to hear any conversation.

Or has my memory betrayed me again? Was that recaptured conversation spread over the outward and return journeys? Have I created a neat, coherent order out of a few disparate, half-forgotten sentences?

I turn my back on the memory of that departing couple and step on to the footbridge. For the first time today, I am moving forwards rather than backwards. After so much retracing of steps, I am setting forth to an undiscovered land. I sense the two heads of Janus above me, guarding an invisible gate on the bridge, his gaze fixed before and behind.

But before I have even passed the cottage, I stop in disbelief. I am looking at a flat landscape, punctuated with small copses of young trees and pools of water, surrounded by weeds. The scene is not new. I have been here twice before, once only eighteen months ago. Lewis and Esther drove me here, but I never knew the exact location. There was no wetlands area here when I was living in Denbridge. It was created on some land quarried for the new ring road, which was only at the planning stage then—I remember signing a petition against the construction. The new landscape was in part an attempt to appease protesters who had predicted environmental disaster.

I walk on uncomprehendingly, unable to assimilate the proximity of two locales which I had known at such different times of my life. As I approach the first of the pools, a mallard flies off, quacking in complaint at my intrusion. I recall my first visit here about fifteen years ago—was it at this very pool?—when Rob and Sally were chasing the ducks, imitating their calls.

'They're both quacking quite convincingly,' I said, impressed.

I remember Esther's response. It was slightly out of character—more reflective, more intellectual than usual. For once, she reminded me of her sister.

'It's strange—that word "quack" really sounds like the noise ducks make. It's called onomatopoeia, isn't it? I wonder if other languages use the same word.'

And I had tentatively made a classical allusion, but without the ostentatious bravado of my embarrassing narration of the Halcyon story.

'Plautus makes a joke about the sound in one of his plays. A character says something like he wishes he were a duck in the water. With a stress on the word "aqua"—the Latin for water.'

Esther smiled politely, but it was Lewis's reaction which interested me. You looked at me very seriously as you spoke.

'I'm glad you still remember your classics, Colin.'

I felt awkward, because I remembered so little. I couldn't even have recounted the plot of the play. But I remember wondering how much you recalled of your studies and whether you were regretting your apparent neglect of them.

Another image superimposes itself on this memory. On my second visit here, as we watched a squirrel disappearing into a clump of trees, Esther suddenly said, 'I wish Denise could have come here. She used to love wild places.'

I didn't know what to say, but now I suddenly realise that she had been almost here—only 50 metres away—and I had been with her. And suddenly the distance of 30 years is conflated into those 50 metres, the experiences separated only by the canal, while the intervening years of my life are of no further consequence. For suddenly I see that I have been remembering everything in the wrong way. My self-centred self-conceit about my possible role in Denise's death has prevented my appreciation of her enjoyment of that walk on the towpath.

I feel a sense of liberation. I am no longer haunted by the avenging Furies, created solely by my own imagination. I was not to blame for Denise's death—only for killing my memory of her by exaggerating my importance in the tragedy.

I continue walking. The sky is darkening now. As I pass the largest expanse of water in the area, a flock of Canada geese takes off, circles once and then disappears into the darkness in a V-shaped formation. I reach the picnic area near the carpark. We played with a Frisbee here once. I feel remote from Denbridge and all its memories.

It is too dark to return to the towpath, so I begin to walk back into town beside the busy main road. Lewis and Esther must have driven me this way, although I don't recognise the surroundings. After walking for half an hour, I arrive at the town. The road is unfamiliar, but I soon find my way to the station.

I have to wait only a few minutes for the next train to London. I sit on board, making notes about my day, intending to copy them into my journal tomorrow…

I picked up my pen.

Saturday 19th October 2002

Caught train to Denbridge. Walked to park. Looked at former homes of my uncle and Lewis. Lunch in pub near old office. Walked along towpath. Crossed river to wetlands. Back to station by road.

So, I thought, the gap had been filled. I couldn't write down all those experiences and memories. It would take too long and it was too late now. That moment of exultation in the wetlands had not remained with me. Yet surely not everything was lost?

I went to the bottom corner of my bookcase, where a small collection of Loeb classics was shelved: red covers for Latin texts, green for Greek. I took down a green volume, but quickly put it back. It was too difficult for me. Instead, I turned to my old friend, Horace. In those early days in Denbridge, he had been an even more loyal friend than you, Lewis. Flicking through the pages, I came to the poem in which the ghost of a drowned man, his corpse lying exposed on the Matine shore, calls out to a passing sailor to stop and bury him. I tried to concentrate on the original text, but my eyes kept straying to the parallel English translation. I was no longer capable of reading it without the English version, but with its help, I was able to make sense of the lines:

Don't leave me here, my prayers unanswered. No propitiatory sacrifices will absolve you. Though you are in a hurry, the delay will not be long. Once the dust has been thrown three times, you may move swiftly on.

Inside the Chest

'Yes, I felt the same way,' I said. 'I adored my grandmother. She only lived around the corner, so she used to babysit all the time. And she'd really spoil us—let us stay up much later than Mum and Dad.'

'I know, mine was like that too—and Grandpa. The thing was, though, they weren't old. Not when I first remember them. They used to meet me from school and take me to the park and we'd play all sorts of games there. They had so much energy. You see, they were only in their fifties. I suppose I never thought they'd grow old and die. Not like some other people's grandparents who've always seemed old.'

'Well, that's nice. You can remember them when they were still young and active.'

'I know, I know. But it's still sad. And then for them to go so close together—one after another in a couple of months.'

'Yes, it's an awful shock for you. But think about it from her point of view. She wouldn't have wanted to go on living—not without your grandfather.'

'I didn't really know my grandmother at all.'

We looked in surprise at Donna. This was the first time she had spoken since sitting down in the pub. I had asked her along at the last minute, hoping she would be able to share with me the burden of Gerry's grief. So far, she hadn't proved very helpful.

'Well, I knew Dad's parents—they used to come and stay with us. But Mum's mother lived in Felixstowe, so we had to go by train. I was always scared.'

'Was she a bit of a dragon?' I asked.

'No, it wasn't that. She was nice. But she had a chest—a wooden chest.' She nodded emphatically, as if this explanation were sufficient.

'A wooden chest?' I prompted.

'Yes, and I was frightened of it, you see.'

'Why? Why was that?'

'I don't know. I can't remember if it was something that happened or if I just dreamt it. Well, I know I dreamt it...'

She blushed with embarrassment at her confusion. I turned away and took a sip of my beer. This was not going well. I had always felt comfortable at work with both Donna and Gerry, but this was the first time any of us had seen each other outside office hours. It might have been a strain under any circumstances.

'What I mean is,' she said, thumping the table with both hands, 'what I mean is, I definitely dreamt about the chest, but I can't remember if it was the first dream which made me frightened of it or if something really happened which gave me nightmares.'

She sighed with relief at having made herself clear. I was intrigued, but worried about where the conversation was leading. Nightmares were surely the wrong topic for Gerry at present. However, when I glanced at him, he seemed excited, and he was the one to encourage Donna to continue.

'What did you dream?'

'It was always the same. We'd all be at Gran's—me, my parents, my sister. We'd be eating downstairs and talking. Then I'd leave them to go upstairs. And I'd just peep into Gran's bedroom—and see that chest. And that would be it. I'd just be terrified. I'd scream, but no sound would come out. And then I'd wake up. And then I'd really scream—at least I would when I was younger.'

'And did you ever open the chest? In real life, I mean. Later on, when you were older?'

Gerry was captivated by the story now. I felt jealous, though guiltily so. I had hoped to divert him from his unhappiness at some time during the evening, but I had intended to be the one to stimulate his interest. Donna had usurped my role. She carried on talking, her eyes fixed on Gerry, as if I were no longer there.

'Not until much, much later. We didn't visit her often, you see. And even when we did, I hardly ever went upstairs. She didn't go up herself during the day—she found the stairs difficult, so once she'd come down in the morning, she wouldn't go up again until bedtime. But I always associated the house with that chest. I never felt easy there. And then she moved.'

'Where to?' asked Gerry eagerly. 'And did she take the chest with her?'

'Yes, she did. She moved into sheltered housing. A tiny place, but very cosy. It was furnished already. Modern stuff—Formica tops and all that. She must have got rid of all her own furniture. She had some nice things too.'

'But she kept the chest?'

'That's right. It was just about the only old thing she did keep. It looked really out of place beside all that modern furniture.'

'So, you saw it when you went there?'

'Oh yes, you couldn't help it. She'd only got two rooms. The chest was in the front room, squashed up between two armchairs. I was more terrified than ever. It looked so huge. And then the nightmares started again. And they were worse—much worse. I was fourteen then. I couldn't scream like a kid when I woke up. But I still did sometimes. I was terrified.'

'Was it still the same dream?'

'Yes. Well, it started the same. I never dreamt about her new home—it was always upstairs at the old house. And I'd go into the room just as before, and I'd try to scream. But then the lid of the chest would open. Can you imagine that? I'd been frightened enough when nothing happened, so what do you think it was like when the lid came up?'

'Did anything come out of it?'

'I never saw anything. The lid opened towards me. You know, the hinge was facing me. So the lid masked whatever was coming out. And then I woke up.'

'You must have dreaded visiting your gran.'

'I did, I did. And she was such a nice old thing too. If it hadn't been for that chest, we could have talked and talked. I feel so bad about it. I never asked her anything. And I didn't take in anything she said to Mum or Dad or Alison. I just used to sit there, trying not to look at the chest.'

She stopped talking and stared in front of her, as though she could see the chest now. I intervened for the first time since her mention of the dream.

'What sort of chest was it? You said it was big and wooden…'

She looked at me in surprise. I felt that she was criticising my pedantic desire for detail.

'That's all it was. Just a big, wooden chest with a carved pattern on it and a rounded lid. You see them in churches sometimes, but I was coming to that.

'It was in Year 10 at school. We'd gone on a field trip. You know, a bit of geology, bit of geography, bit of history. And we were looking at this old church. The teacher had pointed out various things of interest—there was a Norman window in one of the aisles, I remember—and we'd all taken notes. Then we were told to look around on our own. Later on, we'd have to write up everything we'd seen. Mark and I went to the back of the church and drew back the curtain in front of the bell-rope. Mark pulled on the rope and made the bell ring. He got into trouble about that later. But I did something much worse. What do you think was on the floor beside the bell-rope?'

'A wooden chest,' whispered Gerry.

'Right. Just like Gran's. And I opened it. It was unforgivable. It was, well, blasphemy and I knew it. To open that chest in a church.' She was blushing again.

'What was in it?'

'Oh, just some choirboys' cassocks. It seemed to be used as a sort of linen basket. But that wasn't the point. I knew what I'd done. I'd opened the chest, the chest that I'd been dreaming about all my life, and I knew what it meant. I'd killed my grandmother. I knew she was dead.'

Donna and Gerry stared at each other in horrified silence. Then, quietly, Gerry asked, 'And was she? Dead, I mean?'

'Yes, she was. I rang home that evening. She'd died of a stroke.'

'You must have felt terrible.'

'I did, I did. Actually, I soon found out that she'd had the stroke the day before. My parents hadn't been able to contact me. But when I rang Dad, he told me what time he'd heard from the hospital about her death. It was just the time that I'd opened the chest. He said it was a "merciful release". I still remember those words. They sounded so strange coming from him. He never speaks like that.'

'Well, it must have relieved you, anyway. Even if you caused her death somehow, it was probably a good thing in the circumstances.'

'Um, I don't know. I don't think I want that sort of power, whether it's good or evil. I'm not a god. Anyway, it was all nonsense. I said that Dad had heard of Gran's death at about the time I opened the chest. But that was when Mum rang him from the hospital. She'd died two hours earlier—at least two hours. The chest had got nothing to do with it. I felt awful. There was I, all upset about that stupid box, when I should have been grieving about Gran.'

'I know what you mean. But I still think the events were linked in some way. I don't quite know how.' I noticed how eagerly Gerry was looking at Donna: he was entreating her to acknowledge a connection.

'Well, yes, I'm glad you think that. Because I do too. And I don't feel bad about opening the chest now… I'm still sorry about Gran, though. And sorry that I never asked her things—you know, things about her past, her childhood.'

'What happened to the chest?'

'Mum's got it now. She said it had always been in the family and it always should be. So, when I go and stay with Mum and Dad, I see it every day. No nightmares now.'

'And what's inside it?'

'Nothing. Nothing at all. Completely empty. And it was the same when we took it from Gran's house. All a bit of an anti-climax, I suppose.'

'Yes, but it's got memories, hasn't it? Don't you feel it's got memories of your gran's childhood in it?'

'That's right. You understand. All those memories which she never told me, which I never asked for. They're all there—safe in that chest.'

They smiled at each other in mutual understanding. Each took a sip of their drink. I sat silent, feeling ignored and irritated. My own glass had been empty for the last quarter of an hour.

I Shall Never Go Back Again

I returned to my old home last night.

I shall never go back again.

When I moved there, I loved the seclusion—the dark, narrow stairs leading to my small bed-sit. It was a quiet house and Mr Hudson, the landlord, was friendly and co-operative.

But when I decided to leave, I was ready. The room was too small, the shared bathroom too often occupied.

So, I was surprised, some nights later, to find myself unlocking the familiar front door.

After climbing a wide stone staircase, past gold-framed portraits beneath a massive chandelier, I entered a dormitory with twenty bunk beds, most of them occupied by people who stared at me as I began self-consciously to undress.

On other nights, I was searching for something. I would enter each room in turn, hoping, vainly, that one of them would satisfy my quest.

Once, I was standing above a broken flight of stairs, desperate to find the way out. Clutching the rotten banister as I descended, I despaired of ever reaching the ground floor.

I was always scared that I would meet Mr Hudson. When I left, I had assured him that I had not retained a key.

Last night, when I unlocked the front door, he was standing there. He didn't look angry—just disappointed. I had betrayed his trust. He approached me with outstretched arm, but not to shake my hand. I dropped the keys into his palm and left the house for the last time.

Harvest Festival

The sky was darkening as Rebecca and Daniel left their home. Daniel, a little scared, held his sister's hand, but he needn't have worried. Most of the villagers were nearby, all walking in the same direction. Only their mother stayed at home, isolated in her disapproval.

They said hello to their neighbour, Brian, who was walking with his grandmother. He waved to them, but didn't speak. He rarely did.

Everyone was silent as they turned on to the path through the wood. There was no noise, except when a twig cracked underfoot or the bracken swished against a walker's legs. Occasionally, there was a muted cry as a bramble or a nettle encountered exposed flesh. A tawny owl hooted above them.

They emerged on to a straight track, leading through thick hedgerows up to St Catherine's-on-the-Hill. The full harvest moon shone with a red hue, and the church was lit up, its tall tower silhouetted against the dark woodland which rose to the top of the hill behind it. The church bell was tolling.

Passing through the lych-gate between the two ancient yew trees, the walkers approached the door which opened into the south aisle. The rector was waiting to welcome them, but there were three other people—two men and one woman—who were less welcoming. Dressed all in black, they were holding placards aloft:

'This is the house of God. You have made it the home of Satan!'

'The light of Christ, Not the powers of darkness!'

'No pagan rituals in a Christian church!'

Inside the church, the products of harvest were everywhere. Baskets of carrots, parsnips and runner beans stood on the table amidst the hymn and prayer books. Apples formed a circle around the base of each pillar and around the font. There was a punnet of tomatoes in every pew; a huge marrow adorned the lectern; potatoes were lined along the windowsills. Bales of hay covered every inch of the central aisle, creating a thick carpet on the stone floor. Corn effigies hung from the rafters in the chancel. Rebecca had plaited straw into a tube to form a small corn dolly at school the previous week, but these were the size of full-grown adults.

The festival seemed a celebration of death as well as life. The corpses of pheasants and rabbits hung from the pulpit and the choir stalls; a stag's head had been placed on the altar, its antlers masking the silver cross behind it.

Rebecca and Daniel had been awarded a special privilege. As the other worshippers filed into the pews, their father—the churchwarden—stepped over the hay to greet them. He led them to the west end of the church and opened a small door near the massive stained-glass window. It depicted Jesus on the shore of the Sea of Galilee, watching as his disciples dragged in their nets, which were almost breaking under the weight of so many fish.

The children followed their father up the narrow staircase to the organ gallery. The organist, waiting to accompany the first hymn, smiled at them as they looked around in astonishment. They had been up here before, but usually there was just a small balcony in front of the organ, from where they could look down to the nave. Now two panels of wood were covering the whole aperture, sloping downwards to form a groove which ran from east to west, immediately above the nave. More fruit and vegetables—apples, pears, potatoes, onions, swedes, turnips—had been placed on the panels and had slid down into the groove.

Above the children was a roof boss, which couldn't be seen from the floor below. It depicted a wild human face, surrounded by foliage. Tendrils of leaves stretched over the forehead to dangle in front of the eyes.

'Now,' said their father, 'the lever is here.' He indicated a latch on the balcony. 'In a few minutes, the bell will stop ringing. When it starts again, you must lift the lever. That's all. Do you understand?'

They nodded. He hugged them both and retreated down the stairs. They waited, expectantly. At last, the bell stopped ringing. The organist began to play a familiar hymn tune. Could they hear the words which the congregation was singing below or were they just remembering them?

We plough the fields and scatter
The good seed on the land,
For it is fed and watered
By God's almighty hand...

Afterwards, someone—the rector, they presumed—started to speak, although they couldn't make out a word he said. Occasionally, the congregation responded with "Amen" or "And with thy spirit". Then the bells sounded again—a peal of five bells rather than the previous tolling of one.

'Quick!' said Daniel in a panic. But Rebecca stayed calm. Gently, she raised the lever, and the improvised ceiling began to separate. Immediately, the fruit and vegetables dropped on to the bales of hay beneath. The organist resumed her playing.

The reaction from the congregation was instantaneous. Everyone stood up, shouting 'Alleluia!' and 'Praise the Lord!' They ran out of their pews to bounce up and down on the hay, dancing to the music of the organ. Some picked up fruit and vegetables which had fallen from above and tossed them to each other; some juggled with apples, throwing them high, almost into the rafters of the hammerbeam roof. And still everyone was shouting and singing.

The rector raised his hand. The bells ceased ringing; the organ was silent; the worshippers stood still. Then, quietly—almost sheepishly—they filed back into the pews, leaving the central aisle an unsightly mess of crushed fruit on the scattered hay.

But one person was still singing, still dancing. Brian—normally so quiet and reserved—was leaping like an acrobat, his legs stretched out horizontally beneath him. Rebecca and Daniel stared down at him in amazement. They tried to make out what he was shouting, but his words were incomprehensible. He danced into the chancel, pushed aside the corn effigies, vaulted over the altar rails and raised his arms to the stag's antlers. Then he backflipped over the rails again and danced along the nave once more. Unintelligible sounds continued to emanate from his mouth. At last, leaping high over the font, he gave a final, ear-piercing scream, before disappearing through the south door.

Now the congregation was speaking again. 'It's him!' one shouted. 'He's the one!' said another. 'The next Corn Lord!' Others called out his name: 'Brian! Brian! Brian!'

Looking down from above, Rebecca and Daniel shared the excitement, but also felt distant from it. They were not overjoyed by Brian's gymnastics and shouting; they were scared. He had been, if not a friend, a part of their lives. Familiar with his taciturnity, they had accepted him as he was and didn't welcome his sudden change.

The rector raised his hand again. Gradually the worshippers became quiet. The rector spoke.

'We thank thee, Lord, for our harvest, for the means of nourishment which thou hast bestowed. All things come from thee, O Lord. Without thee, we are as naught.'

'We thank thee too for sending us thy Corn Lords to guide us through each year's harvest. Tonight, even before we welcome this year's Corn Lord, thou hast already chosen the Lord for next year. So, we can go forward, firm in the assurance of thy continual bounty.'

'Now let us stand to sing our final hymn.'

The organist played the opening bars and the congregation rose to sing.

Come, ye thankful people, come,
Raise the song of harvest home;
All is safely gathered in,
Ere the winter storms begin;
God our Maker doth provide
For our wants to be supplied;
Come to God's own temple, come,
Raise the song of harvest home.

Rebecca was feeling relief. Nervous of the earlier excitement, she felt reassured by the resumption of a normal service. They were singing a hymn, as they did on any other Sunday of the year. It was part of the familiar—and boring—Sunday routine. But her relief was short-lived. She watched, as the verger lit the candles at the east end of the church. Then the rector spoke again.

'And now the time has come to welcome this year's Corn Lord. See his cloak, woven from the last gleanings of the fields. Let us welcome him into our presence.'

The lights were switched off, leaving only the candles burning in the darkness. The vestry door beside the chancel opened and a figure appeared, covered head to foot in a straw cloak. Two antlers rose from his head. Over one shoulder, he was carrying a scythe. There were cheers from the congregation, but in the loft above, Daniel reached for his sister's hand.

'Welcome! Welcome!' shouted the crowd.

The Corn Lord was standing on the chancel steps. He lowered his scythe, holding it horizontally, the blade towards the worshippers. Then he raised it into the rafters and with a flick of his wrist, he sliced through the cord holding one of the corn effigies to the roof.

'Largesse!' he cried, as the effigy dropped to the floor.

'Largesse!' he repeated. 'Largesse! Largesse!'

Each time he shouted this word, he cut another cord, until all four figures were lying on the floor or draped over the front pews. The worshippers were stroking the figures, burying their hands in the straw, cheering. The rector raised his hand once more.

'Now let us light the bonfire. Let us burn the four figures and release the corn into next year's seed.'

Rebecca and Daniel couldn't see the west door, but even above the shouting and cheering, they could hear the bars being drawn back. People were pouncing on the corn effigies, grabbing a part of one and charging to the back of the church, as though wielding a battering ram to break down the door. Behind them came the verger with his lighted taper and, last of all, the rector, a mad gleam in his eyes.

Rebecca and Daniel looked at each other; they looked at the organist, who had not played a note since the final hymn. She smiled at them, seemingly unaffected by the chaos below.

'I think you'd better go down now,' she said.

Nervously, the children walked down the staircase. The church was a mess: the bales of hay had disintegrated under the congregation's dancing feet. Strands of hay were scattered across the floor and the pews. The fruit and vegetables from the organ loft had been crushed like grapes in a wine press. Hymn books lay abandoned amongst the detritus.

Through the open west door, the children could see the bonfire, its flames already soaring upwards. The corn effigies were alight and blazing. There seemed to be other figures in the fire too. Faces stared at them through the smoke. Who were they? There was no sign now of the three protesters. Had they been thrown on to the fire? What if Mum were there too? Mum, who had demonstrated her disapproval by staying at home.

They looked for their father, whom they had not noticed during the service. He was coming towards them now out of the shouting crowd around the bonfire. He looked worried.

'Dad!' called Rebecca. 'Where's Mum?'

'Your mother's safe at home,' he replied. 'I think you'd better go home now too.'

'But I'm scared,' said Daniel.

'Don't worry. You can go back with Brian's gran. She'll look after you. And she'll like the company now Brian's gone. Come with me.'

They followed their father around the bonfire to where Brian's grandmother was staring forlornly at the flames.

'Hello, Mrs Carter. You'll take the children home, won't you?'

'Of course I will.' Instantly she was looking cheerful again. 'You come along with me, my dears.'

She grasped each child by the hand and turned to walk back down to the village.

'I'll come home as soon as we've cleared up here,' said their father.

'What was that burning in the fire?' Rebecca asked Mrs Carter.

'Oh, that was just the corn gods. The ones that were hanging in church. They burn them every year.'

'But I thought I could see real people there.'

'You see a lot in those flames. A lot more than was ever thrown on the fire.'

'But no one's been killed?'

'Bless you, no. No one's been killed.'

'What's happened to Brian?' asked Daniel.

'He'll be the next Corn Lord. Next year, if I'm spared, I'll see him in the church with his straw coat, his antlers and his scythe. Haven't you been to the Harvest Festival before?'

'No,' said Rebecca. 'Mum doesn't really approve, you see. She didn't want us to go this year, but with Dad being churchwarden, she agreed at last.'

'Your mother's a good woman, but she don't hold with the old ways.'

'But where's Brian now?' asked Daniel.

'Oh, he'll be back soon. They always come back. I know I'm not to worry, but you can't help feeling anxious.'

They were entering the wood now. The old woman seemed as pleased to hold on to the children as they were to grasp her hands.

Suddenly, a shape approached them. They all stopped. They all screamed.

'It's all right, Gran. It's only me.'

Mrs Carter let go of the two children and opened her arms to greet Brian.

'Oh, I'm so pleased you've come back. Let's get off home now.'

Forgetting the other two, she grabbed Brian with her right hand and began marching through the wood. With an anguished moan, Daniel took her other hand, while Rebecca hung on to him. Both felt resentful that Brian had ousted them on this terrifying night. The path was too narrow for all four to walk abreast, but they didn't loosen their grip, even though they were trailing behind.

At last, they reached the village. The dark streets were deserted. The other villagers were still by the bonfire. There was silence, except for the distant sound of hoof beats.

Suddenly, Mrs Carter remembered her responsibilities. Turning to Rebecca and Daniel, she said, 'Just you come along with me now. I'll bring you safe home to your mum.'

The lights were on in their house when they reached the gate. The two children released their hands and ran to the front door, just as it was opening.

'Oh, thank God you're safe!' said their mother. 'I've been so worried. I should never have let you go.'

A Brief Rebellion

'Oh God, Claire! You're not seeing that old woman again today, are you? It's Saturday.'

'I know, but I had to cancel my visit last Wednesday. This is the only day I could manage.'

'But what about us? When do we have time to see each other?'

'Don't be so dramatic, Craig. I'll only be with her for three hours—at most. We can still go out this evening.'

'That's not the point. Why do you have to see her every week? You don't even like her.'

'I *do* like her. OK, she's a bit boring, but I've made a commitment. When I signed up with the charity, it was agreed that I'd go and see her once a week.'

'Yes, but you didn't have a boyfriend then. What about your commitment to me?'

'I *am* committed to you. But that doesn't cancel out other commitments. Anyway, do you want to see me later or not?'

'Oh, let's forget it.'

I was angry: angry because Craig was trying to control my life; angry because he was right about Ann. I wasn't looking forward to visiting her. And I hadn't been honest with Craig. It was Ann who had rung to cancel our meeting on Wednesday. She had "company", she said, and we had decided that I should go to see her today instead. I hadn't wanted to disrupt my weekend for her, although I didn't tell her that. Now I was thinking that I would rather not see either Ann or Craig.

Ann had rung me twice today to make sure that I was coming. I was already a few minutes late and I knew that she would be at the window of her first floor flat, peering down to see me when I turned the corner. I resented her intrusiveness, wanting to cherish those last few minutes of my own company. I turned up a different street, intending to enter her own street from the other end, to approach her home from an unexpected direction and, maybe, avoid her spying eyes.

Why had the charity paired me with Ann? When I first volunteered, I was looking forward to meeting an old person, listening, perhaps, to their reminiscences about their wartime childhood. Instead, I had to put up with Ann's accounts of her visits to the doctor, the state of her feet, her complaints that no one ever came to see her (even though her neighbour seemed to look in every day). Presumably, most of the old people I was imagining didn't need charitable visits. They would be grandparents, content to chat with their families. Poor Ann had no family. She and her husband had been unable to have children. She was reliant on neighbours and visitors like me. 'That's not the same,' she would say, and I sympathised with her. Our visits could never replace a husband who was with her all the time.

But I *did* like her. She was always so pleased to see me. If only we could have more interesting conversations.

Then there was the tea. It was generous of her to provide the plate of cup-cakes, but I didn't want them. I had to eat at least three or she would criticise me, tell me that I needed to eat more, that I was too thin. I always left her feeling bloated and worrying about my teeth. I wished I could persuade her that a cup of tea was enough.

I was not familiar with the far end of her road. It was a busy area. I passed a row of shops, a laundrette, a café. On an impulse, I stopped. I walked back to the café, entered and ordered a coffee. Then, sitting down, I turned off my mobile, wallowing in a sense of guilty liberation. No one knew I was here: not Ann, not Craig, not anyone. Of course, there would be explaining to do afterwards. I would have to ring Ann to apologise. She would be worried, disappointed, angry. Perhaps she would let me visit her later that afternoon—if so, she would make it plain that she was doing me a favour. As for Craig, I wasn't worried about him. His "Oh, let's forget it" would soon be forgotten. I could see him again tomorrow—if I wanted to.

'Do you mind if I sit here?'

The café had become crowded. There were no free tables. The woman who addressed me was young—maybe only 20. I smiled at her and gestured to the chair opposite me. Then I took a book out of my bag. I didn't want to be disturbed by any small talk.

However, although I kept my eyes fixed on the book, occasionally turning a page, I couldn't concentrate on what I was reading. Craig and Ann. It was strange how two people, with so little in common, could have become so inter-related. I had told Ann about him; she had listened and even given me some advice: 'Don't rush things'; 'Don't commit yourself too soon.' These were not words of great wisdom and yet I found them helpful. However irritating Ann might be, she was not totally self-centred.

The young woman opposite me was typing on her laptop, stopping frequently to gaze into the distance. Our eyes met and she smiled nervously.

'Sorry, I hope I'm not disturbing you.'

'No, of course not. I can see you're busy.'

'Yes, it's an essay for uni. I've got to submit it on Monday.'

I paused, remembering my resolution not to engage. Then I decided that good manners demanded a response.

'What are you studying?' I asked.

'Psychology. But I'm thinking of giving it up.'

'That would be a shame. Are you finding it too difficult, too boring…?'

'I don't know. Just a bit pointless, I suppose. This term, it's mainly social psychology. I know it's important to get away from the individual, but it's not really what I was expecting. This essay's on consumerism.'

'Really? I didn't think you'd be doing that in psychology. Were you hoping to be a counsellor or a therapist or something like that?'

'Well, yes. I used to think that—until I started this course.'

'Is it too academic for you? Did you want something more practical?'

'Yes, I suppose so. Something which would help me understand the people I meet—understand myself, even.'

I thought about this. Would a psychology course have unravelled my feelings about Craig and Ann?

The woman shut her laptop.

'Well, I won't disturb you any longer. It was nice talking to you.'

I watched her leave. She was only a few years younger than me, but our preoccupations were so different. Her worries about an essay and her university course seemed so mundane. Then I smiled at my presumption. How could I, based on a few minutes' conversation, know anything about the complications of her life? She would probably think that my inability to reconcile my relationships with Ann and Craig was trivial—that the means of resolving the problem was obvious.

I finished my coffee. My brief holiday was at an end. It was time to ring Ann, to apologise for being late, to ask if I could come and see her now. I wasn't looking forward to her criticism, but I would have to endure it. I rang her number.

There was no answer.

I rang again, giving her a chance to reach her handset. Still no answer. Putting on my jacket, I hurried out of the café and ran along the road to her block of flats. I rang her bell repeatedly. Then my mobile rang.

Relieved, I took it out of my pocket, only to see that the call was from Craig. I switched the phone off. Why had I listened to him? If I had arrived here at the appointed time, I would have been spared this worry.

I rang the other bells on the first floor. At last, someone answered on the intercom.

'Hello. I'm trying to contact Ann Jeffries.'

'Oh, you can't do that. She's in hospital.'

'Oh no! What happened?'

'I don't know exactly. She had a fall. I've got her spare key, you see, so I was able to let the ambulance men in.'

'Thank God you did that. Do you know how she was?'

'Well, she was talking. But she didn't look good when they carried her out.'

'Do you know what hospital they took her to?'

'Yes, it was St Mark's.'

I travelled there by bus. I had so many unanswered questions. Who had called the ambulance? When had the accident happened? I was so afraid that she had gone to the window because I was late and had fallen then. Yes, I know I was thinking of myself. The cause of her fall made no difference to Ann.

I went to the main reception and asked where Ann was. Fortunately, I knew her date of birth, so the receptionist was able to locate her and sent me to the ward. Then a nurse directed me to Ann's bed.

She was dozing, so I sat and waited, feeling more and more anxious. There was a large, purple bruise on her face. Eventually, she opened her eyes and greeted me with a smile.

'Hello Claire. Have you come to take me home?'

'I don't think you're ready to go home yet, Ann. How are you feeling?'

'I'm in a lot of pain, but I'm all right. But I need to thank you. You saved my life.'

She was confused. It wasn't surprising at her age. To be transported by ambulance, wheeled through corridors on a trolley and deposited in a strange bed would have unsettled anyone.

'Yes, if you hadn't made me wear that button thing around my neck, no one would have known about me.'

I understood now, although she was exaggerating my role. The charity had arranged for her to have a panic button installed. All I had done was to persuade her to wear it and not leave it on her bedside table. We had tested it together and heard a reassuring voice asking Ann how they could help her.

'What time did all this happen?'

'It must have been just after 12—soon after I rang you. I was getting my lunch and I dropped my plate. Then when I tried to pick it up, I crashed down after it. And I couldn't get up again. But I remembered my button and soon an ambulance came. So, it's all thanks to you that I'm here.'

I didn't think I deserved such praise, but I was relieved that I wasn't to blame—Ann had fallen nearly two hours before I was meant to arrive.

'Have you broken any bones?'

'I don't know, dear. My back hurts a lot, but I could be worse.'

She seemed to be complaining less than normal, despite her fall. I went to find a nurse who could tell me what was wrong with her.

'She's not too bad. She's cracked a vertebra, but there's nothing we can do about that. Only time will heal it. Otherwise, she's just got a lot of bruises. And she's suffering from shock, of course. We'll keep her in for a couple of nights, but she can't stay here long. She'll need to see a physio, but after that she should be ready to go. Are you her next-of-kin?'

'No, I'm just a friend. I don't think she has any family. There's a nephew somewhere, but he's never around.'

'Well, she'll need a lot of support once she's home. A carer should be able to call each day—help her to wash. But that's all. Will you be available to help?'

'I work full-time, but I suppose I could help out most evenings.'

'Good. You'll need to get in touch with the occupational therapist. I'll give you the number.'

What was I committing myself to now? I returned to Ann's bed.

'Hello again. You should be going home in a day or so. The nurse says I'm to help look after you then.'

'Oh, that will be lovely, Claire. It's so kind of you. I hope your Craig won't mind.'

'Don't worry about him,' I said.

Compare and Contrast

9/8/62

We set out for Scotland at 8.13 a.m. Dad did most of the driving. We stopped for a picnic lunch in a layby in Lincolnshire and then continued our journey north. We arrived in Ripon at 4.28, having travelled 194 miles and passed through the counties of Norfolk, Lincolnshire and Yorkshire. We pitched our tents in a campsite which was a field attached to a timberyard. I put up one tent all by myself while Dad showed Laura and Robin how to assemble the other. After supper we went for a walk by the river. When we got back, Dad made us all cocoa. Then Robin went into one of the tents and got into his sleeping bag. The rest of us stayed up talking. Then Laura and I went into the other tent while Dad joined Robin.

Thursday 9th August 1962

We had loaded up the car the night before, so we were able to set off on our holiday just after 8 o'clock. Mummy and Uncle Roy shared the driving while Lucy and I sat in the back. We didn't say much to each other. We had lunch in a layby. When we were getting near Lincoln, Uncle Roy told me to look out for the cathedral and I soon saw it at the top of a high hill. In the evening we put up our tents in a timberyard in Ripon. Then Mummy cooked fish fingers, potatoes and peas on the primus stove. After that we went for a walk by the river. The sun was setting over the fields. The path was winding and we kept getting different views of the cathedral. When we got back to the tents, we drank cocoa. Then we cleaned our teeth and got into our sleeping bags.

I am smiling as I read these journal entries. I notice how each of us exaggerated the role of our parent while downplaying that of the other. As far as I can remember, the adults shared the driving and the domestic chores equally. I can't suppress a feeling of pride that my version is more evocative: the account of the views of Ripon Cathedral is—I think—more interesting than the number of miles we had travelled.

I didn't dislike Lucy, although—as a nine-year-old boy—I had no interest in getting to know a girl four years older. I didn't dislike "Uncle" Roy either. I just didn't want him to marry Mum. The two of them had come to stay with us only six weeks before the holiday. The move had seemed both sudden and permanent. I realised later that it was experimental—an experiment that failed. Just two days after our return from Scotland, Roy and Lucy went back to live in their old flat, which they had never attempted to sell. I can confidently say that I was not responsible for the failure. I don't think that Mum really wanted to live with another man after Dad's death.

I notice that—unlike Lucy—I didn't mention our sleeping arrangements. I had resented sharing a tent with a man I barely knew and whom I didn't want in my life. However, I was usually asleep when he came to bed, so I wasn't greatly affected by his presence. I wonder now how much the adults liked the arrangements. I never thought of them as lovers who would want to be sleeping together. The possibility of marriage hadn't suggested to me any sexual liaison between them.

10/8/62

Dad cooked porridge for breakfast. We took down the tents and loaded up the car again. At 9.27, we continued our journey north, passing through the counties of Yorkshire, Westmorland and Cumberland in England and through Dumfriesshire, Kirkcudbrightshire and Wigtownshire in Scotland. At 5.27, we arrived at Glentrool in Kirkcudbrightshire, having travelled 188 miles. We pitched our tents in a large campsite near Loch Trool.

There is a thick cardboard page with eight photo-corners next to the diary entry. I remember Lucy taking numerous photographs during the holiday, particularly in the early days. She must have moved back to the flat before she had the film developed. I think a relative had given her the diary. It was specially designed, with the words "Holiday Journal" embossed on the cover. I can see now how sensitive and tactful Mum had been. She didn't want me to feel left out, but nor did she want to belittle Lucy's present. She had given me a large notebook, with no spaces for photos.

I am surprised that Lucy didn't take her diary with her when she and Roy moved out. If she had forgotten it, surely Mum would have posted it to her? Perhaps she had left it as a farewell gift for Mum to show that, despite her imminent departure, she had enjoyed the holiday. If so, it seemed a selfless present. I would not have donated my own journal. That was too important for me—a part of my identity, my personal history. I had always kept it, each time I moved house, even though I had rarely looked at it.

Whatever the reason, Lucy's journal had stayed in Mum's home until I found it when clearing the house after her death, fifty years later.

Friday 10th August 1962

After breakfast, we took down the tents and put everything back in the car. Then we set off again. We ate our sandwiches by the side of a small country road in Westmorland and then continued north into Scotland. At last we arrived at a campsite near Loch Trool. There were lots of tents and caravans as well as a shop and a large building for washing, with plenty of toilets and basins. After we put up our tents, Mummy cooked us sausages. Then we went for a short walk along a narrow road.

Toilets were always a worry for me. I had been nervous using the single water closet at the timberyard, worried that Roy or Lucy would be complaining that I was taking too long. I remember my relief on seeing the luxury of the washroom at Glentrool.

11/8/62

After breakfast, we had a look at the loch. Then we went for a drive in the car. We went first to the village of Glentrool, where we did some shopping, and then continued to Bargennan, before returning to the campsite for lunch. In the afternoon, we walked up some of the hills around the loch. Dad and I climbed a steep hill called Doon, which is 806 feet high, while Laura and Robin rested lower down. We got back to the tents at 6.07 p.m.

Saturday 11th August 1962

In the morning we clambered over some of the rocks at one end of the loch. The loch was long and winding, so we couldn't see all of it. We watched a heron standing very still at the edge of the water. Then we got into the car and drove to the village to buy some food. On the way, we stopped to look at the River Minnoch. The brown water was flowing fast over rocks and boulders and there was a waterfall. When we had done the shopping, we went to Bargennan and looked in the church. It was a Church of Scotland and so had no altar. Then we returned to our tents and ate bread and cheese for lunch. Afterwards we climbed among some nearby hills and saw a lot of waterfalls. It was very windy. Now we were higher up, we could see the whole of Loch Trool from one end to the other. As we walked back to the tents, we saw two red grouse. Mummy cooked omelettes for supper.

I am glad that I included extra details: the fast-flowing Minnoch, the elevated view of the loch. I don't recall Lucy's and Roy's ascent of Doon. Probably it didn't take them long.

12/8/62

After breakfast, we walked to the loch. We went behind some boulders and changed into our swimsuits. Robin can't swim, so he just paddled, but the rest of us swam a long way. I was out of my depth most of the time. The water was cold and we ran back to the tents afterwards to get warm. After lunch, we went by car to Bruce's Memorial. Then we climbed Buchan Hill, which is 1,617 feet high. After a short rest, we walked back to the car. We got back to the tents at 6.28.

Sunday 12th August 1962

In the morning we went to the loch, changed into our swimming costumes and bathed in the water. It was very cold. Then we returned to the tents for lunch. After that we drove to Bruce's Memorial. This is a large stone monument with writing carved on one side. It celebrates Robert the Bruce's victory over the English. We then started to climb Buchan Hill. We crossed Buchan Burn by a bridge and began to climb steadily. About halfway up, we saw a female red deer. From the top we could see Loch Trool and the campsite and, in another direction, the Long and Round Lochs of Glenhead. We then walked down to the car and drove back to the campsite. Mummy cooked fishcakes.

I remember how self-conscious I was at being unable to swim. Lucy was wearing a blue swimming costume and she seemed to swim for miles. I console myself by thinking how much better I had described the ascent of Buchan Hill.

13/8/62

At about 6.00, I squeezed out of my sleeping bag without waking Laura. I walked to the loch and stood there, staring at it. I have had enough. I am hating this holiday. Robin is too young. Laura is OK, but she is too absorbed with Robin and Dad. I can't talk to her about anything important. I don't like sharing a tent with her. I want privacy and independence. I wish we could go back home. At least I have my own room there, although it's not really my home. I want to go right back to our own flat. I want Mum to move back in with us.

The early morning sun was shining across the lake, leaving a trail of gold glinting on the surface of the water. I wished I could walk across this, walk back into my old world.

I went back to the tents, where Dad had just started preparing breakfast.

After breakfast, we drove to Bruce's Memorial again. Then we climbed Mount Merrick, which is 2,764 feet above sea level and the highest mountain in the Scottish Lowlands. We had a good view from the summit. Then we climbed back down to the car and returned to the campsite at 7.17.

I feel shocked by this diary entry. Lucy had seemed so composed—almost one of the adults. It never occurred to me that she too was feeling overwhelmed by the unwanted arrival of two new members into her family. I had been thinking only of myself. Her writing implied that she was unhappier than I was, for—despite my discomfiture—I had enjoyed the holiday amongst the lochs and the mountains. And the day we climbed the Merrick was the best of all. I remember the sense of achievement when we finally reached the summit. I was on the top of the world, feeling the sun and the wind, looking down on wisps of clouds, seeing a buzzard soaring above me, using the indicator on the beacon to identify distant mountains and islands. Both Mum and Roy had praised me for completing the long walk, there and back again.

I read my own version:

Monday 13th August 1962

After breakfast we decided to climb the Merrick, which is the highest mountain in the Scottish Lowlands. As it was going to be a long walk, we took our lunch with us. We parked the car by Bruce's Memorial again. Then we walked beside a burn until we reached the foot of the Merrick. We crossed the burn and began to climb. About three quarters of the way up we had lunch. Then we climbed to the top, but when we got there, we saw that there was a still higher peak to be climbed. Eventually we reached the top of this and we really were at the top of the Merrick. It was a bright, clear day and there was a marvellous view in every direction. To the west, we could see the Rhinns of Galloway and, beyond that, Ireland. To the north was Ayrshire and, beyond that, the Firth of Clyde and the Highlands. To the east was Loch Doon and to the south was Loch Enoch (which some people say is the most beautiful lake in the world) and Clatteringshaws Loch. After a good look around, we started the long climb down to the car and drove back to the campsite. Mummy cooked scrambled eggs for supper.

Did Lucy experience none of this? Did the climb up the Merrick amount to nothing apart from the number of feet above sea level? Perhaps I had been at fault. Should I have shared my own sense of wonder with her? I thought of my nine-year-old self and realised the impossibility. How could I have determined the direction of a relationship which didn't even exist?

14/8/62

I got up early again before anyone else was awake and walked to the loch. I gazed at the sunlight reflected in the water. The glistening rays seemed to swirl up and form a human figure, floating above the surface.

'Mum,' I said. 'Come back to me, please.'

'Lucy, I can't. You've got Laura now. She's a good woman.'

'I don't want a good woman. I want you. You're my mum.'

'No, Lucy, I'm no good for you now. You're better off without me.'

'That's not true, Mum. I want you back.'

The tears were streaming down my cheeks. Then the sun went in and Mum disappeared. I dried my tears and went back to the tents for breakfast. Afterwards Dad drove us all to the Rhinns of Galloway, a peninsula on the west coast. We ate our sandwiches on the shore and had a walk on the beach. Then we drove back.

I would have been frightened by Lucy's vision if I had read about it as a nine-year-old. Even today, I find it shocking. She sounded on the edge of a nervous breakdown and I had had no idea about it. How much did Mum and Roy know? Maybe Lucy had deliberately left the journal at our house, desperately wanting us to read it so that we could appreciate her suffering. Maybe Mum *had* read it, but she never said so. We didn't talk much about Lucy and Roy after they moved out, although I knew Mum was in contact with Roy for some years. They exchanged Christmas cards if nothing else.

I don't think I ever asked Mum about them. I was afraid that she would tell me that they were about to move in again. I remember that she mentioned that Lucy had gone to university, so I know that she survived her adolescence. What happened to her afterwards? I have no record—only this journal hidden away in a shoe box with other assorted papers.

Lucy had written a very brief, matter-of-fact account of the rest of the day. What had I recorded?

Tuesday 14th August 1962

Mummy let me sleep late after our long walk. After breakfast we decided to go to the coast. First we drove to Newton Stewart to do some shopping. Then we went through Wigtown to Port William, a fishing village. There was no sandy beach there, so we drove around Luce Bay to Glenluce. Then we crossed the isthmus on to the Rhinns of Galloway, which is a peninsula. We drove beside Loch Ryan to the sea. We saw a large number of shags, some ringed plover, redshanks, herring gulls and great black-backed gulls. We had lunch in the car and walked on the beach. Then we drove back to the campsite. Mummy cooked fish fingers again for supper.

"Isthmus". "Peninsula". Of course, I didn't know those words. I can remember Roy looking back from the front seat of the car to teach me them. Later I proudly transcribed them into my diary. Strangely, I don't remember either the isthmus or the peninsula themselves. But I remember the birds. I had never seen a shag before and I was very excited. I don't think I was bothered if Lucy shared my excitement.

15/8/62

It rained all day. I spent most of the time lying on my sleeping bag, reading. We tried sitting in the car—all four of us—to play some card games, but there wasn't room. I envied other campers with large frame tents, where they could sit inside on chairs without touching the canvas. After lunch, Dad and Laura made

Robin and me go for a walk together. We walked a short way along the road but didn't talk much.

Wednesday 15th August 1962

It rained all day. Lucy and I went for a short walk in the afternoon. We didn't talk much.

As an adult, I like to walk in silence with a companion if I am confident in the relationship. Other silences are awkward and embarrassing. I see it as my responsibility to introduce topics of conversation, however unimaginative. The overwhelming silence must be quelled.

With Lucy, I didn't enjoy the silence, but neither did I think it was my duty to overcome it. I just accepted that we didn't want to talk, didn't want to be together.

I think now that I should have spoken. She should as well, but maybe her state of mind made that impossible. She was missing her mother. Would I have understood that? I missed having a father, I felt jealous when schoolfriends talked about their own fathers, but I didn't miss my father as an individual, because he died when I was too young to remember him. I have a vision of him in the garden, cutting the grass, but I don't know if I really saw him or whether Mum had told me that this was what he used to do. I have no recollection of any interaction between us. And while I recognised a void in my life, I felt secure in my diminished family unit and didn't want the space violated by an interloper— a potential surrogate. If I had known Lucy later, we could have discussed our different circumstances, but at the age of nine, I lacked the ability to empathise.

16/8/62

I got up early again and walked to the loch. The sun was behind the clouds and I could see nothing on the water. I just sat on the grass, looking. Then the sun came out and glistened on the water. I saw Mum again, suspended above the surface in the sun's rays. 'Mum!' I cried. But the sun disappeared again and I was alone. I couldn't stand it. I waded into the loch in the direction that I had seen Mum. I had forgotten how deep the water was. Soon I was out of my depth and turned back to the shore. I sat there, shivering in my drenched clothes. At last Dad appeared. He looked angry and frightened and he shouted at me. Then he led me back to the tents.

Later we went for a drive. We stopped to look at the Grey Mare's Tail and walked to the Black Loch. Then we returned to the car and drove on to Woodhall Loch where we had lunch. Afterwards we drove back, stopping for a walk in a fir plantation. We got back to the camp at 8 o'clock.

I have a vague, incoherent memory of that day. I can picture Lucy, soaked to the skin, but I don't know why. What had I written?

Thursday 16th August 1962

Mummy and I had breakfast alone, because Uncle Roy and Lucy had gone for a walk. Mummy looked worried. At last they both came back. Lucy was wet all over. Uncle Roy laughed and said she had fallen in the loch. She went into her tent to change. Later we went out in the car. We stopped to look at a waterfall called the Grey Mare's Tail, which is about forty feet high. From there, we walked past another large waterfall to the Black Loch. We then walked back to the car and drove on. We went past Loch Ken and stopped by Woodhall Loch for lunch. Afterwards we turned back the way we had come and stopped near Clatteringshaws Loch to look at Bruce's Stone, which is not the same as Bruce's Memorial. We then drove on and had a walk in a forest. We saw a golden pheasant and, as we were coming back, a barn owl. We got back to the tents at about 8 o'clock.

So, I hadn't understood what was going on with Lucy. The adults were protecting me, pretending that nothing unusual was happening. I don't recall the car journey. In my memory, the events have been conflated with those of the trip to the coast two days before.

17/8/62

I don't think Laura slept much. I could sense that she wasn't going to allow me out of the tent before her. She asked me why I was unhappy, but I didn't say anything. When we were washing up after breakfast, I heard her speaking to Robin. She was telling him that he must try to talk to me, but Robin said he didn't like me. Laura looked cross and embarrassed.

Later we took our lunch on to Mulldonach, which is 1,827 feet high. At the top, Robin pushed me. I don't know if he wanted me to fall down the mountainside. I was never in danger, because he is too small, but I felt furious. We got back to the tents at 5.53. Later I told Dad that I wanted to go home.

I don't believe her. At least, I don't think I believe her. The problem is that I have no memory of the day at all. I remember the name "Mulldonach". An old man in Glen Trool village once stopped to talk to us. He had an ornately carved walking stick and he used this to point to the mountains all around us, naming each of them: Mulldonach, Mullwarchar, Buchan, Merrick. His mouth extended to utter each "ch"; I realised I could never pronounce that sound properly. I know that we walked on many of those mountains. I can picture the acres of purple heather, stretching down towards Loch Trool, but I don't remember climbing Mulldonach in particular. I suppose Lucy might have reported my conversation with Mum accurately—or nearly accurately—but surely I would never have pushed her? There are three possibilities: I accidentally bumped into her while I was looking at the view from the top; she invented the incident; or I have suppressed the memory of a deliberate shove. Would my diary entry reveal anything?

Friday 17th August 1962

After breakfast we decided to climb Mulldonach. At first we went the wrong way, but when we realised that the path had faded away, we stopped and ate our sandwiches. Then we turned back and started to go up the right way. From the top, we had a good view of several lochs and mountains. We got back to the tents at about six o'clock. After supper we had a walk by the River Minnoch.

Of course, I hadn't written about any antagonism towards Lucy, but my account doesn't suggest any conscious suppression of inappropriate behaviour. I gave the impression that I was enjoying myself, which is how I remember the holiday.

18/8/62

We dismantled the tents after breakfast and loaded the car. I was glad when we drove out of the campsite, although I didn't want to have to sit next to Robin. I ignored him and spoke mainly to Dad. When we reached the border with England, we drove to the Lake District and put up the tents in a campsite belonging to a farm just above Ullswater.

I was *not* glad when we left Loch Trool. It was a shock to me, because I had thought that we would be staying almost a week longer. I don't recall the journey south. I'm sure I didn't say much, but I can't remember an uncomfortable silence. I notice that Lucy didn't record the number of miles we travelled or the counties we passed through. Perhaps she was interested only in getting home. If so, she was to be disappointed.

Friday 18th August 1962

In the morning Mummy and Uncle Roy decided it was time to go back to England. We took down the tents after breakfast and loaded up the car. We took a different route and ended up by Ullswater in the Lake District. We parked in a campsite which was a farmer's field. We walked up to the farmhouse to pay and to buy some milk. There were three collies at the farm called Nell, Nip and Fly. After we had put up the tents, we had supper and then went for a walk along the road beside the lake.

I hadn't known what was happening. I evidently thought that the adults had made the decision to drive south, not realising that Lucy had persuaded them. I was pleased when we pitched our tents. I didn't know what we were going to do, but we were in a campsite very different from the timberyard in Ripon, which had been merely a staging post on the journey to Scotland. Here, by the lakeside, we could linger perhaps; from here, we could explore a new landscape. I remember the dogs: two were black and white and the other was brown. They were all friendly and one insisted on following us around.

19/8/62

Before breakfast, I told Dad that I was going to walk to the banks of Ullswater. I stared out over the lake. I hoped I would see Mum, but the water was still. Dad followed me and we talked about the holiday. He said we could go home whenever I wanted, but he would like us to stay here for a few days. I agreed. We walked back to the tents. Later we drove to Haweswater and ate our sandwiches there. Then we walked to Small Water Tarn. It was very windy. The wind blew across the water, sending sheets of spray towards us. We crouched down to avoid being blown over. Then Dad, Laura and Robin started to walk back, but I stayed for a few minutes. The wind blew again. In one part of the lake, the spray shot upwards to form a human shape. 'Mum!' I called, but it wasn't

Mum. It was my friend, Joanna. 'Jo,' I called out. 'What shall I do? Should I tell Dad that we've got to go home—back to our own flat without Laura and Robin?'

'No, Lucy. You've got to try harder. Make friends with Robin. Take an interest in what he's interested in.' The wind dropped. The water was calm. I ran after the others but kept behind them as we went back to the car. Then we drove back to the tents.

It is all so long ago. I have no recollection of Haweswater, but I can still remember Small Water Tarn: the wind driving the spray across the surface of the lake; the four of us crouching down on the bank, trying to keep clear of the blast. I remember a combination of fear and laughter. I knew we were not in danger, but the force of the gale was so strong. When the wind subsided, Roy took my hand and pulled me up. We were both laughing with the excitement. Looking back, I can see that I was becoming closer to him. Maybe I could, at last, have accepted him as Mum's husband, as my stepfather. Lucy as my stepsister, however, was a different prospect. What had been happening to her? I don't remember her reaction; I don't remember her staying behind at the waterside. If I had known about her mental state, would I have behaved differently? I think I was too self-absorbed at that age. I would have been frightened by her hallucinations, but I wouldn't have been capable of helping.

Saturday 19th August 1962

After breakfast we went in the car to the village of Bampton. Then we drove along a narrow road to Haweswater where we parked the car. It was raining, so we stayed in the car as we ate our lunch. We looked at the lake. Uncle Roy said that when the water is low, you can see the remains of a flooded village, but we could see nothing now. When the rain stopped, we went for a walk. We crossed a beck and walked up a steep footpath. We crossed two more streams by stepping-stones. At one time, there were waterfalls on either side of the path. At last we reached Small Water Tarn. There were steep, rocky hills on the far side of it. The wind was very strong and it sent up a lot of spray from the tarn. We turned back and walked down to the car. Then we drove back to the tent.

The reference to Roy confirms what I have been thinking. He was trying to win my confidence and I think he was succeeding.

20/8/62

After breakfast, we drove to Dale Head Farm and parked the car. Then we walked to Angle Tarn where we had lunch. Afterwards, we returned by a different route and passed a herd of deer. I remembered what Jo had said and I asked Robin, 'What sort of deer are they?'

'Red deer,' he said, without looking at me. It was no use. Just before we reached the car, I told Dad that I wanted to go home.

Had I really been so rude? I remember how excited I was as the path brought us nearer and nearer to the deer. They were aware of us, but they didn't seem bothered. They knew—I suppose—that they could out-run us if we came too close. Perhaps I was so intent on looking at them that I was offhand when Lucy spoke to me. I'm sure I didn't want to be rude, but my response must have confirmed her ill-feeling towards me.

What worries me now is the knowledge that Mum must have read Lucy's journal. She probably left it in our house with the express purpose that Mum should read it. What impression had it made on Mum and why had she never mentioned it to me? Had she been thinking for fifty years that her son was a rude, selfish, unwelcoming boy? Why hadn't she given me the chance to defend myself? And what would my defence have been at that time, before oblivion had conveniently come to my aid?

Sunday 20th August 1962

After breakfast we took the car to Dale Head Farm and then started to walk to Angle Tarn. We ate our sandwiches on the way. There were small islands in the tarn. We went back to the farm by a different and much longer route and we got very close to a large herd of red deer, several of which were stags. We stopped for a rest at Prison Crag and looked down at Hayes Water. We then went on to the car.

I have an elegiac recollection of that day. Did I sense that it was to be the last full day of our holiday? Or did our return home the next day reformulate my memory?

21/8/62

We took down the tents after breakfast and loaded up the car. Then we began the journey home. I insisted that Robin should sit in front, next to the driver. I sat in the back with Laura when Dad was driving and with Dad when Laura was driving. We got home at about 8.00.

How humiliating that my behaviour had caused a change in the travel arrangements. I remember sitting next to the driver, but I thought the adults were giving me a treat, so that I would have a clear view of the road ahead. It never occurred to me that Lucy had refused to sit next to me. I don't recall much of the journey except for our lunch break in Wensleydale. Opposite us, on the other side of the valley, were the square, grey towers of Bolton Castle. Roy told me that Mary Queen of Scots had stayed there.

Monday 21ˢᵗ August 1962

In the morning we took down the tents and loaded up the car. Then we started to go home. We ate our lunch beside the road with a good view of Bolton Castle. We got home at about 8 o'clock.

I wonder what that night was like for Mum and Roy. They must have shared a bed for the first time for a fortnight. Did they sleep together as lovers or were they distant—argumentative even? Half an hour ago, I was congratulating myself that I was not responsible for the rift. Now I see that I was the main culprit.

My journal ended there. However, Lucy's had one, final entry.

22/8/62

After breakfast Dad and I loaded up the car again and took most of our belongings back to the flat. It was lovely to see it again, although it looked empty and smelt fusty. We opened the windows and spent most of the day cleaning. We unloaded the car and put all our stuff in order. Then we drove back to Laura's house. We packed the rest of our luggage into the car and then we all sat down to eat our final meal. Dad and Laura tried to be cheerful, but I felt very awkward. I went to bed soon afterwards. I shall be glad when we leave for the last time tomorrow. I feel sorry for Laura, because I liked her and I think I could have lived with her. But I am so glad that I shall never have to see that horrid little boy again.

Jupiter Semele Bacchus

Yes, dear boy, sit down, sit down. You're new to the Pelham, aren't you? About time we had some fresh blood. Good to know the young are still interested. I can't see gentlemen's clubs lasting much longer. Don't even know how much longer I'll be coming. Money, you see. Not much left. Still, I'll carry on as long as I can. This place has the best cellar in London. Don't have many pleasures now, except for wine.

Odd, you know. Never touched a drop when I was your age. Didn't need to. But things change. I wouldn't have set foot in a place like this then either. Wasn't born into it, you know. I come from a very ordinary family and went to an ordinary school. That's where it all started, I suppose. How old was I? Eight? Nine?…

Mrs Thomas was the teacher. I hadn't meant to scare her. She wasn't a bad sort. Of course, I knew I shouldn't have done it. Mother had told me often enough. But until then, I'd thought it was something on a par with… well, you know, picking your nose: something everyone did, though it was frightfully bad taste. I hadn't anticipated the effect on Mrs Thomas.

Thinking about it afterwards, I realised how restrained she'd been. She didn't scream or shout; she just turned white and backed away from me, saying in a loud whisper, 'Don't do that again. Don't ever do that again.'

It was different in the playground twenty minutes later when some of my classmates were gathered around me.

'What did you do to old Tommo? Show us, come on!'

I tried to shrug them off, but three of them were too persistent: George, Gail and… Harry. They led me behind the bike sheds and threatened to sit on my head if I didn't show them. Reluctantly, I obeyed.

Harry and Gail just stood there, screaming. George didn't make a sound. He simply fainted. Then we all screamed. Teachers came running from all directions. Fortunately, we didn't have to explain anything. We just pretended

152

George had fainted for no apparent reason. Everything was soon calm again, but I scarcely spoke to the other three afterwards. I still regret that. Harry was the best friend I ever had.

I did a lot of thinking after that. I tried to remember the first time it had happened; it must have been a long time before—maybe I was still a baby. I remembered Mother being very angry several times, but further back still—unless it was a dream—I seemed to recall her being frightened too—hysterically frightened. Now I realised that I was capable of doing something which wasn't simply naughty; it was something outrageous—something other people couldn't do. From that moment, I knew I was no ordinary schoolboy; I knew I had power.

My first thought was that I should act upon this new-found power. There were two people I would have loved to see screaming like Harry and Gail, even if they didn't faint like George. There was Jackson, the school bully—he'd locked me in the toilets once—and Mr Willis, my form-teacher. I smiled at the thought of their frightened faces, white and open-mouthed, fear dribbling out of them. I could hardly wait for the first hint of provocation.

Then I thought some more and I found myself licking my lips at the cunning of it. I didn't need to do anything; I didn't need to see those pathetic tyrants recoiling from me in terror. It was enough to know that I *could* reduce them to that state. How could their threats have any impact on me with all my power? Wasn't that power still stronger if it were never used?

How right I was. I was a changed person. Freed from my former timidity, I could do whatever I wanted. No one could stand in my way, for I could conquer anyone instantaneously. I watched with amused detachment as other pupils confessed fearfully to not having done their homework or waited in trepidation for exam results. Nothing made me afraid.

It was the same ten years later when I left school. Terrifying ordeals for my peers were to me merely diverting games. How could I be cowed by a panel of interviewers? They were all in my power. Behind their confident personas, I could see the incipient panic, primed for me to activate it.

Your glass is empty, dear boy. An excellent vintage, this. As I said, I never touched it at that time. What need had I for Dutch courage? Where was I? Oh yes, I'd just left school.

I didn't waste time on university. Nothing was going to slow my ascent to the top. No, I started as a journalist on the local paper. But only a year later, I was with "The Dispatch". Funny, you know, I was never that good a journalist.

I wrote competently enough, but I had no style. All I had was confidence, flowing from the knowledge of my hidden power. I was twenty-seven when they took me on at the BBC. Even then, I was still mainly a reporter, but after I'd interviewed a few people on radio, my talent was quickly recognised. I told you that job interviews never made me nervous—it was the same when *I* was the interviewer. It was just ordinary people at first—someone who'd survived a fire or won the pools. But oh, the day when I had my first politician—some cocky little junior minister. Thought he could do some free propaganda and impress the PM. Most put out when I ordered him to answer my question. Got quite uppity with me, but I wasn't standing for that. I thought of Mrs Thomas all those years ago; I relished the idea of tipping him over into a similar terror.

He never got his promotion after that. The PM pensioned him off with a knighthood. That calls for a celebration, I think. Astonishingly good wine.

There was no stopping me then. Every important politician had to sit down opposite me; each left sounding stupider than when he started. And then there was television, of course. How they all dreaded my interviews in front of the cameras. Did you ever see me with... What's-his-name? Chancellor-chappie? No, you're too young. Anyway, he walked out mid-session. Tried to make a dignified exit, but it was no use. They said that interview lost the government the election. You see how powerful I was? Not that I cared which side won. The other lot were just as scared.

So, you're wondering what happened to my career after that? Why did it peter out so quickly? I'll tell you, dear boy, in one word: women. Oh yes, you think, with my confidence, I'd have no problems in that department. You're right. Not for me the fear of rejection, the worry that she would know dozens of better-looking men. I could have had any woman I wanted—and I did. But there was always something lacking. There was never any intimacy, because it could never be an equal relationship. Not with my power. I'd get a bit of sexual release and that would be it. Then, during the day, my work would take over. That didn't suffer. Not until I met Lorna...

I'm sorry? Yes, just a drop more. You see, I was rather fond of her. I don't know what she thought of me, but she seemed to want to get close. We were in bed in my flat and she... she started talking, asking me about myself. I told her about my job, my parents—the usual boring things. But she wasn't satisfied.

'You're keeping something back,' she said.

'No, I'm quite ordinary. I'm just lucky to have a successful job.'

She was quiet for a minute. Then she said, 'I want you to promise to do something for me.'

'Anything,' I said.

'I want to see you as you really are.'

'But this *is* as I really am. I'm just an ordinary bloke.'

'Don't patronise me. I've seen your interviews. Why are they scared of you if you're so ordinary?'

'It's technique, that's all. I've worked at it, you know.'

'You're lying.'

She got out of bed, turned her back to me and began to get dressed. Her anger pervaded the room. In two minutes, she would be away, out of my life forever. Why didn't I let her go? I'd no wish to terrify her. Anyway, I'd got so used to exerting my power without revealing it that it seemed a self-betrayal to reverse the decision I had made after my great discovery. But seeing her on the verge of leaving, I couldn't help myself. I shouted, 'All right, I'll show you!'

It was the first time for twenty-five years—the first time since I lost the friendship of those kids in the playground. I knew that I would lose Lorna too, but once I'd started, what a sense of relief I felt. It was as if all those years of self-control had been leading to this moment.

She turned when she heard me shout. For a moment, she looked… she looked startled. That was all. Then she said contemptuously, 'Go to hell!'

She picked up the rest of her clothes and walked out of my bedroom, slamming the door behind her. I heard her putting on her shoes, then the sound of the door opening and banging shut. Her footsteps faded into the distance.

As for me, I got back into bed and stayed there, motionless. Occasionally, a car drove past outside. Otherwise, silence.

Still I lay, devastated. Had my whole career been founded on an illusion? My interviewees had been frightened merely by my confidence of power; the power itself had been non-existent. One short "Go to hell" would have revealed my impotence to a million viewers. Could I ever set foot in a television studio again?

I did, as it happened. I was able to survive on my reputation alone for a long time. Somebody would sit opposite me, quivering with fear, unaware that I was equally nervous. Gradually, though, people noticed the change; they found they could get away with waffle and evasiveness unchallenged. Even then, my career wasn't finished at once. While viewers were less impressed by my technique, politicians began to demand to be interviewed by me. No, what finished me, dear boy, was this—I'd started drinking.

Yes, another glass, I think. I'd never touched it before, but once I'd started, there was no stopping me. I was warned once at work, but to no effect. And then there was the time I was drunk in front of the cameras—completely drunk. They had to sack me, of course.

We got through that bottle quickly, didn't we? Never mind, we'll get some more in a minute. It was after that I joined this club. Always despised such places before. Not my sort of people. But I adapted. Learnt the lingo. Soon felt like home. You see, there's one great advantage of places like this—one very great advantage: no women. That and the wine, of course—delicious stuff. Money's a problem, though. Fancy another bottle?

No, that's all right, dear boy. You go home and leave me. I enjoyed our little conversation. Very nice listening to you. You go home. I'm just going to have a quick word with my friends over there. Goodbye, dear boy.

Gentlemen, good evening. Well, that's most kind of you. Just a drop to keep out the cold. Funny thing, you know. Never touched it as a young chap. Didn't need to. You see, it all goes back to my school days. How old was I? Eight? Nine? I didn't mean to scare Mrs… Mrs… Dammit, can't remember her name. Very good teacher. Didn't mean to scare her. Never wanted to scare her…

I Used to Play Here

I didn't go to the park until the last day of my visit. I had been to see several friends of my parents—friends who had been kind to them in their final illnesses and were now old themselves. I had spent time in the city centre, browsing in second-hand bookshops, sitting in cafés, looking in old churches.

But the park was the sacred place of my pilgrimage. I entered by the familiar iron gates, walked through the ornamental gardens and passed the bowling green and tennis courts. I had played there often on summer evenings long ago.

Near them was the children's playground: swings, see-saw, roundabout, slide. The slide seemed so low now. I had been scared when I first climbed up it.

After a short, grassy track, I was in the wood, the wild stretch of the park. I heard a great spotted woodpecker, drumming against a tree trunk; a fox stared at me momentarily, before disappearing into the undergrowth; a robin sang from a hazel tree. I forced my way through brambles and nettles, to the circle of seven old oak trees, their leafy branches stretching out as if to link arms with their companions. Children used to run around these trees, always in the same direction, always anti-clockwise. Sometimes, Paul and I would join them after school, winding in front of one gnarled trunk and behind the next. We ran in silence, obeying some unwritten law.

Two boys were running around the trees now as I approached. One raised his eyes to glance at me and I shuddered.

I was staring at myself.

Not Too Late

Usually, when they came home from the hospital, Ros would sit in the kitchen with her mother, drinking coffee and chatting for half an hour. Tonight, though, she went straight to her bedroom and shut herself in. Homework was her excuse. It was true that she hadn't started the English essay which was due the next day, but really she just wanted to be alone, especially as Frank, Mum's boyfriend, would be arriving soon. Anyway, Grandad was so much better—he might be home in a week.

She sat down and read again the title of the essay: "Demonstrate the changes of mood and diction employed by Tennyson to depict Ulysses' resolve to triumph over the adversity of old age." Why were essay titles always so difficult to understand? She gazed at the words for a few minutes, but her thoughts were still on Grandad in his hospital bed and Mum in the next room, waiting for Frank. She slapped her cheeks in an effort to concentrate and began to re-read the poem.

It little profits that an idle king,
By this still hearth, among these barren crags,
Match'd with an aged wife, I mete and dole
Unequal laws unto a savage race.

It was no use. The poem sent her straight back to Grandad and to Gran, sitting meekly beside him: that strange, wizened, almost silent woman, who was always there, wherever Grandad was—always just a little way away from him. Tonight, she had been sitting faithfully by his bedside, just as a few weeks before she had been sitting by the swimming pool, watching him compete in the Senior Citizens' Diving Contest. What was her history? According to Mum, she had never been any different.

Ros forced herself back to the book:
I cannot rest from travel: I will drink

158

Life to the lees: all times I have enjoy'd
Greatly, have suffer'd greatly, both with those
That loved me, and alone.

But wasn't that Grandad's great problem? He had never been able to rest. Sport had been his life, but it hadn't been a relaxation; he hadn't been capable of taking it easy. Even when not competing or training, he used to pace up and down, recounting his sporting triumphs to anyone who would listen: football captain at school, boxing champion in the army, highest run-scorer for his cricket-club in his sixties. You could never talk about yourself; he was always thinking of his next conquest. Whenever he heard of a sporting event for the elderly, he had to take part in it, whether it was cycling, sailing or rock-climbing.

I am a part of all that I have met;
Yet all experience is an arch wherethro'
Gleams that untravell'd world, whose margin fades
For ever and for ever when I move.

Of course, she admired him. It was wonderful to refuse to give up, but couldn't he stop long enough to see what was happening to his family?

How dull it is to pause, to make an end,
To rust unburnish'd, not to shine in use!
As tho' to breathe were life.

Well, since the heart attack, he would have to rust for a while, but she could see how restless he was. Only that evening, he had been moaning about lying stationary—he who had been in the garage by seven o'clock every morning, training with weights and dumb-bells. The nurse had told him that he must be careful from now on, but he had scorned her. He didn't want to live, he said, if he couldn't force his body to its limits. How he would agree with Ulysses:

159

...and vile it were
For some three suns to store and hoard myself,
And this grey spirit yearning in desire
To follow knowledge like a sinking star,
Beyond the utmost bound of human thought.

Ros could hear raised voices in the next room. Mum and Frank were quarrelling. How Ros hated him for messing up their lives. She squashed her fingers into her ears and carried on reading.

This is my son, mine own Telemachus,
To whom I leave the sceptre and the isle...
Most blameless is he, centred in the sphere
Of common duties, decent not to fail
In offices of tenderness.

Well, if Telemachus were blameless, why was Ulysses bent on doing the opposite—running away from his responsibilities? Common duties were so boring—much more fulfilling to go on yet another voyage or try to win yet one more trophy. Couldn't Grandad see what was happening? Why didn't he intervene and show his daughter the damage she was doing? Why didn't he remind her that she was married to Dad and make her kick Frank out? What sort of father was he if he could let her get involved with a man like Frank?

Angrily, she started reading the final section of the poem:

Old age hath yet his honour and his toil;
Death closes all; but something ere the end,
Some work of noble note, may yet be done,
Not unbecoming men that strove with gods.

No, she didn't want him to do anything more. Why couldn't he just die—now, quietly, in his hospital bed?

She realised what she was thinking and hated herself for it. Of course, she didn't want him to die, but she didn't want to hear any more of his absurd aspirations. No, she didn't want him to die; she wanted him to grow up.

Come my friends,
'Tis not too late to seek a newer world.
Push off, and sitting well in order smite
The sounding furrows; for my purpose holds
To sail beyond the sunset, and the baths
Of all the western stars until I die.

This was just desperation, self-delusion, and it was so unnecessary. He wasn't seeking a newer world. It was the same one he'd been seeking all his life. The real new world was the one he was escaping from. But of course, it was more difficult to start talking properly to your wife and family. He wouldn't know how to begin now. What could Grandad say to Gran? He scarcely knew how to talk about anything except sport. Ros remembered his words tonight, when she'd asked him how he was.

"Much better, thanks. Much better. The doctor says I'll soon be out and about again. Then I'll start to build up my strength. Don't worry, I'll be sensible. I know what I can do. Swimming. That's the exercise for a dodgy ticker. But it won't be dodgy for long. I'll be swimming further every day. And I'll let you into a secret. You're looking at the man who's going to be the oldest person ever to swim the Channel."

How proudly he had looked at her, while Gran was smiling wanly at him. Gran knew what was going on, but she would never tell him how stupid he was being, and he was happy to believe that her silence was admiration for his indomitable will.

Tho' much is taken, much abides; and tho'
We are not now that strength which in old days
Moved earth and heaven; that which we are, we are,
One equal temper of heroic hearts,
Made weak by time and fate, but strong in will
To strive, to seek, to find, and not to yield.

Ros shut the book in disgust. Triumphing over adversity indeed!

The flat was silent now. It must be very late, and still she hadn't started the essay. She was tempted to give up and go to bed. Perhaps she could get up early tomorrow and write it before school. But she knew that there was little chance of that. If she went to bed now, she would have to endure Mrs Johnson's sarcasm tomorrow. She sighed, opened her exercise book, wrote the title… and laid her pen down again.

Of course, she knew what she was meant to write. She should contrast the lifelessness of Ulysses' current existence amongst the "still hearth" and "barren crags" with the ceaseless motion of his remembered adventures through "scudding drifts"; she should set his son's slow prudence against his own inexhaustible yearnings. She should point out the images of death and evening in the final lines—the images which he was still intent on conquering. The essay wouldn't be difficult, but how could she write it when she was expected to applaud the character?

Coffee. That was what she needed. It would keep her awake, settle her mind. Carefully, so as not to wake Mum, she opened her bedroom door and tiptoed along the hall to the kitchen. She turned on the light… and screamed.

Frank stood up guiltily.

"Oh, hello Ros. Sorry to startle you. I was about to leave. Just gathering my thoughts before I set off."

They looked at each other in silence. Then he continued.

"The fact is, your mother asked me not to stay tonight. These are difficult times—difficult times for all of us."

Another silence. Ros refused to show him any pity. She spoke coldly, without expression.

"I was just going to make myself a cup of coffee. I've got an essay to write and I need to keep awake."

"Let me make it for you. You sit down and relax for a couple of minutes."

God! He was going to start chatting her up. Mum had given him the boot, so now he was trying to get off with the daughter. The creep!

"Only for two minutes. Then I must be off or I'll miss the last bus."

She collapsed, horrified, into a chair. He had guessed her thoughts even though he had probably intended simply to make her coffee. She felt her eyes filling with tears. Now he would put his arm around her to comfort her, but she didn't want to be touched—she couldn't bear to be touched by him.

He didn't touch her. He had put the kettle on and was very deliberately not looking at her. He carefully spooned coffee into the cup, concentrating as though he were counting every grain.

"What's the essay about?"

"It's English literature. On a poem by Tennyson."

"Can't help you there, I'm afraid. The only one of his I remember is 'The Charge of the Light Brigade'. I hated that poem."

"This isn't like that. It's about an old man. And he's just like Grandad."

"Bad luck. Just the worst time to have to study a poem like that."

"No, no, it's a great poem and it ought to be helpful. It's just my teacher. She's got it all wrong."

"They usually do."

"She wants me to write about how Tennyson shows the old man triumphing over adversity. But you've seen Grandad. There's nothing triumphant about him. He's just—he's just pathetic. But I can't write that. She wouldn't understand."

Frank poured the boiling water into the cup, added milk and sugar, and started to stir. Then he spoke.

"Look Ros, I was never any good at literature—no good at all. But I do read a lot, and there's one thing I know. English teachers go on about all these high-flown emotions—triumphing over adversity and all that. But that's not what I want out of a book. I want something that will help me—help me make sense of—make sense of all this mess. Teachers never understand that—they never understand anything."

All this time, he had been stirring the coffee. He slowed down a little, but still the spoon went around, as he stopped talking for a few seconds.

"That's not fair, of course. I had some wonderful teachers. I'd never have got this job if my maths teacher hadn't made me work. But some of them…" The spoon rotated faster again. "…some of them don't have a clue. They've been to school, then to college, then back to school and they know nothing. Now you, you can write this essay, because you've got the experience. You know what your Grandad's like and what a mess he's made of everything. You've seen me and your mum and dad—we've done our best, but we've all made a right balls-up of our lives. So, write your essay—tell the teacher what the poem means—make her understand—just once in her life. Go on, dare her to give you a bad mark."

He stopped stirring suddenly and passed the mug to Ros, the bubbles still revolving frantically. In silence, he washed and dried the spoon, before putting it away tidily in the drawer. Then, whispering, as if he had suddenly remembered Mum in her bedroom, he said, "Goodnight, Ros. Good luck with your essay."

Ros carried the cup to her bedroom, sat down, took one sip and began writing:

Tennyson does not show an old man triumphing over adversity. He describes a pathetic figure, trying to pretend he is still young, while refusing to accept any family responsibilities...

By the time she took her second sip of coffee, she had already written a page and a half.

Easter 1988

My stomach had been rebelling for two days at the prospect of the Easter weekend, but I hoped that it would come to order now that it had to. When I arrived at Victoria at 10 o'clock on Good Friday morning, I was feeling healthy, though still anxious.

'Hello Charlotte,' said Vernon. 'I thought you said you couldn't come.'

'No, I'll be walking with you today. But I'm busy tomorrow and Sunday. Then I'll join you again on Monday.'

To my relief, Vernon didn't ask any further questions—at that time. He was busy organising the rest of our group. Evidently, we couldn't walk to the start of the march in Hyde Park without his leadership.

There were twelve of us from Anerley CND. I felt awkward, because of my enforced absence the next day. If I had been fully committed, would I have cancelled all other engagements?

As I feared, after satisfying himself that there were no stragglers, Vernon returned to me.

'So, what are you doing tomorrow, then?'

I could sense that I was blushing.

'Oh, I'm going to a christening. An old school friend has asked me to be godmother.' Why did I sound so apologetic?

'You'll make a lovely godmother,' said Eunice. 'You'll take your responsibilities very seriously.'

I was relieved by her approval, although her assurance overwhelmed me with a sense of my inadequacy. Justin was more critical.

'You didn't have to accept when your friend asked you.'

'But I wanted to. It's not just a religious thing. It's important that children should have adults they can turn to—apart from their parents.'

I was sounding defensive. And I didn't know if I would have a significant role in Michael's life. I hadn't seen Emily, his mother, for three years.

165

We had reached Hyde Park by now. As we waited for the march to set off, I listened to the speeches. I realised that I hadn't even thought about the purpose of the march until now; I had been too busy worrying. When I joined CND in 1980—just after university—it had meant everything to me. Leafleting, flyposting, meetings, running a stall, street theatre—I had done them all. I had watched the movement grow with all the publicity. I had felt a part of the revival. I truly believed that change was possible. Now, eight years and two general elections later, the speakers sounded boring and repetitive. All were optimistic after the nuclear treaty signed by Reagan and Gorbachev; all stressed the dangers of Trident. I looked cynically at the crowds. Many older people were wearing badges from the Aldermaston marches of the 1950s and 60s. Was this event just an exercise in nostalgia? Why was I here? Because I thought the issue was important or because I would have felt guilty to stay away? Would I have felt more committed if I were about to march the whole way?

We set off at 11.30, but progress was slow. After an hour, we were still alongside Hyde Park, on Kensington Road. I was walking with Eunice. She told me about her own godson, who had recently married. Eunice was a Christian; her religion and politics seemed totally integrated. She didn't need to censor portions of her life, according to the company she was with. How I envied her. I could never tell my parents that I was taking part in this demonstration, any more than I could tell Emily.

By this time, my earlier confidence in the behaviour of my stomach had proved unfounded. I was feeling queasy and began to doubt whether I would complete the day's march and even whether I should go any further at all. While Eunice was talking to someone else, I hurried ahead, away from anyone I knew. Should I just disappear at the next tube station to avoid the embarrassment of saying goodbye to my colleagues? It took me an hour to answer this question, by which time we had reached Turnham Green, where we were stopping for lunch. I sat down on a park bench and immediately felt better. After buying a sandwich and a cup of tea, I rejoined my colleagues.

As we re-started the march, I thought again that I had recovered and again I was mistaken. The view across the Thames to Kew was impressive, but I couldn't appreciate it because of my renewed nausea. I recalled a childhood visit to Kew Gardens with my parents. Afterwards, we had walked along the towpath to Richmond. It was an idyllic memory, untainted by any feeling that I should have been somewhere else.

I was walking mainly with strangers now, not wishing to talk to anyone. I hurried ahead to avoid a noisy contingent who were chanting slogans, including the inevitable:

Maggie, Maggie, Maggie! Out! Out! Out!

Five years ago, I used to join in, but now the words seemed inane. I preferred the quieter sections of the march, where I could focus on my own thoughts.

Eventually, at 5 o'clock, we reached Southall, the end of the day's march. I was able to say goodbye without any embarrassment, while the others made their way to the community centre, where they would spend the night.

On the station platform and later, in the warmth of the carriage, I felt better again—able to ponder the day's events and my inability to reconcile them with those of the two days to come. This, I was sure, was the cause of my physical discomfort. I thought of Eunice and all the other Christians on the march (I had seen their banners). Why couldn't I tell Emily of my part in it? Twelve years before, on Good Friday 1976, she and I had joined a Procession of Witness through the streets of St Albans to the cathedral. I remembered entering the long, dark building through the great west door. Was today's march so different?

Unfortunately, it was. Perhaps if I had dropped hints of my political activity over the years, we might have been able to remain friends, but suddenly to confess on the day of the baptism that I had just been on a CND march would have been devastating. She had an insatiable yearning for order and tradition, into which I had somehow become assimilated.

When I arrived home, Shoba, my flat mate, took pity on me. She ran me a hot bath, scented with various oils, and made me peppermint tea to soothe my stomach. I went to bed, feeling clean and healthy.

I woke early, tense but well. I had already packed the dress I had chosen for the service; now I just needed to decide what I should be wearing when I met Emily. I knew I was being ridiculous. What did it matter, so long as I was dressed respectably at the church? But I didn't think I could wear jeans in front of her— even smart ones. I chose grey trousers and a blue jumper and ran out of the flat before I could change my mind. After a short bus and tube journey, I arrived at King's Cross an hour before my train was due. Having bought my ticket, I sat in the station buffet, worrying about what to write inside the christening card. I was still undecided when I boarded the train. Eventually, while we were stopped at the next station, I wrote in the card: 'May this special day mark a deepening of faith for us all.' I didn't say faith in what, so perhaps I wasn't being entirely hypocritical.

The train reached Bradwick in the early afternoon. I was a few minutes early, so I waited in the car park until Emily drove in. She jumped out of her car, arms outstretched.

'Charlotte! Thanks so much for coming to support me. And thank you for agreeing to be Michael's godmother.'

'My pleasure,' I said. 'It's a privilege.'

For the first time, I realised how important my presence was for Emily. I had been thinking only of me, of whether the responsibility fitted in with my self-image. Now I saw that Emily believed she needed me.

I listened as she explained the programme for the rest of the day—it sounded sufficiently full to avoid any embarrassing silences. She drove us to the town centre, parked the car and led me to the supermarket, where we bought some plastic glasses and discussed drinks for after the baptism. Should we offer wine? Most of the congregation would be arriving by car. Perhaps it would be wrong to serve alcohol. Her nervous uncertainty put me at ease. I suggested fruit juice, non-alcoholic wine and water. She agreed gratefully. We bought crisps and biscuits, before returning to the car. Then she drove to the bus station, where we were to meet her mother. I understood that her anxiety was partly a concern that the arrangements would meet her mother's approval.

The coach arrived and parked next to the railings. As her mother emerged, we stepped forward to greet her, but her hug (for Emily) and her handshake (for me) were constricted by the narrow corridor of metal. Emily and I backed away to allow her mother to step out into the space of the station.

Mrs Edwards, the widow of a Royal Navy captain who had taken part in the D-Day Landings, had always been very conservative, but unassuming and anxious to please. She had seemed elderly, in both appearance and attitude, when I first met her twenty years before; now she didn't appear much older. I was fond of her. She politely asked me about my parents, as Emily drove us home.

I had not been to the house before. It was small, but tidy. The front door opened on to a narrow hall, leading to the kitchen. The three of us turned left into the sitting room, from which masculine voices were booming. These fell quiet as we entered and three men stood up to welcome us: Terry (Emily's husband), his brother, Mark, and their father, Gordon. Michael lay in his pram in the middle of the room. Mrs Edwards and I shook hands with everyone, and we admired the baby. Then Emily and her mother disappeared into the kitchen to prepare tea.

I had liked Terry the few times we had met, but now he seemed to have become part of a triumvirate of male authority. They were discussing proposals to ban cars from the centre of Bradwick and all three were appalled at this infringement of their rights as motorists. They predicted damage to the trade of the high street shops; they wondered how fire engines and ambulances would cope in an emergency; they threatened to defy the law. Fortunately, they were so busy agreeing with each other that they never asked me for my opinion—not that I knew anything about the town centre, although I was in favour of pedestrianisation in principle. Instead, I played with Michael. I didn't have much experience with babies, but I was pleased that I could make him laugh by pulling his fingers.

Just then, the doorbell rang and I jumped up.

'I'll get it,' I called out, anxious to escape.

I opened the door to find David, Emily's brother. Another man, I thought, but at least one I had known a long time. He greeted me with a kiss, to my surprise and pleasure. I led him into the kitchen and stayed there, hoping I would not be unwelcome.

The kitchen was not large enough for four people. Mrs Edwards was buttering bread, so I offered to relieve her. She agreed, though rather doubtfully, squeezing herself against the fridge while chatting to her son about his drive from Peterborough. I was careful to spread the butter into the corners of every slice, guessing that I was being watched.

Tea was an important tradition for the Edwards family, especially if shared with guests. Lots of bread, butter and jam, a choice of home-made cakes. As we carried the plates and cups into the sitting room, Emily apologised that she had not had time to bake a cake—the plethora of bought ones were a good substitute. In deference to Mrs Edwards, Terry's family was polite and respectful. I enjoyed the tea, although I struggled with the etiquette: jam had to be spread on the side of the plate first and then transferred to the bread—a messy process. As we ate and drank, Emily, glancing repeatedly at her mother for approval, outlined the plans for the evening. She explained the order of the service to the godparents— Mark, David and me—and made sure we knew the exact moment when we would be needed.

'You don't have to worry about memorising the vows—they're clearly printed on the service sheet.'

'Shout 'em out, Mark!' said Gordon. 'Loud and clear.'

Mark looked embarrassed. I could see that he was nervous—nervous of the service and of his father. I relaxed. I wasn't going to have any problems with either godfather. Mark was scared and David seemed to like me.

'And now,' said Mrs Edwards, 'I would like to give my godson his christening present.'

She handed over a Bible (Authorised Version) in a handsome red binding.

'Well, Mark and I are giving silver—thirty pieces of it,' said Gordon. 'Not really—only one piece.'

He presented a christening mug, engraved with Michael's name.

David's present—a photograph album—had Michael's name on it too.

Now it was my turn. I gave Emily the card. She read the message, thanked me and passed it to her mother, who nodded approvingly. Then I gave her a second envelope.

'Sorry, it's not a very imaginative present, but I hope it will be useful.'

'Charlotte, that's really generous,' said Terry. 'We keep meaning to open a savings account for Michael. Now we can make a first deposit.'

'I haven't made it out to anybody yet. I wasn't sure…'

'Make it out to me!' roared Gordon.

'Dad!' said Terry. I could see he wasn't scared of him.

There followed a long debate about what name should be used on the cheque. I enjoyed this pointless discussion. Eventually, I made out the cheque to Emily's and Terry's joint account.

'Good, that's settled,' said Gordon. 'Never too soon to get 'em thinking about money.'

I hadn't intended to instil in Michael an early love of capitalism. Nevertheless, I was pleased that my gift was appreciated.

It was time to change for the evening service. Emily took Michael upstairs to get him ready, while Mrs Edwards and I followed David to his car, so that he could drive us to our hotel. I sat on my own in the back, but David asked me questions from time to time. At the hotel, we checked in and went to our separate rooms. I had a shower and put on my dress, hoping it didn't look creased. I wore a simple necklace and a black jacket. My shoes were almost flat; high heels would have been too flamboyant. I stood nervously in front of the mirror, then panicked and rushed downstairs, worried that I was late.

Mrs Edwards was there, but not her son. She praised my appearance, which boosted my confidence. I returned the compliment. Then David appeared, apologising for being late.

I felt relaxed as we walked into the car park and got into the car. We waited until we saw Terry's and Emily's car at the entrance. Then we followed their lead.

The church, about five miles away in the village of Plumley, was secluded amidst the yew trees in the churchyard—very peaceful in the dimming light. Having parked the cars, we took the refreshments to the back of the church. These included a magnificent cake, baked by Emily, with "Michael" written in blue icing on top. Gordon insisted on carrying the "wine".

'Wouldn't trust anyone else with this!' he said.

Emily smiled at me and put a finger to her lips. Meanwhile, a group of girls—Michael's fan club—ran to meet him.

We settled ourselves in the pew nearest the font and waited in the darkening church.

Above me was a small, dark shape, flying up and down the nave: a bat. I was about to point it out to Mrs Edwards, who was sitting beside me, when it occurred to me that she might be scared of it. Other members of the congregation had noticed it too and were laughing—apparently it was a regular worshipper—but I was right. Mrs Edwards was talking agitatedly to David and pointing upwards.

The service was not simply a baptism; it was also the Easter Vigil, incorporating the Service of Light. We were invited to leave the church—now in total darkness—and take candles into the graveyard, where the vicar was about to light a bonfire. From this, he lit the Paschal Candle and, as we processed back into the church, the light was passed to each of us. It was exciting—almost a pagan ritual. There followed a few prayers and hymns. I struggled to keep my candle alight, while finding the page in my hymn book with one hand. Then the baptism party was asked to congregate around the font.

We turned to Christ, repented of our sins and renounced evil. The baby was baptised with water and oil (newly blessed by the bishop) and a candle was lit for him. I had known that this would be passed to me to hold; I had not known that I would already be carrying another candle, as well as a hymn book and service sheet. I fumbled all these into one hand and took the new candle in the other. Next, the whole congregation, as part of the Easter service, were asked to renew their baptismal vows, so, for a second time, we turned to Christ, repented of our sins and renounced evil. Finally, everyone was invited to approach the font and make the sign of the cross on our foreheads, before returning to our pews for the concluding prayers and hymn.

After the blessing, Terry asked everyone to stay behind for refreshments. David and I immediately got to work, opening bottles and filling glasses (Mark, the third godparent, had seemed reluctant to help). We worked well together; I felt relaxed. Everyone seemed to be enjoying the drinks, apart from Gordon:

'Non-alcoholic wine? If I'd known, I wouldn't have carried the bottles so carefully.'

Soon it was all over. We cleared up and walked through the churchyard to the cars. I had found the service moving. I didn't know if I was moved for the right reason, but I didn't know what the right reason was. David drove us back to the hotel, his mother asking if he was sure he was safe to drive—was the wine really non-alcoholic? As we said goodnight to each other, Mrs Edwards invited me to share their breakfast table the next morning, but assured me that she wouldn't mind if I preferred to be on my own. Touched by her sensitivity, I accepted her offer willingly and said goodnight.

Although it was only 10 o'clock, I went to bed immediately and pondered the events of the day. Emily had been so grateful for my help; David had been lovely; their mother, who used to scare me, I found endearing. Terry seemed nice too and Mark was harmless: when separated from their father, neither was any threat. Even Gordon was friendly enough, although rather loud and overpowering. I felt that I was being sucked into their existence—respectable, pleasant, unchallenging—but a lifestyle incompatible with my activities of the day before.

I slept.

I woke up at 7 o'clock. Again, I had to be well-dressed, because we were going to the 9.15 Easter Communion Service. I wore the same clothes as the night before. When I went down to breakfast an hour later, I was glad to see that David and his mother were wearing the same clothes too. The breakfast room was locked, so we sat anxiously in the foyer. At last, the doors opened and we went to our table. I had coffee and scrambled eggs on toast. We talked of how an extra quarter of an hour would have been useful, but it couldn't be helped.

After eating, we returned to our rooms to brush our teeth and fetch our suitcases, which we carried to David's car. As he drove us to church, it occurred to me how much time we were spending in cars. I couldn't drive; in London, I travelled everywhere by public transport. I felt this set me apart from the others, though no one commented on it.

It was a bright, sunny day. The churchyard, where we waited for Emily, Terry and Michael, had lost the solemnity of the previous night. As their car turned into the car park, Michael's admirers ran across the grass to take turns in holding him.

Emily and Terry were singing in the choir, so the rest of us found an empty pew, where Mrs Edwards nursed Michael. It was a joyful service. The vicar said repeatedly, 'The Lord is risen,' and we replied, 'He is risen indeed. Alleluia!' I felt alienated in a way I hadn't felt by the baptism the night before. The rejoicing seemed artificial and complacent. The certainty expressed in the prayers, the hymns, the sermon contradicted the bewilderment and confusion in the Gospel reading of Mary Magdalen's meeting with Jesus in the garden.

I was sure that David and his mother didn't agree with me, although I was pleased that—like me—they refrained from waving their hymn books in the air during the chorus of "Thine be the glory".

After the service, we posed for photographs in the church porch. This would have been difficult in the darkness of the night before. Then we all drove back to Emily's and Terry's house for coffee. The atmosphere was more relaxed without Terry's father. We sat quietly, chatting about the two services. Mrs Edwards had been worried about the sharing of the Sign of Peace. She was relieved that she was expected only to shake hands with other worshippers—not to hug them.

Emily said she needed to prepare lunch. Terry suggested that the rest of us should go for a walk in the park. I noticed how easily the couple had accepted traditional gender roles. Nevertheless, I was happy to join him, David and Michael. Mrs Edwards said that she would prefer to stay and rest.

The park was beautiful, with oak trees just coming into full leaf and dogs vainly chasing the squirrels. At the pond, some swans took food out of our hands, much to Michael's excitement. We took turns to push his pram. I was glad he was with us; his presence avoided any awkward silences. I was impressed by how proud Terry was of him.

David asked me about my life in London. I felt nervous. I didn't want to reveal anything about my political activities, but neither did I want to seem to be evading his questions. I talked about my work and, fortunately, he appeared interested, asking me detailed questions. He was easy to talk to. I wondered if he would want to meet me again, but I was relieved (if a little disappointed) that he didn't suggest this. We were getting on well, but I didn't feel that I could accommodate him in my current lifestyle.

Lunch was ready when we returned to the house. I had given up meat years before, but, of course, I hadn't confessed this to Emily. I hated biting into the steak and kidney pie, but I loved the apple crumble we had for dessert, so my compliments were not entirely false.

After lunch, David was keen to leave and he offered to drive me to the station. Emily asked me to go upstairs with her first, so that she could talk to me in private.

'Charlotte, thank you so much for coming. It's really important for me that Michael should have you as a godmother. We don't know what the future will bring. There may be difficult times ahead for Terry and me. I know I can count on you to support Michael whatever happens.'

'Of course, I'll be there for you,' I said, 'but I don't think I'll be needed. You and Terry are solid.'

We embraced and went downstairs, where David was saying goodbye to his mother, who would be leaving later. I wished everyone well and got into the car next to David.

It was only a short journey. He kissed me when we parted and waved as I walked into the station.

I couldn't read much on the train. I felt worried about what I'd done and what I'd promised. The interrupted CND march focused my mind on the difficulties. Could I really provide the support Emily was asking for? Could I do so without entirely jettisoning my political beliefs? I reached King's Cross, feeling rather melancholy, and went by tube and train to Crystal Palace, where I walked in the park, seeking comfort amongst the ducks. They only reminded me of the swans in Bradwick Park that morning. I was hoping that Shoba would be at home to look after me, but she was out. I washed some clothes, had a snack and went to bed. My alarm was set for 6 o'clock.

I woke punctually. I was out of the house by 6.15 and at Victoria by 7. However, I didn't reach Paddington until an hour later, because of delays on the Underground. The march was to leave Reading for Aldermaston at 8.30: I wouldn't be there in time. I sat on the cold train to Reading and arrived at 8.45— late, frozen and lost—I had no idea where Prospect Park, the assembly point, was. I bought a street map and took it into the buffet to study it over a cup of coffee. I located a Prospect Street and I also worked out a route to Burghfield, where the march was due to stop for an early lunch. I decided to find the park if I could and then pursue the march.

Soon I saw a signpost directing me to Prospect Park. There was another one 100 yards further on, then a roundabout with no signposts showing anywhere nearer than 12 miles. I rushed down various roads in turn, feeling self-conscious as I gave up each to return to the roundabout. I decided to forget the park and make straight for Burghfield.

The first part of the journey was exciting: along the towpath by the river. The busy Basingstoke Road was less enjoyable. I crossed the motorway by a footbridge and turned off on to a country road. I was still feeling anxious, as I didn't know which part of Burghfield the marchers would be going to. The Royal Ordnance Factory there didn't officially exist and wasn't marked on my map. Nevertheless, I knew that it didn't exist over a large expanse of land, whereas the village, though publicly recognised as a physical entity, was small. As I walked alongside the non-existent wire fence, looking at the non-existent telegraph poles, I recalled earlier demonstrations. I had been here on an all-night blockade five years ago. Would I have the energy to do that again? I walked on and turned into a road signposted to Aldermaston.

Ahead of me was an elderly couple, wearing anoraks and walking boots. I guessed that they would be joining the march and wondered if I should continue behind them. I wasn't sure if I wanted to talk to anyone yet. But they were walking so slowly that it was difficult not to catch up with them.

'Hello,' I said. 'Are you going to the march? Do you mind if I join you?'

Like me, they had arrived too late at Reading, but they knew the route and so, despite their slow pace, they had made good progress. They were impressed that I had walked the first stage. To my relief, they didn't question me about what I had been doing for the last two days. Both had been campaigners most of their lives and had taken part in the Aldermaston marches in the 1950s.

'How does it feel to be doing it again after all these years?' I asked.

'It's strange,' said the woman, 'but I think the continuity's important. We have to keep campaigning for peace, even if no one seems to be listening. Mind you, Frank's been involved longer than I have. He was a conscientious objector during the war.'

'Really? That's impressive.' I was silent for a minute. Frank could never have lived my divided life. You couldn't be a CO one day and then pretend to be a patriotic soldier when you met your conservative acquaintances the next.

'I think you were very brave,' I said at last. 'In some ways, braver than the men who fought.'

'I would never underestimate the bravery of those soldiers,' said Frank. 'Never. And remember—they were fighting fascism. It wasn't an easy decision for me. I still believe I was right, but would I have thought the same if the Nazis had won? I like to think that I would, but I don't know. There are no easy answers. I don't even like easy answers. They're one of the weapons of fascism.'

'So, what happened to you? Did you go to prison?'

'No. I knew people who did. But I became a medical orderly in Tooting—helping people injured in the Blitz. Some friends criticised me. "You're helping the war effort," they said. I can respect their viewpoint. As I said, there are no easy answers. But I couldn't accept that people were being burnt alive and not help them. Some doctors didn't want me on the wards at first. But they soon changed their minds when the burn victims came in.'

By now, we had come to a wood. Gorse and dry bracken covered the ground. Through the trees, we could see people. A track led us to a large crowd, who were eating sandwiches in a clearing by a lake.

'Well, I'd better join my group now,' I said. 'Thank you for your company. You've given me a lot to think about.'

I quickly found the two members of Anerley CND who had walked all the way: Vernon and Geoff. They greeted me with hugs. I asked them about the march; fortunately, they didn't question me about the baptism.

We started the final, three-mile stretch to Aldermaston. I was beginning to reclaim my identity as an anti-nuclear activist, but I felt something of a fraud amongst so many who had walked the whole route. (Others had joined that morning, so I didn't need to worry.) Song sheets were passed around and I joined in the singing, while trying to look as if I wasn't. At last, we reached the fence of the Atomic Weapons Establishment. There were demonstrators all around it, all clapping us (which made me feel even more fraudulent). At 2 o'clock, everyone made a noise: shouting, yodelling, banging tambourines. I felt self-conscious again, but I clapped a little as a token gesture. The noise went on and on and some people started dancing. I liked the festive atmosphere, although I was worried that everyone would lose self-control and start trampling each other underfoot.

Eventually, the noise subsided. Geoff had by now rejoined his wife in a different part of the crowd. Vernon had booked a seat on a minibus back to London and he said he could find a place for me on it too. I was grateful, as I had feared that I would have to walk back to Reading. He led me around the outside of the base, pointing at the banners and the messages pinned to the fence. I am fond of Vernon, but he can be overbearing. He was in a state of elation after completing the march and was shouting out witticisms to anyone who might be listening, while I cringed beside him. I was relieved when we found the minibus. Although other marchers were on it, Vernon had decided that he was in charge and I felt guilty by association. I hoped no one thought he was my boyfriend. However, the journey was uneventful and I was dropped near my home at 7 o'clock.

The last four days had been intense: two separate compartments of my life had nearly collided, but I had survived the impending disaster. Probably, I would continue as a peace activist, although without the enthusiasm of a few years before; I would continue to see Emily and honour my responsibilities as a godparent, but I hoped that my visits would be infrequent, to avoid too much embarrassment. Probably, nothing would change.

Return to the Island of Opposites

'Not like you to be reading a kids' book, Dad.'

'No, that's true. But this book's special. I read it over and over again when I was a boy.'

'And you've still kept it after all these years?'

'No, this is a second-hand copy I've just bought. I turned out my old one when I left home. Didn't think I'd ever read it again. I don't suppose I even thought about it again until we moved here. You see, it's set here—in Thrilby.'

'Really? Does it mention our street?'

'I doubt if our street existed when the author was writing. But she writes about the town centre—the bus station, Leigham Park, the market. And the children were all at the Alfred Fairbrass School, though it's given a different name. But what really interested me is an island on the river. That's where the action takes place. And I've been looking at the map. The island is really there.'

'What happened on the island?'

'Well, it's a fantasy story. The children spend a lot of time there. But the weather's different from the mainland.'

'It has its own micro-climate?'

'Yes, I suppose so, though I didn't know that word when I first read it. The kids are playing on the island on a summer's day, while there is snow on the riverbank. Then, later on, they're on the island in a winter storm while the sun is shining across the water. And it's exciting because they're stranded there. The river is in flood. It's too dangerous to get back to the mainland.'

'Sounds OK for a kids' book, but I don't think I'll bother to read it.'

'I think it's the kids' relationships which are interesting. When they're stranded, they're not very nice children. They're not the resourceful kids who can build rafts and light fires without matches. They just shout at each other and don't know what to do. So, I think there's a psychological angle to the book.'

'Oh, that's deep, Dad!'

'Well, I suppose I've got to justify reading it. Anyway, I have to look at that island. Would you like to come with me?'

'I don't think so, Dad. I'll leave you to enjoy your fantasy alone.'

I stood on the bank, scowling at the island. It was located exactly as described in the book—just five minutes from the main road. But the country track no longer existed. It had been replaced by a concrete path, with houses on one side, the river on the other. Even the river was different: no longer clear and fresh, but a repository of rubbish, where beer cans and an abandoned supermarket trolley were wedged in the mud against the bank. The island itself was inaccessible. In the story, the children had reached it via a tree trunk spanning the water. As they struggled past a branch halfway across, the climate of the island would magically change. Even if there had been a way on to it now, it wasn't the idyllic paradise which the author had portrayed. Thick undergrowth of brambles and nettles would have made the children's games impossible.

I wished I hadn't re-read the book. I had hoped to recapture my childhood delight, but I needed more than that. I needed to experience the characters' emotions, to live their active lives. The reality of the scene stifled that possibility.

I walked a little further along the path, passing the end of the island. Then, looking back at it, I suddenly felt a surge of excitement. I might be able to reach it from the other bank. I couldn't see clearly from this distance, but there seemed to be a series of stepping-stones or objects of some kind: metal cans, a green recycling bin, an upturned chair formed a makeshift, unstable causeway to the island.

I hurried back to the main road, crossed the bridge and looked for a way to the stepping-stones. There was no riverside path on this side. I passed the first house and turned down the next road. The river was invisible behind the houses, but I soon found an alley which led me to the bank. The 'stepping-stones' looked very precarious. Would I be able to cross them safely? Worse, two motor bikes were leaning against the wall of the nearest house. Their owners, dressed in leather, were sitting on a rock in the bay of the island, drinking and smoking. Seeing me looking at them, one of them called out:

'Come across if you like. We'll fish you out when you fall in.'

'Or we might not bother,' said the other. They both laughed.

I gave a perfunctory wave and walked home.

A nocturnal visit, I thought. That was what was needed. The fictional children had crept out of their houses one night, terrified that a creaking stair might waken their parents. My fear would be that I would disturb Jason. That might be worse. The children's parents would simply have sent them back to bed; my son, if I were lucky, might favour me with a shake of the head and a sardonic smile. However, he could be very serious and responsible at times and might decide that I needed help from a doctor or social worker.

I chose the next Friday night. Jason was going out in the evening. I knew he would be back early, but I hoped he would be tired. I was still up when he came home. After chatting to me for a few minutes, he said goodnight and went upstairs. I waited for half an hour, before putting on a thick coat, picking up a torch and tiptoeing out into the street. It had been too easy.

The "stepping-stones" were not so easy. Trying to keep my balance while training my torch on the next object, I nearly slid into the water twice. But at last, having steadied myself on a slippery oil can, I prepared for the last jump to the shore, craving the feel of dry land under my feet.

'Welcome, I have been expecting you.'

For a few seconds, I feared that I had encountered one of the bikers again, but this was the voice of an older, calmer man. I kept the beam from my torch directed at my feet. It seemed rude to shine it in the stranger's face.

'You have travelled far, my friend.'

'Well, not that far. Less than a mile, I think.'

'I speak not of measurable distance.'

'Sorry, I don't understand.'

'You have crossed running water.'

'Yes, but I do that every day. I cross the bridge on my way to work.'

'But not by the stones. And not to the island.'

'That's true. But so what?'

'You are entering a new plane of existence.'

I felt a sudden sense of terror. 'What are you talking about? You don't mean I've died, do you?'

'No, my friend. You have travelled backwards, not forwards. You are returning to your youth.'

I was silent. His words did not reassure me. I felt even more frightened.

'But I sense a resistance. You are unwilling to jump to the shore.'

I looked down at my feet, balanced unsteadily on the can.

'Are you ready to surrender all your adult responsibilities and make the final leap?'

What responsibilities did I still have? Since Dawn moved out with our two young daughters, there was only Jason left. Loyal old Jason. I loved him; I was proud of him. But at 16, he didn't need me. Should I make the last leap to the Island of Youth? Wasn't that what I had wanted since I started to re-read the book?

'You are still hesitating, my friend. There is just one short step to take.'

'I know, I know, but what would I be jumping into? Is it my own youth or shall I be joining the children in the story?'

'Is there a difference, my friend? Weren't you with the children every time you read the book? Every time you thought about the book?'

'Yes, I was with them, but I was also an onlooker. I was a part of the group, but I was also separate from them. Isn't that what happens when we read fiction?'

'It is. And now you have the chance of complete union. Isn't that your desire? To be a whole person, totally integrated, with no regrets, no yearnings for something different?'

He had identified the exact cause of my feeling of dissatisfaction when I re-read the book. I had been unable to recapture my youthful enjoyment of the story, because I had outgrown that innocent facility of totally immersing myself. Yet wasn't that part of being an adult? And did I truly want to become one of that group of children? They had seemed pleasant enough during most of their adventures, but they had grown horrible when they were stranded on the island, unable to cross the tumid river. I remembered Roger, the oldest. How patronising he had sounded when addressing a colleague as "my friend". I wasn't surprised that Tom had thrown himself at him, punching him in the face. Then the others had started egging the two on, cheering each hit, while Roger laughed, mocking Tom's feeble efforts: 'Go on, my friend, hit me again.'

'Well, my friend,' said the stranger, 'why don't you take that final leap?'

Suddenly I decided. Turning clumsily on the can, I stepped on to the packing case behind it. Then I jumped on to the recycling bin. I was progressing quickly, but the next "stepping-stone" was small and slippery. I had hoped to make a dignified escape to the bank; instead, my right foot sank into the water. My left foot followed and I ended up wading, knee-deep, to dry land. I hoped the stranger had not seen anything in the torchlight. He would certainly have heard the splashes.

I squelched home.

The downstairs lights were all on. As I unlatched the gate, the front door opened and Jason called out in panic:

'Dad, where have you been?'

'I just fancied a night-time walk.' I tried to sound calm.

'I was so worried about you. I was going to call the police.'

As I approached him, I saw that he was holding a book.

'What are you doing with that?' I shouted.

'I was just skimming through it while I waited for you—trying to take my mind off your disappearance.'

'Well, throw it away. I don't ever want to see that book again.'

There I Saw One I Knew...

As I approach the station after work, I pass Russell again. As usual, he pretends that he hasn't seen me.

We were never close friends, but I valued his acquaintance when we were colleagues. I was shocked when he left so suddenly and upset that he didn't say goodbye or give me any explanation. Why had he left?

The train is about to depart when I arrive. I jump aboard just as the doors are closing and hurry towards a vacant seat. Then I stop. Who is that I would be sitting next to? Surely it's not Erica? I turn away. I liked her, but we haven't met since we were students. I can't cope with the complicated unravelling of our life-stories. Anyway, it probably isn't her.

I alight at my stop, my eyes fixed on the ground.

As I pass the Crown, I say hello to a man I often see. I can't remember why we started greeting each other. Was it simply because our paths crossed so frequently or did I know him better long ago? Did we once work in the same building?

I have walked a few steps further when he calls out.

'Do you fancy a drink before you go home?'

I follow him into the pub. He buys me a pint and we carry our glasses to the table where Russell and Erica are seated, engrossed in animated discussion.

There's No Place

The journey was so familiar. Out of the windows of the train, I recognised a church, the distant view of a manor house, the ever-growing housing estate on the edge of a town, a factory chimney near a station. When we looped around the estuary, I counted the egrets, shelducks and coots. Since moving to London two years earlier, I had made this journey back to my parents every few months. Always I felt the pressures, the responsibilities of my London life dropping off me, as I returned to my old home, where Mum and Dad would be in charge once more, where meals would be cooked for me once more, where I would be a boy once more.

But this time, I wasn't going home.

My bicycle was in the guard's van. When I reached Delchester, I would not walk through the city on my usual pilgrimage, revelling in the old sights and smells. Instead, I would be cycling away from the city—a 15-mile ride to a birthday party for Rupert's sister.

I hadn't told my parents about this trip. I felt I was betraying them, coming so near home before deliberately turning away.

It was not that they would have minded. Why shouldn't I spend a night at a birthday party with a friend? I wouldn't even have needed to explain the nature of the friendship, particularly as I wasn't sure myself. I could have slept on the floor after the party, got up early and cycled home in time for breakfast with my parents.

Except that I couldn't have done that. These were two separate worlds. Now was not the time for them to collide. Perhaps it never would be.

It was growing dark as the train neared Delchester. The Holiday Inn—a well-known beacon—was lit up on the hill above the city. In five minutes, I would be at the station. Picking up my rucksack, I walked unsteadily along the corridor to the guard's van, unlocked my bike and put on my helmet. When the train stopped, I was the first to alight.

While I was leaving the station, I was looking wistfully towards the high street where I would normally be walking. But as I mounted the bike, I felt excited by my clandestine adventure.

The first part of the route was well-signposted. I rode quickly, suppressing my sense of treachery and wondering—almost for the first time—what the party would be like. I would know nobody apart from Rupert. How would he introduce me—as a partner or a casual friend? What would his sister and her friends think of me? What would be my status in the household?

I felt scared as I left the built-up area. There were no streetlamps on the country road. My front light seemed feeble—I could see only a tiny portion of the road ahead of me. I had never ridden at night outside the busy streets of London. There was little traffic here, but I felt a sense of panic whenever a vehicle overtook me or approached me from in front. Would the drivers see me?

'Lingford welcomes careful drivers.' I was nearly there now. I cycled into the centre of the small market town, surprised by my delight at the return of the streetlamps and the well-lit houses. I had learnt Rupert's instructions by heart. 'Turn left at the market cross. Cycle for two miles. Number 17 is the third house on the left as you enter the village of Worksby.'

The road was dark again, but the journey didn't last long. I almost missed the sign announcing Worksby; it was half buried in the hedge. The first houses appeared almost immediately. They were modern buildings; I felt sure that there would be older ones further on. I stopped at the third house, checked the number and locked my bike to the fence. I walked to the front door and rang the bell.

A young girl in a pink party dress and yellow ribbons in her hair opened the door.

'It's my birthday,' she said.

'Happy birthday,' I replied. 'How old are you today?'

'I'm six,' she said. 'Have you got me a present?'

'I've got a banana.' I searched in my rucksack. 'It's rather squashed, I'm afraid.'

'That's OK. I like squidgy "nanas".'

'Do you know if Rupert's here?'

'Yes, he's my brother.'

This was strange. I had thought Rupert's sister was about his age—not eighteen years younger.

'Who is it, Holly?' A woman came to the door. 'Oh, hello. I'm sorry, we're running a bit late. I'm just clearing away the tea things and then I've promised that we'll have a last game of Musical Chairs.'

'Can I help you clear away?' I was bewildered, but I thought I should try to be helpful.

'That would be great. Just dump everything in the kitchen.'

She led me into the sitting room, where ten children were jumping up and down excitedly. Plates and glasses were scattered on the floor, with a few half-eaten cup-cakes. A jug of orange squash was lying on its side on the table, the liquid dripping off the edge. I stacked up the plates and took them into the kitchen. I returned with some kitchen towels and wiped up the squash. I put the remains of the food in the bin and carried the glasses into the kitchen.

'Thank you so much,' said the woman. 'You've been really helpful. Come on, everyone! It's time for our last game. You know the rules. When the music starts, you start to dance. When the music stops, you have to find a seat. But there are ten of you and only nine chairs. If you can't sit down, you're out.'

She turned to me. 'I'll work the CD player, so can you take the chairs away one by one?'

'Of course,' I said. 'Always happy to help.'

The music started. The children danced. When the music stopped, they all screamed as they ran for the chairs. One boy was left standing. He looked sad, almost tearful. But the woman didn't waste any time. The music started again; I removed a chair. The music stopped; another child was without a seat.

By this time, other adults were entering the house and standing by the sitting room door, watching.

'Mummy!' cried the first unsuccessful child, as he ran into her arms, cheerful once more. Some of the remaining competitors were waving to their parents; others were concentrating on the game. Soon only two children were left sitting: Holly and one other girl. When the music re-started, I picked up the chair further from Holly, ensuring that the birthday girl was the winner. She raised her hands in triumph.

By now, most of the children had been reunited with their parents, who were thanking their hostess and saying goodbye, while their offspring told them excitedly about the evening. Soon I was alone with the woman, Holly and a small boy.

'Sorry,' said the woman. 'Which is your child? There's no one left.'

'I don't have any children,' I replied. 'I'm here because Rupert invited me.'

'What do you mean? Rupert, do you know this man?'

'No,' said the small boy, 'but I like him.'

'Who are you? What are you doing here?' The woman was shouting now.

'My name's Martin,' I said.

'Yes, but what are you doing at a kids' party? Are you a paedophile? Were you trying to abduct one of the kids?'

'No, you don't understand.' Of course, she didn't. I didn't understand either.

'I need to phone the police. Kids are in danger from people like you.'

'Wait. I can explain everything,' I lied.

'Well, explain it to the police. Holly, Rupert, come with me,' she ordered, as they left the room.

Just then, the doorbell rang. No, the police couldn't be here already! Or had one of the other parents rung them? I heard the woman open the front door.

'Hello. Sorry we're late,' said a familiar voice. 'We're here to collect Martin.'

'I'm here!' I called out, in relief. I went into the hall to greet my parents. They looked younger—much younger.

'I hope he's behaved himself,' said Mum.

'Oh yes, he's been very helpful,' replied the woman. 'He cleared away all the tea things for me.'

'You're honoured,' said Dad. 'He never does that at home.'

'Well, we'd better be off,' said Mum. 'Have you thanked Mrs Porter, Martin?'

'Thank you for a lovely party, Mrs Porter,' I mumbled.

'You're very welcome. You must come again soon.'

I followed Mum and Dad to the car. I recognised it from my childhood: a blue Morris. I remembered the number plate without looking at it: RVG 159D. They had sold the car fifteen years before.

I climbed into the back seat. My parents got into the front. Mum started to drive.

I felt the pressures, the responsibilities of my life dropping off me, as I returned to my old home, where Mum and Dad would be in charge once more, where meals would be cooked for me once more, where I would be a boy once more.

Where the Footsteps Led

'Sit down, Chrissie. So, you want to talk to me about your thesis? Have you chosen a topic yet?'

'Yes, but I hope you won't think I'm being cheeky.'

'Sounds intriguing.'

'You see, I've read your own thesis. And, well, I'd like to write about…'

'You want to write about Robert Eltham?'

'Yes, I'm not going to disagree with anything you said, but I thought, maybe I could add something?'

'Certainly. I wrote mine nearly 20 years ago. A lot's happened since then. There was that new biography by Watkins. And then one of Eltham's notebooks was discovered. That was exciting. Did you hear about it?'

'Yes, I read the transcription online.'

'Good. So, there's definitely more to write about him. Now, what's your focus going to be? Have you decided?'

'I was hoping to relate his work to particular places that he would have known. You see, most people concentrate on the meaning of his allegorical writings—I thought you did that brilliantly—but I believe that every poem is rooted in a particular place. For instance, *Voices* is set in Lincoln. He's standing on the top of the hill next to the cathedral—just as he did when he lived there as a boy.'

'Yes, I can see that. And you think you've found a setting for every poem?'

'No, not yet. But I want to.'

'OK, that sounds interesting. Write an outline of your plans and we'll take it from there. And no, you're not being cheeky. I'm looking forward to working with you.'

Vince had essays to mark, lecture notes to prepare, but after Chrissie left his office, he just sat at his desk, eyes half-closed, pondering.

He liked meeting students individually. He was skilled—or so he believed—at encouraging them to unleash their responses to literature; his office was a safe place to experiment with new ideas and arguments.

He sometimes worried that he was too fond of the students' company—particularly the women—but he was able to reassure himself that his conduct was always scrupulously professional.

Certainly, Chrissie was attractive, as he had noticed when delivering lectures. She was petite, with cropped blond hair and hazel eyes. But what struck him during this meeting was her expansive gestures as she tried to quell her embarrassment at encroaching on his literary territory.

However, it was her choice of topic—not her appearance—which had dictated his response. As soon as she mentioned Eltham, he found himself transported back 20 years, to the summer term of his first year at university…

…It was 7.15 when he finished his coffee—time he left the café if he were to meet the members of the Robert Eltham Society at the station. Or should he catch the tube home? It would take him 90 minutes. Did he really want a late night?

He loitered near the station, still undecided what to do. A few other people were waiting at the ticket barrier. Were they members of the society? Until three days before, he wasn't even aware of its existence. When his tutor advertised the event, he had awakened memories of snatches of Eltham's verse which Vince had read at school. These verses had stayed in his mind, even though critics had dismissed them as frivolous when compared with the long, allegorical poems, which he had never read.

Were these station-lingerers aficionados of Eltham? Were they dilettantes like him? Or were they waiting for friends for an after-work drink? Vince looked in vain for his tutor; he had hoped to impress him with his presence.

A scholarly-looking man, with long white hair and beard, arrived, a dilapidated folder overflowing with papers under his arm. Suddenly, he was surrounded by people—Vince included—as if an invisible sheepdog had rounded up assorted passers-by, interrupting their journeys home.

There were introductions: Joshua (the bearded secretary), Cristobel (tonight's speaker), Karen and Peter (committee members). They discussed the route to the pub where the meeting was to take place. Peter proposed a 347 bus, but he was overruled. Karen suggested the direct route beside the main road.

Joshua and Cristobel wanted to lead the party along a woodland track past Samuel Pearson's cottage, which Eltham had visited 200 years before. There was a delay of ten minutes before everyone set off up the High Road. The sky was darkening; the moon was almost full. Vince felt irritated by the lack of organisation, but also excited at the prospect of a strange evening.

A man walking beside him fantasised about how Eltham might have met John Garnett, who had been living near the wood at the time when Eltham walked there. Vince laughed in appreciation at the thought and mentioned how much he liked Garnett's house, which had been converted into a museum. His companion agreed enthusiastically. They discussed Garnett's work at length, realising that his shadow had dwarfed that of Eltham, whose writing they were meant to be celebrating.

Ahead of them, Joshua had stopped. He turned to explain that the Highwayman was only half a mile down the road. Anyone who wished could go there directly; he and Cristobel would lead the rest of the company along woodland tracks to Pearson's cottage. Most chose the latter route. Vince felt a nervous expectation as they veered off the main road on to a narrow, dark footpath. They passed a few houses: one, they were told, had belonged to a judge who, after moving in, remained ensconced there without ever re-emerging; another was built by a nineteenth century architect as his home, although it was a plain, dull building, with none of the exciting features of the houses he had been commissioned to design. At the end of the track was Pearson's cottage—a small building, little changed since the days when Eltham used to walk there, all the way from his home in Spitalfields.

Joshua and Cristobel next turned on to a still narrower path, which wound through a patch of dark forest. Vince's previous thoughts of an early night had vanished; now he was immersed in the mysteries of this land, with its legends of woodcutters and charcoal burners, highwaymen and gypsies. The conversation had ceased by tacit mutual consent. They moved in silence, except for the sound of their shoes, rustling through the leaf-mould.

The walk ended too quickly for Vince. They emerged on to the main road and there was the Highwayman pub—their destination. It had been a coaching inn in Eltham's day. Had he ever drunk there? Probably not—Vince didn't think of him as a drinker. He bought half a pint of beer and followed his colleagues up a rickety staircase to the room that had been booked for their meeting.

Joshua introduced the speaker.

'Cristobel's book is an account of a series of walks in the footsteps of writers from the Romantic period. But as she describes each walk, she doesn't focus exclusively on the writer in whose steps she is treading. Her attention is as likely to be caught by a modern multi-storey car park as by the medieval church tower, which would have been so prominent in the writer's time. And what Cristobel sees brings back memories of her own life. So as the walk unfolds, perhaps we are learning more about Cristobel than the writer in question.'

Joshua talked at length. Vince wondered why he was telling them all this, instead of letting Cristobel speak for herself. At last, his introduction reached its end.

'And now, Cristobel, would you read us a few pages from your chapter on Eltham?'

Although she had been presented to them at the station, Cristobel had not so far made much impression on Vince. Beside Joshua's eccentric energy, she had seemed a nonentity. Yet when she stood up, she caught his attention immediately. She was short, perhaps 50 years old, with grey hair. She looked severe, but smiled when she started to speak, making exaggerated gestures with her hands.

'I'm going to read the beginning of the chapter. Robert Eltham lived in Spitalfields and this is the start of his walk to Pearson's cottage.'

Vince had hoped that she would read the section about the end of the walk. He had been so moved by that woodland path that he had wanted to hear how she described it. Instead, he listened to her comments on an area of London he had never visited. But as she spoke, he felt that he was entering her world. Her voice was quiet and soothing. Her expansive gestures seemed to embrace her audience. She conjured up images, some of which Vince quickly forgot.

She talked about Christ Church, Spitalfields. She was standing in the lofty nave, gazing at the white pillars, the round arches, the clerestory. She talked of Hawksmoor, the architect. She described the excavations in the 1980s, when nearly 1,000 bodies were exhumed. She walked out of the west door, down the church steps, across the road and into the market, where she wandered around the arts and crafts stalls, paused for a coffee, before turning a corner into…

Vince stayed in the market, hearing the stallholders shouting to passers-by in their cockney accents. When he forced himself back to Cristobel, she was walking up a flight of steps to a front door. Did this happen in 2002 or 1813? He waited for the door to open, but Cristobel shut the book and read ten lines from a poem by Eltham, in which he described a market, dominated by a mansion. There was the bustle of buying and selling. Gradually, the audience realised that the customers and stallholders were bargaining for human souls.

There was silence. Then everyone applauded. Vince was cursing his lack of concentration, desperate to learn more about that flight of steps and the door about to open.

'Thank you very much,' said Joshua. 'That was an exciting reading. Now, does anyone have any questions?'

Several hands went up.

'How do you approach your writing? Do you do your research before or after the walk?'

'I immerse myself in the writer's work before beginning the walk. That way, I can try to look around me with their eyes, noticing things which would have interested them. I don't read about the topography or the folklore of the area until after the walk.'

'Why do you write about recent buildings, which Eltham couldn't have seen?'

'I suppose I'm trying to show that his writing is still important to us today. For instance, he wrote *A rebuke to Lord Surfeit* in 1792, the year in which Mary Wollstonecraft's *Vindication of the rights of woman* was published and the year after Thomas Paine's *Rights of man*. We need to know about those writers to understand Eltham, but we also need to compare them with what's happening today.'

'Who are the other writers in your book?'

'My longest walk was tracing John Clare's steps from High Beach Asylum in Epping Forest to his home in Helpston near Peterborough. It's all of 90 miles and it took me a week. Then I walked with Dorothy Wordsworth in Grasmere and with her brother in the Alps. I walked...'

Vince's concentration lapsed again. He was wishing that he had thought of doing walks like these. Perhaps he could do some from a different period. Maybe he could follow TS Eliot across London Bridge, along King William Street to St Mary Woolnoth Church. No, somebody was sure to have done that. He needed to choose a more obscure writer. How about...

Joshua was speaking once more.

'I would like to thank Cristobel again. I'm sure there are other questions and you'll have a chance to ask these later, but I'm going to bring the formal session to an end now. Cristobel has brought some copies of her book, so if you'd like to buy one, please come up and she'll be happy to sign it.'

Everyone clapped again. Vince joined the queue for the book signing. Those ahead of him were all asking the speaker detailed questions about her work. He didn't dare ask her anything. His wandering mind had made him miss so much of what she had said that he might easily have asked her a question she had already answered. Could he train himself to concentrate, he wondered? If not, should he abandon the degree course? Could he ever produce any worthwhile work if he couldn't concentrate?

When his turn came, he picked up the book from the diminishing pile and almost thrust it, with the money, at Cristobel. She signed it. He said, 'Thank you'—his only words to her. Then he hurried self-consciously down the staircase and left the pub. The walk back to the Underground was short and uneventful; it had none of the mystery of the dark, woodland footpath.

He had picked up the book unthinkingly; now, on the tube train, he wanted to treasure it. He reached into his shoulder bag for it. He took out his newspaper, sandwich wrapper, notebook. Cristobel's book was not there.

He was annoyed rather than disappointed. He was not concerned that he had lost a signed copy, but he had been anxious to read that section with the flight of steps leading up to the front door, as well as her description of the walk they had made that evening. Now he would have to wait until he bought or borrowed another copy.

He never did.

Over the next few weeks, he looked in every library and bookshop he could find, without success. He searched on the internet. Not only could he find nothing about the book; he couldn't even trace the existence of a Robert Eltham Society.

Later, he spoke to his tutor. He denied having advertised the meeting, but encouraged Vince to write his thesis about Eltham. Unlike the other Romantics, not much had been written about him. Vince read everything he could find. The thesis was well-received; eventually, he re-wrote it as a monograph. He didn't think he inspired the resurgence of interest in Eltham, but he certainly contributed to it. When a Robert Eltham Society was established, he was asked to be its honorary president.

And now Chrissie had invaded the world of Eltham.

Vince knew that his role was to encourage her to develop her own ideas about Eltham, to work out her own approach to his writings. He should intervene only if she asked for help.

But that wasn't what he wanted.

He wanted her to be the new Cristobel, to replicate the book which had been snatched from him. He wanted her to climb that flight of steps to the front door, to reveal what was on the other side of it.

And maybe, 30 years from now, Vince—an elderly, bearded academic—would introduce Chrissie to the members of the society at the underground station and together they would lead the procession through woodland paths to Pearson's cottage and on to the Highwayman pub.

Thirty-Nine Today

It had not been a bad day—all things considered. After all, I wouldn't have chosen to spend my birthday in the office. You bring in cake and have to stop work while everyone asks your age and expresses the perfunctory incredulity when you divulge it. Then they ask how you will be celebrating tonight and all agree that an Italian meal in Crystal Palace with friends will be very nice. No, of course, I would rather have stayed hidden behind my computer for those ten minutes, but this was one of the duties which must be endured at work and I had successfully endured it.

Then I was on my way to the restaurant. Something to look forward to at last. But the crowds at the tube station, the platform almost overflowing, the threat of delays. Still, it could have been worse and when I arrived at Victoria, the Crystal Palace train was already there—with some empty seats.

I sat down, opened my book and relaxed.

'Whoa-oh! Come on, you lads!'

I kept my head bowed over my book as the youths crowded noisily on to the train, just as it was starting to move off. I was determined not to attract their attention, but as one of them barged clumsily into me, I looked up involuntarily, then stared in amazement. It seemed so incongruous: this tough football supporter, with denim jacket open to reveal his bare chest, was carrying a large bunch of pink carnations. I tried to pretend I hadn't seen him, but I was too late.

'Wotcher Nick!' he shouted, giving me a friendly punch on the shoulder. 'Happy birthday, mate! Thirty-nine, eh?' And he pushed the carnations into my hands.

'Thank you, thank you, thank you, thank you,' I muttered in embarrassment, wondering how many more times I would repeat those words before I could gain enough composure to restrain the opening and closing of my mouth. I leaned forward, trying to think of some polite topic of conversation, but I needn't have worried. My well-wisher had already turned back to his friends, as if no longer aware of my existence. I returned to my book, but I couldn't concentrate. I was glad when the train stopped at Battersea Park and the youths shoved their way off, once again ignoring my repeated murmur of thanks.

A young woman boarded the train and sat down opposite me. I sighed with relief—I would not be disturbed now. Out of the corner of my eye, I noticed with some amusement that she too was holding some flowers. What a coincidence. Then my heart missed a beat.

'Hello Nicholas. Happy birthday. The start of your fortieth year, isn't it?'

She handed over her yellow chrysanthemums and, before I had time to thank her, took a book out of her bag and began to read.

Reading was impossible for me now. Not only was I too confused and unsettled; in addition, with two bunches of flowers, I had no hand free to hold the book. I sat, rigid, clasping the stalks.

As we approached Clapham Junction, the woman made no move until the very moment that the train stopped, when she suddenly snapped her book shut and hurried off, without even glancing at me.

Her seat was taken by a businessman. As he sat down, I looked at him anxiously and, sure enough, as well as the regulation briefcase and umbrella, he was holding a bunch of gladioli, the red shoots beginning to force their way through the green points. He looked relieved to see me, happy to be free of his encumbrance.

'Ah, Mr Fox,' he said, handing over the flowers. 'Happy birthday.'

'When three combines with three times three,
That which thou art is what thou shalt be.'

Then he opened his briefcase, removed a photocopied report and began to mark passages with an orange highlighter pen.

Three bunches of flowers and still six stations to go. Was I going to end up with nine bunches? I tried to straighten the flowers, fearful of dropping some of them. As the train drew in to Wandsworth Common, I noticed the ranks of rose-bay willow herb decorating the embankment.

The man, without looking at me, put his papers neatly into his briefcase, stood up, glanced at his watch, brushed an invisible speck of dust off his jacket and left the train.

Suddenly, the carriage was full of people, jostling and tripping over each other, blocking the corridors, squeezing on to seats—five people on seats designed for three. And all of them—all of them were carrying flowers. There was even a tiny baby, wearing a daisy chain as a coronet, while strings of convolvulus were entwining their white flowers around an old man's walking stick. Never had a carriage been festooned with such colours. And everyone was talking—shouting, whispering, declaiming, singing—everyone was talking about one subject:

'Darling, what divine dahlias!'

'Do you like my marigolds?'

'A for azalea B for begonia C for chrysanthemum D for delphinium…'

'I would give you some violets, but they withered all when my father died.'

'My love is like a red rose that's newly sprung in June.'

'Buddleia for a butterfly, lavender for a bee.'

'Lavenders blue, dilly dilly Lavenders green…'

'Would you rather be a lily-of-the-valley or a love-in-the-mist?'

'Well, I went around on Christmas Eve, to take her a cyclamen, like, but she wasn't in, you see, so I left it with her George. And do you know, when I got home, blowed if she hadn't just been and left another cyclamen with my Sid.'

What was I to do? Presumably all these flowers were for me, but I couldn't carry a tenth of them. The people next to me were looking expectantly—any moment now they would wish me a happy birthday and start loading me up with flowers. I thought it best to pre-empt their greetings.

'Those tulips,' I said to the elderly woman squashed up next to me, 'are they—are they for me, by any chance?'

There was complete silence inside the carriage. The sound of the wheels was audible for the first time since the crowd had boarded the train; for the first time, I realised that we had left Wandsworth Common. Then, suddenly, everyone was shouting.

'He's after my tulips!'

'Thief! Thief!'

'Pervert!'

'Maniac!'

'He'll be wanting my marigolds next.'

'And my geraniums.'

'As if he hadn't got enough flowers of his own.'

'If they are his own. It's my belief they're stolen too.'

'Oh, those poor gladioli. Fancy being clutched in those nasty, sweaty, filthy hands.'

'I wouldn't trust him with chickweed.'

'Grab them off him. And the carnations. And the chrysanths.'

'Get him off the train. He's polluting the atmosphere. My sunflower's wilting already.'

I was only too willing to hand over my three bunches of flowers, but that didn't seem enough for them. I was punched and shoved from one person to another; my feet were trodden on, my shins kicked.

'All right, I'm going!' I screamed. 'I can't move any faster.'

Indeed, I could not. The crush seemed impenetrable. At last, I was dragged towards the doors, but these were blocked by more furious passengers, brandishing assorted bunches of flowers. When eventually the train stopped and the doors opened, several people nearly fell out on to the platform. Then they hurled me out instead, the doors shut again and the train continued its journey.

Bruised and battered, I stood up. Despite aching all over, I was not badly hurt and I felt relieved to be free from that frenetic crowd. I was very dazed and it was a few minutes before it occurred to me that I was at an extremely strange station. If I had had time to think, I would have expected to be at Balham, but this was no station I had ever seen before. The platform was merely a long slab of concrete—no notices, no seats, no waiting room, not even any obvious way out. You could simply step off it—step off the platform into a vast cemetery. A wind blew across the flat, deserted land. There was no other living person in sight, but the dead were everywhere. Wherever I looked, there were gravestones—some adorned with marble angels, others with tiny crosses. Some were ivy-covered and decaying, others might have been laid the day before. And all of them were decorated with flowers: a wreath garlanded each headstone, while crocuses, tulips and daffodils were growing between the graves. I had never seen such a multitude of colours. Yet despite this abundance, it was a bleak scene, with the cool wind ruffling the flowers. I shuddered.

'Could I see your ticket, Sir?'

I fumbled in my pocket and handed my travel card to the ticket-collector.

'Zones 1 to 4, Sir? This card's not valid here, I'm afraid.'

'Well, how much extra do I need to pay?' I reached into my pocket once again.

'Oh, it's not that easy, Sir. But don't you worry. You'll have the right ticket when the time comes. In the meantime, why don't you get on this train that's coming in now? All stations to West Croydon. And I'll see you again when you've got the right ticket. Perhaps it won't be so long now, Sir. Perhaps it won't be so long at all.'

The train stopped. The ticket-collector opened the door and ushered me in.

'Be seeing you soon, Sir. Oh, and by the way, have a very happy birthday.'

He handed me some flowers and shut the door behind me before I could thank him. As the train drew away from the platform, I looked down at my latest present—just a small, discreet clump of blue forget-me-nots.